THE RAVEN

THE SECRET CHRONICLES OF LOST MAGIC

ADERYN WOOD

Edited by Pam Collings
pam@tbbooks.com.au

Cover Art by Tairelei
www.deviantart.com/tairelei

Cover art stock care of:
www.deviantart.com/la-catalina
www.deviantart.com/frankandcarystock
www.deviantart.com/mimose-stock
www.deviantart.com/cindysart-stock
www.deviantart.com/moonchild-lj-stock
www.deviantart.com/malleni-stock
www.obsidiandawn.com

A NOTE ON THE SERIES

'The Secret Chronicles of Lost Magic' is not strictly a series, rather it is a collection of standalone novels all set in the same universe. Essentially, each book in the Chronicles showcases a significant historical event in the world known as Larth. Readers will note that each book begins with a brief letter by the Sage Vivlian of Wyllt, who thus connects the stories, and Vivlian herself will appear as a major character in the fourth book of 'The Secret Chronicles of Lost Magic'.

As the novels are standalone stories, it is not necessary to read them chronologically, though there may be some small benefit of doing so, and here is the correct order for those interested readers:

Book One: *The Raven*
Book Two: *Dragonshade*

ABOUT THE RAVEN

The Raven is the first book in a collection called 'The Secret Chronicles of Lost Magic'. To find when the next Chronicle will be released consider signing up to Aderyn's monthly newsletter.

To my parents

ear Albinus,

I HOPE this scroll will find you well and not drowning in the political machinations of our revered tower.

I have settled here in Dyserth. A stone cottage in the forest has become my new dwelling. The villagers tell me it once housed a Cathuchin hermit. There is room for a garden, and Salomon has busied himself over the summer building a stable for my mule. Importantly, I now have the soltiude I require to inscribe my travels and all that I have learned, and I have completed the first of such chronicles for you to archive.

I discovered the tale of Iluna within the Annals of Christoph, located in the Grande Librarie in Rhone. That great tome harboured one small passage that mentioned Iluna's story in mere passing, and within those lines one term caught my eye – dumai'shange – skin changer. A footnote gave me a possible location to the source of the anecdote. And, so it was I traveled to the Arlesatain Mountains, and to the small village of Breue d'Arle.

At first the villagers reacted with heavy suspicion when I asked about the dumai'shange. Almost a month I stayed, before their leader, an old wizened grandmother, decided that I'd earned her trust with my songs and stories. One night during the full moon, she told me Iluna's tale in full.

The following day she beckoned me to trek with her through the mountains to a secret cave that she claimed was the very one in which Iluna had stayed. It was centuries old with wall paintings like none I have seen, chronicling strange events from ancient clans. An odd feeling overcame me in that cave – that undeniable shiver caused by magic.

Later, the old grandmother confided that Iluna still lived, and that she appears in the cave whenever the Blue Comet returns to our skies – every eighty years – to add more paintings to its walls. I surmised she

ADERYN WOOD

referred to Angelus's Comet. I nodded respectfully, but no doubt this was a well-worn fable passed from grandparent to grandchild throughout the centuries.

Within this fable, evidence of strong magic will draw interest from fellow sages, and it is my sincere hope that it does. As you know, references to skin changers are rare indeed. Moreover, the daily practise of magic in primordial tribes also holds opportunities for further study. We've so little evidence about the use of magic in such archaic times.

In the tale, there is mention of dwindling numbers of those born with the gift – the giftborn they called them – suggesting that at one point, in the distant past, it is likely the gifted were common. But gradually over time they have become as rare as black veridian. Indeed, perhaps rarer. This tale verifies that conclusion, but sheds little light as to the cause. The answer, it seems, continues to elude us.

I have recorded Iluna's tale in full in the pages that follow. I look forward to hearing your insights when we next meet. And perhaps, when our paths do cross again, we should not drink so much wine. My head still recovers!

May the Light be always with you,
Sage Vivlian of Wyllt
The Year of our Eternal Lord 374
(2782 - Old Realm Calendar)

2

PART I
WINTER OF THE SKY

IZHUR

*I*zhur stood close to the birthing tree on an outcrop of granite overlooking a forested valley. Mist draped the leafless canopy, clinging to the odd pine tree. The wintry daysun glinted once before descending to its lengthy rest beyond the horizon. Izhur took a shuddering breath. With the daysun now making its descent to Malfiren, Ilun had begun – that dark time when no moon, star or sun walked the sky for an eightnight. The Soragan closed his eyes as his lips murmured an invocation to Ona, the Mother, but the sound of footsteps made him open them again. Lili stood before him, her hands kneading each other into a tight knot.

"What is it, child?" Izhur asked, but he already knew her request.

The young novice's eyes filled with tears. "Amak sent me. She said it's time."

Izhur nodded and gestured for the girl to lead him along the short stone path to the birthing tree.

Men were not supposed to be present during childbirth. It was a female rite. Amak, the clan's medicine woman, and her novice, Lili, saw to such matters. A man was only allowed if he was a Soragan, and only then if something was very, very wrong.

Izhur pursed his lips as he walked the few short steps to the tree. This was his first Ilun as the clan's Soragan. His first birth, too. He wished his master was still alive to guide him, to teach him. Twenty summers was too young to be a clan's Soragan. He hoped he knew what to do.

Izhur followed Lili up the carved steps of the giant oak tree, its leaves long gone with the winter frosts. Snow would come soon. The Winter of the Sky was always cold and dark.

About ten steps up the trunk a tree-dwell made of bark and mud clung to thick lower boughs, the way a hive did. Izhur stepped inside and blinked, adjusting his eyes. Neria lay on the birthing mat, fatigue written on her grey face. Her dark hair clung close; eyes drawn. The bulge of her pregnancy sat low on her abdomen. She had little left.

Amak stood. The medicine woman looked as though she had aged eight winters. The lines around her eyes usually accentuated her smiles, but now they made her appear old and weary. Her tunic was stained and blood dripped from her hands. "The daysun has gone down," her voice almost a whisper.

He nodded. "I will do my best."

Neither of them mentioned Ilun. They were the clan's knowledge keepers: she – the medicine woman; he – the Soragan. They knew the danger that now lurked for human and spirit alike. Ilun was a dark event that occurred every eight winters – during the Winter of the Sky. With no light to frighten them away, the spirits of Malfiren were free to wreak their terror. The first night of Ilun was no time to be welcoming a newborn into Ona's world. Izhur would have to work hard to repel any dark spirits. No easy task. The demons would detect a newborn the way a wolf smells blood.

Neria tried to scream again as another contraction took hold, but her voice rasped like stone on stone. Wolf pelts covered the mud floor of the tree-dwell. Much of Neria's blood had drenched them and the coppery scent filled the modest space. Izhur knelt by Neria's head and wiped her sweaty forehead with the palm of his hand. She was cold.

"I will protect you, and your baby," he said, and Neria's eyes closed, squeezing out a tear.

His voice had shaken, as had his hands.

"Lili, get some lights – as many as you can," Izhur instructed, trying to keep panic from his voice. The girl jumped up and tore down the tree. Twilight now rapidly diminished. They would need light to help keep the Malfir away.

Izhur swallowed a hard lump. He put his leather satchel on the floor of the shelter and took out the implements he required for the task ahead, his hands shaking. He placed two flat stone plates on the floor, both the size of his palm. He took a small clay pot and opened the stopper. The spicy aroma of olibanum and crushed sage filled his nostrils, contrasting with the thick stench of blood. He poured a generous amount on each of the stone plates, and put them on either side of Neria.

Lili came back with a satchel of oil pots. She held one in her hand, already alight.

"Give it to me," Izhur said. He lit a taper then held it to the plates. The crushed spices smoldered and spirals of aromatic smoke danced through the shelter. They would help deter the Malfir.

Izhur handed the oil pot and the taper to Lili. "Light the others – all of them – and place them around the tree-dwell. Try to make a circle."

Lili nodded. Soon a yellow glow lit the mud walls.

Neria cried out again and Amak cooed soothing words as she glanced earnestly at Izhur. He knew the look in her eyes; it was a plea for him to do something, to move faster. A distant rumble sounded outside – thunder. Amak heard it, too. Her eyebrow arched in a question: A winter storm on Ilunnight? Omens upon omens.

Izhur placed his hands on either side of Neria's head and started the song – a deep incantation, a call to Ona, the Mother. Only She had the power to help them on such a night.

His body rocked and he closed his eyes. He focused on his breathing and the words. *'Whenever you're unsure go back to the beginning.'* He remembered his master's advice as he followed it. Breathe. Chant. Breathe. Chant.

Another rumble of thunder echoed. The storm crept closer. An icy breeze whipped through the shelter sending the flames of the oil pots sideways. Neria's strained scream followed. Izhur opened his eyes and wiped sweat from his forehead; his long hair hung in damp tendrils. Amak scowled and shook her head.

He returned his trembling hands to Neria's temples and tried again. Breathe. Chant. Breathe.

He felt it before he saw it, that giddy sensation. This was normal, like a feeling of falling, before his sight opened up to reveal the Otherworld. Its familiar shadowy grey swam before him. Neria's body pulsed dimly as her light waned. Like an oil pot on its last drop, she was dying. Izhur fought the urge to retract out of the Otherworld; his grief would overpower him if he didn't control it.

He focussed his mind and looked around. The Otherworld was clear. No shadows lurked. The Malfir were no threat – yet. He turned his attention to the babe. Neria's womb pulsed with a strong golden light; so powerful, it was like trying to look at the daysun.

Izhur wanted to turn away but forced himself to send his sight further down, toward the bright spirit still nestled within Neria's womb. In the Otherworld, the form of the baby was fluid. The child took no clear shape, and resembled something of a circle of fire. Izhur marveled. Never before had he seen a spirit so bright. It calmed him. Perhaps the Malfir would be frightened.

Izhur had to force the birth. It was the only way. He sent forward his ethereal arm, and saw the luminance of his hand and fingers. He touched the ball of golden light and whispered a chant as he pushed down. Movement and light throbbed and he pushed harder. The glow from the oil pots was visible on this plane, dancing red globes. But another flash struck, to the north – rapid bolts of blue and white. Lightning.

He pushed again. More movement. *Come little one.* He pushed harder. Neria's light faded further, blinking out. Nothing could be done for her now. Izhur had to save the child. He pushed again and an eruption of light threw him back before darkness came.

∞

"THE CHILD IS CURSED. That is as clear as my foot." Ugot spat next to the foot he mentioned. "I can see it. As can you. We know what has to be done."

There were several nods.

The Circle of Eight sat in the Tree of Knowledge, the oldest oak in the Wolf clan's winter lands. It stood away from their family shelters, giving them the privacy they needed to make decisions about the clan's daily existence. Its mud walls weren't maintained as well as the family tree-dwells and an icy breeze cut through thick cracks, making everyone shiver. The Eight huddled close, a single oil pot lighting their faces; old faces mostly, all of them wearing grim expressions.

Flynth, grandmother of thirty healthy children, had glistening round cheeks, wet with tears that refused to stop no matter how many times she shook her head. Neria had been a friend to all of them. They met now to decide the fate of the babe who had suckled as her mother's life force passed away. The storm had been distant then; now it sent its deadly fingers closer. The rumbling of thunder roiled without pause.

Izhur shook his head as he pulled his wolf cloak around him. "This child, she has an extraordinary light." His voice wavered as he spoke. He wanted to explain more, but a peal of thunder prevented him.

"What kind of Soragan are you, Izhur? Even I can see the omens. She is cursed, I tell you." Ugot spat again; his dark eyes scanned the others, searching for agreement. There was more nodding. Ugot was one of the oldest, and despite his renowned lack of wisdom, this gave him some authority.

"Ugot speaks the truth, Izhur. I am sorry to say it." Amak shrugged. "How else can we explain the drought, the fires? Even Neria's death? She was a healthy young woman; her body should have withstood the birth. And what about her father?"

"Osun was careless. Everyone knows not to hunt lions." With even Amak against him, Izhur felt completely alone.

"Still, he died not long after her conception." The medicine woman shrugged again, as though apologising.

Izhur massaged his eyes, his body exhausted. The birth had required much energy. Such focus in the plane of the Other-world was always tiring. He needed rest. Thinking straight was difficult. But he could not deny the omens.

Osun's death was unnatural. On their return from Agria, they had found their summer lands, usually so abundant with life, burned and barren. The whole forest had suffered drought and fire. And now this – the first night of Ilun, the babe is born and Neria died. Ill-omened indeed. But he had seen her in the Otherworld. He could not forget that light.

Ugot stared at Izhur with a look of smug satisfaction. His

protruding brow and narrow eyes made him appear rather stupid.

Izhur ignored him and forced himself to speak. "I have seen her light. I tell you it is strong. She has – power."

"Then she would make a generous sacrifice, perhaps prevent any further tragedy this Ilun." It was Zodor who spoke, his voice quiet but strong. At twenty-five summers, Zodor was young to be such a respected leader in the Eight, but somehow he was the dominant voice. A fine hunter and father of two healthy sons, he was the unspoken leader. Everyone listened when he talked.

Izhur rubbed his temple, not quite believing what Zodor suggested. It had been generations since there had been a human sacrifice in the Wolf clan. His shoulders slumped with the weight of responsibility. Again he wished for his old master. Jakom had been the clan's Soragan for more summers than most could count. He used to be the dominant voice in this circle – as a Soragan's should. His wisdom had kept the clan from falling into danger many times. But Jakom had passed into the Otherworld last winter, and now Zodor seemed to lead the circle and Izhur was the new, untested Soragan.

The Wolf clan was not the clan Izhur had been born into. He had joined them nine summers ago when Jakom selected him as his novice. He had always struggled to belong. The Wolf clan didn't have the same friendly outlook as the people of the Bear, and Zodor had always been cold. But Izhur had to ignore all of that now; he was the Soragan.

"Zodor." Izhur measured his voice and looked down at Zodor's feet, not daring to reveal the frustration that would be clear in his eyes. "The Wolf hasn't made a sacrifice for generations. Not since Jakom was a young prentice himself." He eyed the seven men and women around him. "Many of you were not even born then."

"Then it is well overdue." Zodor's voice remained low and

determined. "Even a hunter such as I can read the omens, Soragan."

Izhur rubbed his temple again, trying to order the many thoughts that jostled for attention in his mind. What would Jakom do? How could he perform such a sacrifice of an innocent? And what of her light?

"She could help us. She could become the most powerful Soragan our clan has known." Izhur pressed on. "Perhaps we could sacrifice an animal – a wolf – like we do in the spring."

Ugot spat for a third time.

Zodor's eyes burned. "You have foretold of another to be our next Soragan."

Izhur grimaced. Zodor's youngest son, Yuli, had a strong light and was born at an auspicious time – during Agria, the festival of Light. It made sense that he could become Izhur's novice in the future. The gift-born seemed to be rare these days. "Your son bears the power; there's no doubt of that, Zodor. But this little girl, she—"

"Izhur, must I remind you that she was born on Ilunnight? How is it you, our Soragan, can ignore that? If she has power, as you suggest, then we would be wise to use her as a sacrifice. The Malfir will be appeased by such a gift. Do I really need to explain this to a *Soragan?*" Zodor's face was motionless.

The man reminded Izhur of rock – strong, silent, still. He would not be moved, and if he couldn't change Zodor's mind there was no influencing the others. Izhur agreed with them, he was no Soragan. Soragans were respected; listened to. They were the leaders in all clans but the Wolf. Izhur was too young. He was no Jakom.

"If any of you object, speak." Zodor looked to each of the elders in turn.

"She must be sacrificed," Ugot said.

"I agree." Jarel put a hand through his grey hair.

Flynth shook her head and more tears fell from her rosy cheeks.

Tod simply shrugged his shoulders and looked to the entrance of the tree-dwell. Izhur couldn't help but scowl a little. Tod wouldn't shut up when they discussed seasonal migrations, but he always shrugged off the tough decisions.

"This is a grave decision." Lral's dark eyes looked at Izhur, and he straightened his shoulders a little. This elder he respected above all others in the Eight, indeed the clan, even more than Amak, for Lral was the oldest and the wisest. "And you are right to defend her, Izhur."

Izhur's breath shuddered. He blinked.

"But I am old enough to remember the last human sacrifice." Her eyes glistened as she spoke. "It brought us safety for many summers and winters. We of the Wolf have not known tragedy for a long time." Her old eyes looked down to the oil pot and a single tear landed on the muddy floor of the tree-dwell. "It is time for us to appease the Malfir once more."

Izhur slouched. He had lost.

Zodor stood. "It has been decided. We will sacrifice her tonight. We call on our *Soragan* to do the task." He nodded at Izhur.

Zodor left, and one by one the others followed. Lightning ripped through the sky as Izhur watched the circle members make their way to their own tree-dwells. Only Amak remained.

She put her warm hand on his. "It is best for the clan, Izhur. We need to feel safe. This is your burden, you are our Soragan now." She squeezed his hand before rising and following the others out of the shelter.

∞

IZHUR TROD CAREFULLY. There was no moon or nightsun to offer him light, and the faint gleam of starlight had been taken when storm clouds blanketed the sky with their dark ink. Lightning streaked through the black curtain of night and, for an instant, Izhur could see his course. The rocky path remained in front of him. He was not yet lost.

The baby in his arms began to cry.

"Shush now," he whispered. But the crack and roll of thunder drowned the voice of man and babe. With each flash, he increased his pace. He had to get this over with. He had to prove his worth.

A powerful wind rushed from behind, pushing like a giant hand. Izhur's long hair whipped his face and he shivered. A fat drop of rain slammed onto his cheek, quickly followed by another on his moccasin. The dark clouds above released their cargo all at once and the rain drilled down, icy and hard.

Izhur's foot slipped on the rocky path that led to the altar. He slowed and held the baby close – her warmth, a strange comfort on his chest. She stopped her mewling and nestled in to the beads that hung around Izhur's neck – the two threads, one of wood, one of azurite – that marked him as a young Soragan.

Izhur patted her back through his thick wolf skin tunic as he walked. But he shouldn't have. He should have remained cold, distant. How else could he prepare to do the task that had been assigned him? This was to be his first sacrifice. The first night of Ilun was presenting him with all manner of challenges he'd never faced before. Even in his time as novice to Jokam, he'd not attended a human sacrifice.

As he walked, he thought back on the meeting with the Eight and grimaced. Zodor and his bespurned influence. The man was a skilled hunter. No one could doubt that, but he knew nothing about the Benevolent Ones. He knew nothing of the Otherworld, and he knew even less about the Malfir. This sacrifice was wrong. Even a Soragan prentice could see that. Still, Izhur would have his own small influence. The corners of his mouth twitched.

Izhur had made a decision, back in his tree-dwell while he hastily prepared. He would not sacrifice this innocent to the Malfir. It would offer the demons too much, and he couldn't bear the thought of them tearing apart her spirit, consuming all the power of her light, only to make them stronger. No, he would give her back to the Otherworld – to Ona.

Jokam had taught him the ritual, of course. And Izhur had prepared the implements back in his tree-dwell. But now it was raining. How was he supposed to keep the oil pot alight?

Never mind that. Just get to the altar.

Again he quickened his step, and again the lightning blazed. Closer. A clap of thunder roared and seemed to shift the rock beneath his feet. The wind whipped his hair into his eyes and his foot hit a large glossy protuberance. Izhur fell, twisted and landed on his back, cushioning the babe's fall.

"Great Mother," he whispered. Lightning flashed and he glimpsed the rain like fine darts pelting toward him from a black void.

He lay on his back a little longer and the baby nestled once more. Her warmth halted his shivering. He had to get up, keep moving.

He stood and adjusted his satchel. The babe moaned. With soft words, he soothed her and returned to the rocky path, limping.

The altar stood in the centre of a large chasm. Made of hard rock, it had been carved out of the granite many winters past by long dead ancestors. A flash of lightning revealed its stature and the gruesome faces that had been carved into its side – two headed beasts with the maws of lions, the eyes of snakes and the ears of bats – silent guardians. Iridescent lines etched into its surface shone blue with each flash of light. The winter altar was a dark, grim place, so different to the altars in their spring and summer lands. It was, after all, a place where they normally sacrificed to the Malfir. An animal every winter was given over; it was the only ritual that Izhur hated. Usually small animals were sacrificed, sometimes a larger beast like a deer or wolf – especially during Ilun. Izhur had never seen a child bled. It happened. He knew it. But to see it – to do it …

He sucked his cheeks and stepped forward, hoping he could send her to the Benevolent Ones rather than to the clutches of the Malfir. Usually, such a sacrifice required the presence of the clan, to offer their support and energy to the Soragan. But the Eight had charged him with sacrificing the child to the Malfir, and this was a task performed by the Soragan alone, lest evil spirits contaminate clan members. The Eight would remain ignorant to Izhur's plan. As long as they knew she was dead, they'd have no knowledge of which realm she'd been given over to. Izhur swallowed. He would have to draw on the energy of nature.

Wind circled the chasm in frenzied chaos, sending rain sideways. It stung Izhur's bare cheeks and he wished for the warmth of his rabbit-skin hood. He stepped carefully lest he fall again.

The altar seemed too large for the baby. Its slick surface gleamed briefly with each flash of light. Izhur laid Neria and Osun's daughter on the center and tightened the swaddling clothes, a vain attempt to keep her dry, warm. He fumbled with the satchel, removing the necessary items: an oak root, a vial of sacred water, the oil pot, and a knife made from bronze magic. Its orange sheen glinted with each lightning strike. Before, back in his tree-dwell, Izhur had sharpened and polished it.

He bent to sink his fingers into the rocky soil and clench a palmful of mud which he put on the altar at the baby's feet. He placed the oil pot near her head, the oak root to her right and the vial of water on her left.

The rain teemed. Small puddles pooled on the surface of the altar. Izhur's wolf-fur cloak hung heavily on his narrow shoulders, saturated. It tugged with each gust of wind, and he gripped the altar to keep balance. He clenched his jaw to stop his teeth from chattering. Lighting the oil pot would be impossible. Even if he succeeded, the rain would drench the flame in an instant.

A thick branch of lightning sparked the rock somewhere up above, and the thunder echoed round the chasm. The baby screamed. Izhur looked up. Angry sparks of light blinked into a dark infinity revealing purple, blue and charcoal mountains of cloud. The sky roiled.

A dark creature, bird or bat, flapped its wings and flew up amongst the clouds and lightning. Its screech echoed around the chasm. Izhur frowned hoping it wasn't another omen.

The lightning would have to do as a replacement for the flame, but he kept the oil pot in its position. Next, he took the knife, his hand shaking. He tested the blade and sucked in a breath when he pricked his skin. A single red steak ran down his hand, mingling with the rain.

The baby screamed, still. Her swaddles had loosened and one little arm waved at him. Izhur closed his eyes and started the chant. "Ona, Goda, Imbrit, Atoll, Mittha, Utun, Tonat, Shephet." Repeating the names of the Benevolent Ones, beckoning them to hear him and accept his sacrifice.

It happened quickly this time. His surprise nearly sent him straight back, but Izhur steadied his mind as he looked through the plane of the Otherworld. All around him the pale silver streaks of rain fell in odd directions. When he looked to the altar, the golden light of the infant burned – her blinding light.

He couldn't help but marvel at its strength. At its centre, a red core gave way to gold circular rays pulsing outward toward him. So much power. What were they giving up?

He steadied himself. He had to do this. He had to show them he was a Soragan – their Soragan.

Izhur forced his hand forward. It clutched the knife, a black shadow that moved shakily with the tremor of his hand. His lips mouthed the chant "… earth, water, fire …" and his voice carried, filling the chasm. He drew from the power of nature, gaining energy from the trees, the rain, even the rock, until his voice boomed, matching that of the thunderous storm. A deep thrill ran through his being like a euphoric wave. He'd never felt so much power before. It would have been all too easy to give in to the rush, to pass over fully, but he focused and calmed.

"Take this child into your bosom." His words echoed. His arm lifted and braced just above the babe's heart. "She is our gift to you."

The world paused, like something had been registered, and then it started again.

Izhur's arm shot downward.

One blue streak darted through the Otherworld and struck Izhur's hand. The knife flew. Izhur was thrown backwards and smacked the side of the chasm. The crack of thunder deafened and his mind snapped back from the Otherworld.

He opened his eyes, and the pain in his back forced them shut for a heart beat. He looked to his hand. There was no mark, no burn, but the lightning had snatched the knife.

What about the babe? She was silent. Had he struck her?

Gradually, he stood. The rain drilled harder. A streak of fire ran down his spine, but he sucked his breath and took a small shuffling step toward the altar.

Lightning came and went and he saw the small bundle on the altar where he had left it. He shuffled closer, one foot in front of the other until he stood above her. Her little hand still waved at him, and for the first time that night, Izhur smiled.

He scooped her up and laughed and let his tears mix with rain.

"It's a sign, little one. A sign!"

He didn't bother with the oil pot or the vial of sacred water. He left his satchel exactly where it sat on the ground. He braced the child to his chest and ran, ignoring the screaming pain in his back. His feet slid on the rocks, but the lightning lit his way. *He was the Soragan.* They had to listen to him. They must listen, for Ona had surely spoken this night.

The tree-dwells stood as he had left them, though the rain now made them glisten with each lightning strike and the large boughs swayed in the wind. The hearth fires burned low, but were still visible through the small cutouts of the shelters. He went to the one at the center, the most privileged – Zordor's tree-dwell, set high in an elm.

Izhur stood at the foot of the tree and filling his lungs, yelled into the pelting rain. "She is no sacrifice! She is no sacrifice!"

His voice screamed in the night. The clan came out of their shelters. Some stood at the entrance to their tree-dwells; others descended slowly and lingered on the ground with a square of hide held above their heads.

"She is not to be sacrificed." Izhur pumped a fist in the air, his voice rasping.

"What is the meaning of this, you fool?" It was Zodor. The great hunter didn't bother with a cloak to protect him from the icy rain. He marched toward Izhur and stood over him in nothing but a short tunic. Zodor's unbound hair whipped around him and his muscles, like carved flint, gleamed in the flashes of lightning that still flicked through the night.

Izhur's eyes filled with fire as he stared up at Zodor. "I tell you, she is not a sacrifice, she is a gift from Ona herself."

"Madness." Zodor's voice boomed. His eyes burned with anger. "The Eight decided."

"The Eight was wrong. I am the Soragan—"

"You are mad."

"I've seen her light."

"You've seen her evil."

A pause stalled them. They stood opposite each other, breathing hard.

"Give her to me." Zodor held out his hands.

"No."

"Give her to me." The hunter grasped for her, but Izhur stepped back. Zodor lifted a fist and struck.

But Izhur struck too and a blue light sparked within his hand. It shot out like a spear of fire and hit Zodor full on the chest. The big hunter was picked up and thrown back.

Clan members gasped and two of the men ran over to kneel by Zodor who now lay limp on the wet ground. One by one, the small crowd turned to look at their Soragan.

Izhur took the moment. His vision swirled as though he trod the fine edge between this world and the Other. "I am Soragan here. I say again – I have seen her light; she is no sacrifice." His voice echoed through the night, and boomed louder than any thunder.

And the clan bowed their heads.

PART II
SUMMER OF THE FOREST

YULI

*Y*uli scratched his ear. A fly buzzed nearby and he swatted at it.

"Be still and learn," Izhur hissed. The Soragan's irritation was obvious, even to a boy who was almost five summers old.

"Watch how she breathes; look how she concentrates." Soragan Izhur's eyes stayed fixed upon the girl.

Yuli shifted his weight and tried to do what he was told. He studied the girl, Iluna. She was just four moons younger than Yuli; he'd known her all his short life. They'd shared his mother's milk as babies because her own mother died giving birth. Yuli's father sometimes said that Iluna had cursed her mother. He said this to Yuli's mother and Ugot and some of the other adults when he thought Yuli wasn't listening. No one liked the girl. No one except for Izhur; although Yuli's mother seemed to have a soft spot for her. Yuli didn't like that. Neither did his father.

The girl stood about five big steps away in a small clearing, as still as a winter's morning. Although she could have been further. Yuli could only count to five. Iluna could count to ahunred. Yuli didn't like that either. His father said she was too clever for a girl her age.

Yuli had to squint through the branches of a small birch to watch. She was trying to summon an animal. He didn't know which animal. He wasn't listening when they'd discussed it earlier. He wasn't listening when Izhur explained to them how it was done. Soragan Izhur would have to explain it all over again for Yuli.

But it didn't look too complicated. All she did was stand in the middle of the forest and look around. He could see her wide nose and mouth. Frog-Face, they called her sometimes. And her messy hair. She always had knots because she didn't have a mother to untangle them for her. The way she cocked her head on an angle because she was deaf in one ear always made her look like a durg. Not that Yuli had ever seen a durg. They were rare; most of them were exposed as babies or small children. But he'd heard the evenfire stories about them.

Anyway, Iluna looked silly, but he swallowed a giggle. He didn't want to get into trouble again. Izhur would give him another long lecture and tell his mother, and then his mother would give him a punishment, like make him wash old Aunt Zelda's under tunics. He hated doing old Aunt Zelda's under tunics; they were stinky.

Iluna raised her arm and turned her hand so that her palm faced the sky. It all looked easy enough, and boring. Lessons with Soragan Izhur were always boring. He shifted his weight to the other foot and slouched.

"That's it, slowly now," Izhur whispered, his eyes still hadn't moved from the girl.

The fly came back, its buzzing echoed through Yuli's ear. Maybe she was trying to summon the fly. Yuli giggled.

"Shhh." Izhur pursed his lips that way he did whenever he disapproved. His narrow eyes would squint, and he would rub his temple. Izhur was always pursing his lips around Yuli.

Yuli sighed and turned his attention back to Iluna for the third time, and froze. Something moved. On the other side of the clearing. There was something and it was big, for the branches and vines of the forest were moving as though a breeze swayed them one way, then the other. But there was no breeze. The day remained as still as a sleeping doe.

Yuli took a small step back. The forest was dangerous. He'd seen his father's wounds. Deep scars and gashes lined his arms and chest. His father was the greatest hunter of all the clans, but even he wouldn't stand still in the face of a wolf or a lion, or a bear! Not without a weapon.

Yuli took another step and a twig snapped.

"Be still, Yuli. Do as you are told." Izhur looked at him this time with eyebrows that met in a frown. His slender nose paled as he pursed his lips again.

Yuli frowned too. He wanted to run back to his mother. She would wrap him up in her arms and he would be safe. But that wouldn't please Father. His father wanted him to be brave, like his older brother, Anton. Yuli swallowed a lump and returned to watching Iluna.

She had both arms out now and her head held high. It didn't seem right, her looking like that – like she was important. Her hair was even messier from that angle, and when she lifted her arms you could see holes in her tunic. She didn't have a mother or a father, so she had no one to mend it for her.

The trees moved again and a deep noise came from the forest. Was it a growl? Yuli felt the corners of his mouth turn downwards and his bottom lip poke out like whenever Anton played one of his nasty jokes. He couldn't help it. He tried to be brave and make himself still. But then he saw fur – grey, no, brown. A wolf? The beast came closer; more rustling. It was too big for a wolf. Another growl sounded, louder this time, deeper, and it was too much for Yuli. He yelped and ran. His little legs pounded the path back to their tree-dwells, his arms circled crazily and he yelled for his mother as he sprinted.

"Yuli, no!" The strained calls of Izhur came from behind, but he didn't stop, he didn't look back.

He kept running and screaming, "Ma, Ma!" Even when he saw the tree-dwells he didn't stop. He raced under the old trees to the clan's evenfire, a large smoking pit. A few people sat in small groups preparing vegetables and seed cakes. Yuli spotted his mother and flew into her lap, ignoring the sniggers from Sita and Uncle Graig.

"Yuli? What is it?" Her voice soothed him instantly. She had been peeling pigeon peas for the coming feast, her hands smelled of comfort and love. Her arms embraced him and Yuli closed his eyes. He was safe.

IZHUR

*I*zhur hurried, grimacing every time the skirt of his long tunic caught on a branch. He had spent too long meditating, trying to find answers to Iluna's growing talents. She'd almost performed a summoning, and not for any small animal either. Invoking large creatures, dangerous predators, was a skill that most Soragans could only achieve after years of practice, or not at all. She would have succeeded, too, if Yuli hadn't broken her concentration.

Yuli.

Izhur frowned. The boy had talent, yes, but it was little in comparison to Iluna's. He was spoiled by his parents, his father in particular. Zodor had filled his mind with self-important nonsense, and if the child was to become the clan's next Soragan, that would not do.

Izhur decided he would speak with Yuli's mother, Ida, about the episode in the forest. She was supportive and seemed to understand Izhur's frustrations with the boy. He nearly always talked to her about Yuli's progress, as he spoke with Zodor rarely, in the Circle, and only when he had to.

Life as Soragan was easier for Izhur these days. Since that

night almost five winters past when he'd stood up to Zodor, the night that Iluna was given to them, things had changed.

Amak and Lral had immediately sided with him, arguing for the clan to keep the babe and raise her as a member. They'd supported Izhur ever since. Elder Jarel had passed to the Other-world two winters ago and Wogul had replaced him on the Circle of Eight. Wogul was Lral's cousin and he supported Izhur without question. But Zodor still had his defenders. Ugot was his ever faithful disciple. As was Tod. And Flynth was too set in her ways to fathom changing her allegiance. The whole clan was divided in their support. It was not ideal, and Izhur blamed the stubbornness and rigidity of Zodor. But as the circle of time kept turning, more people saw Izhur's worth and respected him as Soragan and leader.

Izhur's tunic caught again. A rose thorn, as long as his thumb-nail, had penetrated the soft leather. He untangled it, trying not to tear the hole further.

"Tsk. I'm already late, spurn it to Malfiren!" Sometimes Izhur wished Soragans could wear the short tunics everyone else did in summer. It would be cooler too.

He freed himself of the rose and marched on, quickening his pace and berating himself for losing track of time in meditation.

A scout had arrived yesterday. The Wolf clan's visitors would make it in time for the evenfire tonight. The Bear and Eagle had been traveling over the last eightnight and joined their clans where the smaller river they called 'Little Sister' met with the larger Mittha's River – the great river that connected all eight clans of Ona's people. The Wolf had spent the better part of an eightnight preparing for the feast. The hunters had brought in a boar, two does, rabbits, mountain pigeon and quail. When he'd left with Iluna and Yuli that morning, a large harvest of vegeta-bles, fruit and legumes had already been collected. It sat in baskets dotted around the evenfire pit, awaiting the cooks.

As Soragan, Izhur had duties to perform at the evenfire to

mark the arrival of their guests. He had to get there before sunset. The daysun danced along the horizon. He cursed himself again and moved on at a light jog.

By the time he arrived the daysun had descended leaving a purple sky in its wake and Atoll's star, blinking in the east. He rubbed his temple as he slowed to a walk. The evenfire, a large blaze that served them for cooking, celebrating and warding off animals, gave off a bright glow. The dual aromas of roasted boar and venison spiraled and Izhur suddenly realised he hadn't eaten since dawn.

The three clans had assembled and Izhur blinked at all the people. They easily filled the large circle of space around the evenfire located between a wall of rock that cut off hot southern winds, and their tree-dwells. The Wolf was small compared to the other clans and he was not accustomed to so many bodies. There were at least three one hundreds assembled, waiting for the celebration to begin.

Zodor stood at the front.

"Bollocks of Dragos!" Izhur whispered. He rarely cursed. But when he saw the hunter addressing the crowd, the profanity escaped his lips.

As he drew closer, some of the clan members turned to look at him. Hogath smiled in relief. Villa gave him a frown. That was no surprise; Ugot's wife had never liked him. Izhur had long ago stopped trying to win her approval, along with some of the others in the Wolf clan. Their type always considered people not born in the clan as outsiders.

"We of the Wolf welcome our brothers and sisters from the Eagle and the Bear," Zodor addressed the crowd.

Izhur stepped forward to interrupt. "Yes. We of the Wolf, welcome you."

Zodor gave him a typical hard stare and whispered, "You're here, Soragan. We had to start without you, the daysun—"

"Yes, thank you, Zodor. I am here now." Izhur nodded briskly and turned away from the hunter to face the other members of the Circle of Eight. Amak smiled and gave him a wink. Ugot chewed on a tulu nut and gave him a frown. "Where is your cloak?" he hissed.

Izhur closed his eyes. *Spurn it!* In his rush he'd forgotten his ceremonial wolfskin. He took a breath and opened his eyes. Ugot spat in his typical fashion. He'd have to do it without the cloak.

Izhur turned and faced the three clans assembled beyond the flames of the evenfire. Its heat touched his face. It was his role to welcome them in the name of their universal Mother, Ona. Zodor knew that, just as he knew that Izhur would have come; the hunter should have waited.

"We welcome you in our Mother's name." His voice easily floated over the three clans and would have filled the tops of the tree-dwells too. He called on the buzz of energy to lift it, adding a sense of power. The people bowed their heads. "We ask Ona to watch over us during the day with her all powerful daysun, and for the Benevolent Atoll to watch over us in the darkness of night with his star." Izhur gestured to the east where Atoll's Star shone more brightly, its familiar blue lighting the darkening sky. "We also call upon the spirit of the wolf, who is most clever of hunters and always protects her own. May the wolf extend her protection to our guests this midsummer." Izhur finished the blessings then stepped back into line with the rest of his Circle members, ignoring the hard glare from Zodor.

It was now time for the Soragans of the the visiting clans to extend their own blessing. Belwas of the Bear was to go first, as he was the elder of the two Soragans. Izhur smiled at his old friend. It was good to see a familiar face. Belwas had identified Izhur's gift as a small child. He'd always been a father figure, particularly after Izhur's own father had died from the water sickness before he could even walk.

Belwas gave him a warm smile in return. He wore a bear skin cloak and the hood was made from the bear's head. The eyes had been replaced with the lapis lazuli that was common in the Bear's summer lands. They glistened in the firelight. Belwas turned to speak to the assembly, clutching the large walking staff that seemed to make him more imposing.

"We of the Bear," his voice was deep and melodic and filled the open space even more powerfully than Izhur's had, "call upon the spirit of our totem, the Bear, who is the most ferocious of hunters and a playful mother. May she extend to us her protection and joy this midsummer."

Tyvan took his place in front of the evenfire. Large feathers stood out from his headdress and the shoulders of his cloak. But his skinny frame was a sharp contrast to Belwas's tall robust figure. Tyvan had only been Soragan of the Eagle since the summer before. He wore a single thread of wooden beads that he received when noviced. He was still to earn his azurite beads. That would come with the next Agria in three summer's time. His voice was markedly weaker than Izhur's and Belwas's had been and his nervousness made him waver. But he did his job and called on the spirit of the eagle to protect the three clans with her wisdom and precision.

With the formalities over, a drum sounded and the crowd mingled. The cooks of the Wolf cut the spitted meat with their precious copper knives and took boiling clay pots off the coals, and began serving the hungry crowd. People embraced and carried on conversations they would have started two summers past when the three clans had shared midsummer in the lands of the Eagle, high up in the alps. Izhur smiled when he remembered the children's astonishment at the summer snow.

Kin were reuniting too. There had been many couple-bonds between the three clans over the years. Their close proximity made it easier to visit each other. Not everyone would reunite with family tonight though. Poor Tenila, Belal's wife, had come from the Otter clan whose lands were far away to the south and took at least a moon of travel to get to. She sat off to one side nibbling on a caroot looking decidedly sad. And Ida, Zodor's wife, had come from the Snake; they weren't much closer.

Izhur looked for Belwas. The old bear was the closest person he had to family. He walked toward the evenfire and saw the large Soragan chatting with old Petral. He stalled, not wanting to get involved. Petral was a boor and Izhur had no wish to succumb to a lengthy rendition of the old man's rheumatism complaints.

The laughter of children came from behind him and Izhur turned to see Yuli chasing three girls from the Eagle clan. They screamed and laughed as they ran around without a care. One of the girls collided into Aunt Zelda's vast bottom as she bent to get her second serving of seed cake, and nearly knocked the large woman off her feet.

Yuli threw something at the girl. It hit her fair on her forehead, spoiling the band of feathers in her hair. The girl's mouth opened in shock and she picked the thing up and threw it back. Izhur squinted. It was a cut of meat from the feast, fatty and moist. It fell short of Yuli and he poked his tongue at the girl before bending to pick it up again.

"Yuli!" Izhur gritted his teeth. "Come here, now."

People turned to see what the problem was and Izhur altered his scowl, smoothing his features. Yuli poked his bottom lip out, but dropped the cut of meat and strutted over to Izhur at once.

"Do you think Shephet gave us the forest animals for you to throw their meat around like a plaything?"

Yuli's bottom lip extended almost as far as his round belly. "We were just having fun."

"Fun? Is that what you call it? Throwing good food around. Scaring poor Aunt Zelda."

Yuli frowned and bowed his head.

"Yuli." A familiar voice.

Izhur turned to see Ida. His breath caught a little the way it always did when he saw her. She was easily the most beautiful woman in all eight clans of Ona's people. With hair that shone like the silk spun by spiders, and skin as smooth as the buds of spring. Izhur checked himself. He was Soragan. Coupling was not an option for him. Not that it would have been an option at all. Ida was Zodor's wife.

"Go to the tree-dwell." Her voice was quiet but stern as she looked at her son.

Yuli pouted again and stomped his feet. "No! I was only having fun. How come the girls don't get into trouble?"

"Yuli, the tree-dwell. Now!" Ida remained calm, but there was fire in her eyes.

"But I'm hungry." Yuli's voice changed to a whimper, the way a child half his age might talk when scolded. But it was hardly convincing. His mouth and cheeks were still stained with the honey glaze that sweetened the meat.

"You need to listen to our Soragan. Treating our sacred food in such a way is wasteful. If you were hungry you should have sat respectfully. Now go. We shall talk more, later."

Yuli stomped his foot again, but turned and headed off toward the tree-dwells.

"Izhur, I am sorry."

Izhur shook his head. How was it that Zodor was such a pig-headed rock and yet his wife was full of wisdom? She could see the flaws in her sons, even though she loved them fiercely, like a she-wolf.

"It is not your fault."

Ida smiled and Izhur's heart fluttered again. "I spoil him too much. Did he disobey you? I will punish him. Aunt Zelda would appreciate her tunics being washed again."

Izhur smiled. Aunt Zelda's laziness was renowned. She had swarms of children, grandchildren, nephews and nieces, all of whom she used to do her chores while she grew fatter with every summer.

"He was excited to see the other children. Perhaps I was too harsh."

Ida looked to the ground. "And what of your lessons today? Yuli ran out of the forest like a frightened rabbit. I assume he disobeyed you in some task again."

"No, he didn't disobey." Izhur lied, not wanting to get into the complexities of what they were doing exactly. The clan had allowed Iluna to be part of the Wolf all those years ago, but no one trusted her, or befriended her.

No one except for Izhur and Ida, and old Agath, of course. But Ida had to hide her affections. Zodor detested the girl and his sons had inherited his hatred. No one approved of Izhur teaching Iluna. But he'd convinced the Eight that, if he didn't, it would be dangerous. This had only scared them more. Now clan members often performed a sign of warding to repel evil – crossing their thumbs and touching four fingertips together in an arch – whenever she walked past. It was a problem. But at least they did it behind her back. Iluna seemed to remain ignorant of their fear.

"He just got scared. No need for him to wash Aunt Zelda's smalls." *Although the boy could do with some hard physical work.*

"Scared? Was there trouble?" Ida's eyes widened.

"No trouble." Izhur lied again. He really wasn't sure how much trouble there could have been, if Iluna had succeeded in the summoning. It was reckless of him to allow it but his excitement often got the better of him. "Sometimes lessons of the Otherworld can frighten small children."

Ida nodded. Everyone had nightmares about the Otherworld and Malfiren as children. This wasn't helped by the popular evenfire stories that adults would tell at night.

"Let me know if I can help. His father is keen that he becomes Soragan one day."

"I will."

"And Iluna, I've noticed her tunic is worse. It has more holes than a hive." Ida glanced around and lowered her voice.

"Tomorrow I will give you another for her – an old one of Yuli's. He has grown out of it."

"Thank you, Ida. I will give it to her. She will be grateful."

Ida smiled again before leaving Izhur to watch the sway of her hips as she walked toward the evenfire.

"Thinking of missed opportunities?"

Izhur jumped and turned to see Belwas grinning down at him before nodding toward Ida. His bear cloak now gone, he stood in a simple light tunic; the multiple colours from the many beads he wore around his neck reflecting in the evenfire light.

Izhur blushed. "Belwas. It's good to see you."

The two Soragans embraced and Belwas put a meaty hand on Izhur's shoulder as they walked over to the feast laid out beside the evenfire.

"Love. It is a difficult sacrifice for us Soragans." Belwas winked. "Believe me I know what I'm talking about. I had a tumble in the bushes before I bent my head for these heavy rocks." He grasped the beads.

Izhur shook his head, unable to stop a grin. "I'm not yearning for love, Belwas."

Belwas winked again. "Well, you should be. Oh, those heady days with Bolga; I'll never forget her quivering bosom."

A short laugh escaped Izhur's throat. "Quivering bosom?"

Belwas looked around. His thick curls glinted in the firelight; there was more grey than black now. "Let's stow away to your tree-dwell before we get dragged into another boring conversation. Talking to old Petral about his piles almost had me falling asleep. It's been a long journey. I need some comfort. And we can talk more freely about your love life then." He turned back to Izhur. "Or Bolga's quivering bosom."

Izhur laughed again. "Come with me then, you old Bear."

∞

"STILL LIKE IT STRONG, BELWAS?"

"Oh, yes, and do you have any of that rose stuff? Such a rare treat for us of the Bear."

"I do, my friend." Izhur finished pouring the mint water into two clay cups and reached to the upper shelf of his tree-dwell for the jar of ground hips. Strictly speaking, they were for healing, but Belwas had a sweet tooth, and Izhur knew how his old friend enjoyed nature's gifts. It would help his fatigue, too. It had been a long journey for the Bear. Travelling a full eightnight from dawn to dusk in the height of summer was no easy task. Even for the young.

Izhur added the rose hip powder, along with mountain honey, and stirred.

"This will refresh you."

"Thank you, Izhur."

Izhur sat on a cushioned wolfskin next to Belwas. The two Soragans sipped the cool brew in silence, the scent of mint and rose filling the modest space. Three oil pots were dotted around – one on the ground before them and two higher on the shelves, revealing the small collection of clay jars – powders and potions typical of a Soragan's store. Izhur reclined and allowed himself to relax, listening to the summer crickets as they sang a night song. A breeze, as light as a butterfly's touch danced through the tree-dwell, cooling them.

"How was the journey?" Izhur asked after a time.

Belwas shrugged as he massaged one foot with a fat hand. "Good. Plenty of game on the way. No injuries or illnesses to speak of. The children behaved themselves. A bit boring really."

Izhur laughed. "Don't tell me you were wishing for ill luck!"

"Nothing too grave; just something bad enough to make an old Soragan feel useful again. There wasn't even a nightmare to interpret."

Izhur's smile faded. "Be careful of what you wish, Belwas."

Belwas eyed him beneath his large brows. "You're right. I should be happy that my own nightmares have let me alone for so long."

Izhur frowned. "You've had nightmares?"

Belwas grimaced. "Yes, and they all had the unshakeable sense of premontion about them."

"You've seen something ill-omened? About your clan's future?"

"Well, I'm not sure."

"Tell me about them."

Belwas stroked his beard with a fat hand. "It was the most difficult, unclear set of images, Izhur. The dreams were filled with bloody destruction, great chaos and horror." His bushy brows met in a frown. "I find them impossible to interpret."

"Can you identify the people in them?"

Belwas shook his head. "The dreams were strong in their emotions. I could feel the horror and sadness, but it was difficult to see what was happening."

"And you haven't had the dream since you left your river lands?"

"No, I haven't had the dreams since we left Agria."

"Agria? Why didn't you mention it then?"

Belwas shook his head again. "Because it wasn't until later, in my meditations, that I realised what the dreams were."

"You're convinced they were a premonition?"

"Yes, the trouble is I can't fathom what. There were two images that were clear, and consistently vivid in the dreams. Two animals always appeared."

"Animals? Totems perhaps. What were they?"

Belwas looked at him. "A raven and a wolf."

Izhur frowned. The wolf was Yuli's totem – and it was considered a very fortunate omen to have the same totem as one's clan. But the raven? A shiver shook him. Such a totem would be most unlucky.

"Well, never mind all of that," Belwas interrupted Izhur's thoughts, his voice back to its usual jolly tone. "How go things for you? Last we met you hadn't long taken up your new position in the Wolf. Zodor still seems to cause you concern."

"You noticed some tension between us?"

"I've been a Soragan for more than thirty summers, Izhur. These old eyes don't miss much."

Izhur sighed. "It's been difficult. I've had to work hard to gain respect. They didn't accept me at first, the way they accepted Jakom."

"Jakom was very old. Older than me even. I've never seen anyone with the like of his power. Not even the Grand Soragan."

"I agree. Everyone respected it."

"Yes," Belwas assented. "But he was once like you, Izhur. He struggled at the beginning, as we all do."

Izhur blinked. "I can't imagine that. I can't see him ever faltering or not knowing what to do."

"Well, he did. Just as I did. Wisdom comes with experience, and age, most regretfully."

Izhur shook his head slowly as he refilled their cups. "What if I were to tell you that here, in the Wolf, is a Gift-born whose light is even greater than that of Jakom's?"

Belwas snapped his gaze to Izhur, eyes wide.

Izhur cleared his throat. "Belwas, I need to tell you about our return here from the last Agria. I need to confide in you."

The old Soragan took a sip of tea and nodded. "You have my ear, friend."

"When we returned that summer, our forests had been burned. It was clear that a long drought had taken its toll. We guessed that a lightning strike set off a fire in the grasslands south of here and the burning went deep into the forest."

"Really? Well it doesn't look that way now. It's all green as ever in your hinterlands."

"The forest regenerates quickly. Sometimes we burn sections of it ourselves to enable this regrowth."

"Fascinating."

"Yes, but that's not what I want to tell you." His eyes met Belwas's. "That year we'd had much bad luck. One of our little ones had broken his leg coming out of a tree."

"It happens. I'm sure Amak fixed it well."

"She did." Izhur nodded. "And then in the winter our clan suffered the sickness that took Jakom and Istia."

Belwas's eyes closed. He and Jakom were close friends.

"In the spring one of our best hunters, Osun, died, fighting off a lion. Even now I can't fathom how it happened. He was a wise fighter, not foolhardy. His woman, Neria, was pregnant."

"Yes," Belwas interrupted. "I remember her at Agria; she had many friends."

Izhur nodded. "It was the following winter, the night that marked the first of Ilun. That's when her baby came."

Belwas leaned forward. "Ilunnight?"

"Neria had struggled with the labor all night and day. When the daysun went down Amak summoned me. I had never attended a birth before, and it was my first Ilun as Soragan." Izhur's eyes reached out for comfort in his old friend. "A storm approached, but I persevered. I couldn't save Neria, but ..." He rubbed his temple. "The baby – I saved her, and she had the strongest light I have even seen – in anyone."

"Indeed? And she lives now?"

"She does. She is a member of our clan. Well, if you can call it that." Izhur hesitated. The truth was Iluna had barely been accepted at all. She lived with the clan's tamatu, or low one, old Agath. Their tree-dwell was out in the forest and they had very little to do with the clan. Izhur and Amak were the only ones who interacted with Agath at all. He cleared his throat and continued. "But that is where Zodor and I disagreed; in truth we still do. He ordered her to be sacrificed."

'Sacrificed?" Belwas frowned. "We haven't sacrificed a human for many winters. And who is Zodor to ask that of you? Such an order must come from the Eight, not an individual."

Izhur clenched his teeth. "As I said, he had great respect amongst us. He was our unspoken leader for a time. He still wields much influence."

"But so do you now. I have seen that."

"Yes, it is true. But it is all because of her." Izhur let out a sharp breath. "I tried to enact their order, to carry out the sacrifice. I went to the altar. I had everything prepared. There was a storm. I couldn't light the oil pot. I thought the lightning could stand in place of fire. So, I conducted the ritual. But when I raised my arm, ready to strike, lightning bolted to me and the knife was thrown from my hand." Izhur bent his head. "I never did find that knife."

The old Bear's eyes widened before he lifted his cup and finished the brew in one great gulp. "How old is she now?"

"She will be five soon, this winter. They named her Iluna." Izhur finished his own drink and wiped his mouth. "I've been training her, along with Yuli. She has much talent already."

Belwas inclined his head. "Tell me."

"Today, she nearly summoned a mountain lion."

Belwas's mouth fell open and he blinked. "I best take a look at this child." He squinted at his cup. "Now that was very refreshing, but I think our conversation requires some stronger elixir." He pulled out a leather cask from his satchel. "Care for some alza?"

ANTON

*J*t was Anton's idea to play Circle in the forest meadow, well away from the adults. At seven summers he was the eldest, the leader. He faced the other children – three fellow Wolves, two Bears and two Eagles.

"We need elders – a Soragan, a medicine woman, and a hunter. I, first son of Zodor, the Great Wolf," he said, as he beat a fist to his chest, "I will be the hunter." He pointed the stick he held at Hennita, a younger girl from the Bear. Their parents had arranged their couple-bond. But that wouldn't happen for ages. "You will be my wife, so you will sit on the Circle as our family elder."

Hennita smiled and skipped to his side, her dark curls bouncing.

"Who wants to be the medicine woman?" he asked next.

Botha, a little Eagle girl who had become friendly with Hennita shot her hands up. "Me, I wanna be medicine woman."

Anton nodded and Botha skipped to Hennita's side.

"Yuli." Anton turned to his brother. "You should be our Soragan."

Yuli smiled and waddled his head as he walked to his big brother's left side.

"The rest of you are elders. Let's sit."

Anton decided they were a clan about to make a long journey to winter grounds.

"We have to shoose," Yuli announced to the others. "Do we go here?" He used the long stick to point at a map drawn in the dirt. "Or here?"

"Choose, not shoose." Anton grabbed the stick from his brother. "There's been snow and hungry wolves here." He drew a crooked circle in the dirt. "So we will go here." And the stick moved a little way south to a rough looking square.

The two girls from the Bear clan giggled.

"Why do you laugh, wife?" Anton growled.

Hennita looked at him wide-eyed. "Nuthin."

"She's not your wife."

They all turned to look at the intruder who had interrupted their game.

Iluna perched in the shadows, one leg bent in a triangle.

Anton frowned. "Go away, Frog Face, no one wants you here."

Iluna thrust her chin forward and shrugged her shoulders. "She's still not your wife."

"Go away or I cuss you." Yuli pointed his finger toward her the way he thought that cursing occurred.

"It's curse, Yuli, not cuss," Iluna replied.

Anton gripped the stick and walked up to Iluna. "You must go away. We're holding a Circle meeting. You're not one of us. You're nothing."

Iluna stumbled back, but lifted her head higher. "I will be part of the Circle one day. I will be Soragan."

Anton laughed. "You'll never be Soragan. You'll probably wind up a witch."

The other children sniggered.

"Yeah, a frog-faced witch!" Anton's best friend Caldon bent over as he laughed.

"And she *will* be my wife." Anton pointed toward Hennita. "We've been promised."

Iluna turned and walked back into the forest. Anton watched her go, his eyes squinting.

"So where we go, brother?" Yuli asked, looking at the map.

"Ya, where we go?" Hennita giggled.

Anton threw the stick toward the forest. "I want to play a new game. Let's hunt witches."

∞

Next summer, his eighth, Anton would begin his training as hunter. He was already tall and strong, and his father had been teaching him from a young age. His natural skills led him to practise the hunt, even as a young boy. And now, during midsummer, he had other children to impress, including his future wife.

Anton tracked Iluna to the waterfall, but then lost her trail. Yuli tugged at his arm and was about to speak, but Anton put a stiffened finger to his younger brother's lips.

"Quiet, the witch is close."

He back-tracked to the last clue of Iluna's path through the forest – a broken branch on a cypress. His eyes scanned the ground. He saw it then, a footprint, pointing toward the rock pool. She must have gone swimming. He looked to the waterfall and smiled. He had learned her secret.

"Can we go now?" Hennita whined. "I'm hungry."

Anton's first thought was to scowl at the girl, but then a plan came to mind.

"It's hot. Let's go swimming before we go back. It will cool us."

43

The other children clapped their hands. Three ran the short distance along a rock path and jumped into the pool before Anton had a chance to tell the the rest of his plan.

"Yuli, Hennita, Caldon and Botha come here." He gestured for them to huddle close. "The witch, she is behind the waterfall, let's get her."

Yuli's eyes widened. "Ya, let's get her," he repeated.

"This is going to be fun." Caldon wore a wicked smile.

"I dunno." Hennita looked at her feet. "I'm hungry."

Anton sighed. "Hunters don't care about their hunger. We have to get the witch, remember? We have to keep our clan safe."

Anton had never seen a witch in real life. He knew of them from the evenfire stories the elders told. Witches were gift-born who turned against their clans and brought forth ill omens. They had to be found by hunters and brought to justice or they would steal babies in the middle of the night and cook them over a fire while they danced naked in the moonlight. Witches had black teeth and black eyes, and drank blood where they could. Iluna's teeth were white, and Anton had never seen her drink blood. But her eyes were blacker than night. As was her messy hair. And he'd heard the whispers about her. Everyone knew she was a witch. Everyone except Soragan Izhur.

"You swim to the left; you to the right," he instructed the children. "Caldon, you come with me. We're going through the fall itself."

They entered the pond slowly. Before he swam, Anton bent to pluck several pieces of reed from the shore and tucked them into the waistband of his loincloth.

Diving and splashing water, he played with the children at first. It was good to put your prey at ease. Then he signaled to the others to move closer. He took a deep breath and plunged. Ice water tickled his skin. The temperature dropped in the depths of the pool. He kicked his legs and pumped his arms and his body moved toward the waterfall. A jet stream of blue and green bubbles danced just above him. He swam through and sharp water prickled his skin.

Another kick and he was on the other side.

He jumped out and inhaled with a great gasp. After a moment he caught his breath and smiled as his eyes met Iluna's.

"I..." He coughed up a little of the water he'd taken in. "I knew you were here, witch. I have you now; the hunter has you."

Caldon emerged beside him.

Iluna's eyes squinted. She said nothing. She turned to her left, but stopped short when she saw Yuli.

"I cuss you," the boy said again, and held his hands the way he had done moments before.

Iluna sighed and turned to the right, but Hennita appeared; a scowl on her face. Botha stood beside her. Both girls were older than Iluna and Botha was much heavier. Iluna was trapped.

Anton smiled. "You are to come with me for your judgment," he said.

Iluna lifted her chin. "Who will judge me?"

Anton hesitated. He hadn't thought of that. He was really only interested in the hunt.

Iluna smiled – a smug smile.

Anton grimaced. "My father will decide." He spat the words. "Grab her," he shouted to the children. "Let's take her back to the tree-dwells."

Iluna ran between him and Yuli, and dove into the water.

Anton shouted, "Get her," and quietly cursed the ineptitude of his brother.

He plunged into the water after her. She was a strong swimmer, but he was stronger. He saw her foot. Grabbing it, he pulled and her body flung back like a wounded duck.

He surfaced and grabbed her under the chin. She let herself float in his arms while he treaded water. "That's right, I have you now," he said.

He steered them closer to the shore and stood when he felt

the rock underfoot. But Iluna kicked, hard, backwards. Anton let her go as his hands went to his groin in an attempt to quell the sharp ache from her kick.

Iluna laughed and ran off, while Anton stumbled in the shallows. Then his anger took hold and overpowered the pain. He jumped out of the rock pool and sprinted.

She was smaller than he, and slower. Following her trail was easy. He just had to keep running, like a wolf.

"I'm coming for you, witch," he shouted and lengthened his stride.

Fronds and branches slapped his face; they stung, but they'd slow her down more. Soon he heard her – her steps, her breathing. She was panicked.

Smiling, he increased his speed. And then he saw her, running for her life, deep into the forest.

He had never been this far without an elder before. But he was a hunter, and a tracker. He could find his way back to the tree-dwells.

He focused his mind back on his prey. Iluna tripped and fell. He stalked closer.

She lay on the ground, still wet from the pool. Her breathing came hard and fast. Her eyes were closed and her lips were moving. What was she saying? Was she praying to some evil spirit?

Anton stepped closer. "I have you now, witch, and I'll take you back for judgment." He grabbed the reeds he had fastened to his waistband and snapped them together.

Iluna's eyes remained closed, and still her lips moved.

"Praying to your demons won't save you now." Anton bent down and held her wrists together. He tied them tight, the way his father had showed him to bind a boar for carrying.

Still the girl whispered as he reached for her ankles, her voice more urgent. All around him the noise of the forest grew. It was as though the insects answered her summons. The high pitch of the cicadas reached a deafening crescendo. Anton put all his effort into resisting the temptation to put his hands over his ears and run. Mosquitoes bit into his skin so much that small trails of blood made their way down his arms and legs.

"Is this your work?" he asked as he slapped at stinging insects. "Keep it up, witch. I'll just tell Da."

Anton bent to pick her up, but a growl came from the forest – a deep, resonant growl. Anton lifted his head, and tried to still the pounding of his heart. He scanned the trees. A movement caught his eye, then something golden. It came toward him, a dark circle at its centre. An iris. It was an eye; a creature watched him. Only one creature had such an eye.

Mountain lion.

Anton ran for his life.

ILUNA

*I*luna sat on the reed mat in the cool of Izhur's tree-dwell with a bowl of summer hazelnuts she'd collected from the forest after Anton had run away. She smiled as she remembered Zodor's son scampering along like a frightened rabbit, mosquito bites covering his skin. She grabbed another handful of nuts and began cracking their shells with a rock, putting the small kernels into a clay bowl. Izhur would be pleased; they were his favourite.

"She needs to be punished, Izhur. That girl needs to know her place in our clan."

She stopped her work and cocked her good ear. Zodor's voice was quiet, making it difficult to hear. She crawled closer to the entrance.

"I think she's well aware of her place, hunter. You and your sons take pains to remind her of her status every day. One wonders why you feel so threatened by a tamatu."

Iluna frowned. She'd never heard Izhur call her that before. Others did, all the time. Especially Yuli and Anton. Her and Aunty Agath were both considered tamatu because they had no family – a sign of ill-luck. Every day she was reminded of her rank when she woke in the small tree-dwell in an old birch well away from the others. Tamatu. It meant lowly one, and once named as such a clan member never lost the title.

Zodor's voice hardened; they were closer now and easier to hear. "My sons are the pride of our clan. Anton is already an able tracker. And we have secured the hand of Donnol's daughter for him. A strong connection for the Wolf. As for Yuli, he will be our next Soragan. You have said as much yourself."

Iluna crept to the round cutout in the mud wall of the tree-dwell and peered down. Zodor towered above the slender frame of Izhur. But the Soragan stood his ground.

"I have said he shows talent." Izhur rubbed at a temple with his two forefingers. Iluna knew his body language like she knew the pattern of the night stars. Izhur was always rubbing his temples around Yuli.

"Whether Yuli will be our next Soragan will only be formally recognized at the coming Agria in three summers … if he proves his worth."

Zodor's stance altered. His shoulders rose, fists clenched.

"Still, it seems the girl has committed some sleight worth looking into. You say she assaulted your boy?" A different voice contributed to the conversation, but the thick branch of the elm blocked the view. Iluna guessed he was an elder from one of the visiting clans.

"Kicked him. Hard. In the groin," Zodor said.

"A girl two summers younger than Anton, the great hunter-to-be, assaulted him physically?" Izhur asked.

Zodor snarled. "It was more than that. She used – her gift."

Izhur threw up a hand. "Of course she did. Your boys are always saying that. Calling her a witch along with tamatu and Frog Face. I wonder where they get it from."

Zodor's nostrils flared as his big chest moved up and down with short breaths.

"Let's question both parties, Izhur," the third man spoke.

"Then we can determine a just punishment. If one is required, of course."

Izhur pursed his lips.

Zodor's fists tightened.

"Would that suit you, Zodor?" The old man's voice had a calming tone – too calming. He was using the gift to soothe the hunter. Iluna sucked her breath. Who was this person? It could only be one of the visiting Soragans.

Zodor nodded once. "I expect your judgment by evenfire." He walked away, muscles gleaming in the hot afternoon sun.

Izhur exhaled loudly, and Iluna did the same.

"Well, let's up and see her then."

Iluna scampered to the back of the shelter and focused on stripping more nuts.

The grunts and groans of the old man sounded as he clambered up the steps to the tree-dwell.

Iluna turned her back to the entrance.

"Haven't you considered caves? They're much easier to get into."

Izhur laughed and Iluna knew he stood behind her. "There are few caves in our lands, Belwas. So we make our own caves in the trees."

Belwas. He was the fat Soragan from the Bear clan. He'd shared Izhur's tree-dwell some nights. Everyone was laughing about his loud snoring.

"Iluna." Izhur's voice was gentle, caring.

She turned around, still holding the little clay bowl with the hazelnuts.

Izhur smiled. "Iluna, I want you to meet someone."

Belwas puffed his way into the tree-dwell and chose a fat cushioned wolfskin to recline upon. The bough of the tree moved under his weight, swaying the way they did on windy days.

"This is Soragan Belwas."

Belwas had big curly hair that was black and grey, a large

round nose and a beard that didn't hide a double chin that wobbled when he moved. He wiped his sweaty forehead with the back of his hand and then smiled at Iluna and nodded before looking up to Izhur. "Some water, Izhur."

Izhur went to the shelf and poured a cup of water from a clay jug.

"Thank you. I miss the afternoon breeze of our grasslands. And the cool caves by the river." The old man gulped the water and held the cup out for more. "Now, let's have a look at you, young one," he said, as Izhur refilled his cup.

"You're going to punish me, aren't you?" Iluna asked quietly.

"Well, nothing wrong with her hearing, Izhur. Even if she is half deaf as you say." He drank another gulp of the water, before putting the cup down.

Iluna took a deep breath. It wasn't fair. Anton had been mean. She'd only protected herself. She could feel her bottom lip tremble and bit it down.

Belwas raised a finger. "Listening in on the conversations of elders is enough in itself for a punishment."

Iluna's eyebrows tremored. "I'm sorry, Soragan."

"I am not going to punish you for your curiosity, child. Now, tell us what happened."

"They were chasing me, calling me witch. Anton tried to tie me up like a boar."

"Children are cruel indeed. But what sparked them off? Did you say something to them?"

Iluna bowed her head. "Only that Hennita isn't his wife."

"They have been promised, Iluna. What made you say that to Anton?" Izhur asked.

Iluna frowned. "I don't know. It was just a feeling I had, like it wasn't true."

"Come, step closer." Belwas gestured with his hand.

Iluna looked at Izhur, who nodded. "Do what Belwas asks, Iluna. All is well."

Swallowing, Iluna stepped forward. Belwas reached out with one fat hand and grabbed her chin in a lock.

"Look," he said, with eyes trying to meet hers.

Iluna's breath staggered as she looked everywhere about the tree-dwell. The circular swirls of the mud cladding, the unlit oil pots in the corner, Izhur's carving of Goda, the nightsun god on the southern wall – her gaze focused on anything but this old man's eyes.

Belwas tightened his grip on her chin. "I said, look!"

And Iluna did.

His eyes reminded her of the dark brown of moist soil. A growl came, and her vision shifted to another scene, deep in a forest. Something lingered. Brown fur. Claws. It paced back and forth and reared up on hind legs. A bear. It was a bear. Iluna smiled. She liked bears.

"No! She's seen me. Stop! Stop it!" The bear spoke. Strange. She'd never heard one speak before.

"Izhur. Help me. Snap her out of it for Ona's sake!"

"Iluna, come back." Izhur's voice.

A cool breeze blew and Iluna felt sleepy. She closed her eyes.

"Iluna, wake."

Her eyes snapped open. She lay on a fur in the tree-dwell. Izhur stood close and she was comforted. With a deep breath she hoisted herself onto her elbows to see Belwas. He flinched, holding a hand over his eyes.

"You're quite safe, Belwas. But no doubt you see what I mean?" Izhur said; a smug smile danced on his lips.

Belwas cupped two hands over his eyes. "Yes. Yes, I see. All too clearly. Her light, so bright."

Iluna scratched her head and pulled at a knot in her hair. Izhur had often spoken about her light. Not in any great detail. She wondered why it was important.

The old man turned to her, blinking his eyes. "Leave us, Izhur. There are things I must say to Iluna alone."

Izhur gave a quick nod and glanced at Iluna before climbing down the steps. Iluna wished he had stayed, but looked at the old man who still reclined on the cushion.

Belwas rubbed his forehead and met her gaze once more. "You saw me, child. You saw who I am."

Iluna crinkled a brow.

"The bear," he whispered.

She nodded.

Belwas held up a finger. "Tell no one. Not ever. Such knowledge of one's totem is dangerous."

Iluna blinked. "How is it dangerous?"

Belwas shook his head and his chin wobbled. "You are a curious one." His eyes squinted as he assessed her and then he seemed to come to some decision. "If an enemy knows of your totem, they can cast injurious spells."

"But, the enemy would have to have the gift to do that."

Belwas nodded. "Yes."

"And they can even injure Soragans?"

Belwas squinted again. "Most master Soragans would be able to resist such a spell. But one can never be too careful."

Iluna frowned. "But are there really enemies out there? Where are they?" Even though Yuli and Anton were unkind bullies, she didn't think of them as enemies.

"Iluna, there is always a possiblitiy that an enemy exists. We don't need to live our lives in fear, but we need to be accepting of this basic fact. Now, I think I have told you too much, but you must promise not to tell anyone of what you now know of me."

"I won't tell," she whispered. Izhur had told her little about totems. Only that everyone had one and it was his job to keep the knowledge of all the clan members' totems secret.

Belwas studied her a moment longer.

Iluna focused on his big nose. It was less threatening than the brown eyes that seemed to hold her in their power.

He smiled. "I believe you."

Iluna breathed out.

"But we still have the problem of the hunter's son."

"He is mean. All of them are." Iluna bit her lip and her vision started to blur. "They called me a witch." She bent her head and two tears splattered on the bowl of hazelnuts by her foot. She couldn't help it. Why did they have to be so cruel?

"Yes, child. I can see how hard life is for you here. The Wolf have always been a confoundedly pugnacious clan. Still, you used your gift, yes?"

Iluna's lips turned down into a sad smile and she nodded.

"Did you really summon a mountain lion?"

"Yes."

Belwas frowned. "It is very dangerous, child, to summon such creatures. Their natures are difficult to control. Even for the most powerful Soragans."

"I know. Izhur has told me not to do it without him. I am sorry."

Belwas sighed. "You will need to pay a penance, little one. Otherwise the young wolves won't be silent and you'll spend all your days in more misery than is necessary. We'll make it as easy as we can."

Iluna sobbed. She had only tried to protect herself.

Belwas put a fat hand on her small shoulder. "Run and get Izhur for me. We'll settle this today. Best get it all over with."

PART III
SUMMER OF THE SKY

ILUNA

*I*luna blinked against the hot southern wind. Summer had only just begun, but the dead grass of the high plains already crunched under foot, and her tunic stuck to the sweat on her legs. They had been forced to climb up from the cool banks of Mittha's River when it cut through the tall chasm of rock. Up here on the plains there was little in the way of food. Only grass and desert pear grew in the dusty ground. The desert pear was edible, just, but there was even less in the way of game. The hunters brought in the odd plain-hare and quail, but nought else, and Iluna doubted she and Aunty would receive a share of that.

Before their climb she had stuffed her satchel full with berries, roots, nuts, and sorrel leaves that grew in abundance along Mittha's banks. Her meagre store had to last her and Aunty for the next three days. The prospect of subsisting on the salty desert pear was not appealing.

Still, the clan of the Wolf made its slow progress to Agria, the eight-day festival to celebrate the long light of summer. It would be Iluna's first Agria and she couldn't wait to see the days without end when all three night bodies – nightsun, moon and star – would walk the sky. There would be no night.

She'd see the other clans too – watch their art, taste their food and hear their stories. Izhur had told her about the paintings of the Lion clan and the fire tricks of the Ox; some of them could swallow a flame. Agria was also the time when the toolmakers performed the bronze magic and cast copper knives for the Soragans and the cooks, in the heat of the huge evenfire. Izhur had told her that the Grand Soragan, Xaroth, had brought the gift of bronze magic to all of Ona's people after his return from the hermitage that had finalized his prenticeship. The knowledge of how to melt rock and sculpt bronze knives had come to him through a meditation that had lasted an entire eightnight.

And maybe there would be another girl like her, a tamatu, unwanted by her clan. Maybe she would find a friend.

Iluna had her head bent low in an attempt to stop the wind from drying her eyes. She almost stumbled into Aunty Agath who had stopped walking, her hands massaging the small of her back.

"Great Aunt?"

Agath was very old but kind; few people were kind in the Wolf. Sometimes the old woman would talk to Iluna, the way a grandmother might. With no living children or grandchildren, Agath had little more status than Iluna. As far back as Iluna could remember they'd shared a tree-dwell – whether in winter or summer lands – and they always sat next to one another during the evenfire meal, right at the back.

Agath groaned as she rubbed her back. "I am an old woman; too old for this kind of travel. They should have left me in our summer lands. Perhaps I would have gone over to the Otherworld. It wouldn't worry me. I'd welcome it."

"Great Aunt, do not say such things! I would miss your stories."

Agath laughed. "So you say, little bird. I know you like my

stories, but not all enjoy the ramblings of an old woman such as me."

Hot sand whipped up with the wind, stinging Iluna's eyes. She squinted. "Why do you call me that, Great Aunt?"

"What, my girl?"

"Little bird. You always call me that."

The old woman smiled. "I don't know. You are like a little bird. And one day, I hope you take flight from this unhappy clan."

A shout came from the front. Ulof ran toward them, his sweat making his skin shine in the midday sun. He carried nothing and wore only a loin cloth. Iluna sighed; he was probably going to tell them to move faster. That was his responsibility, running from the front to the back of the clan to ensure all were present, before doing the circuit all over again. It took days to move the clan to Ona's Valley; almost a full cycle of Imbrit's moon would have passed by the time they arrived for the summer solstice. They traveled over mountains and valleys, through plains and forests, loosely following the path carved out by Mittha's river. It was Ulof's job to ensure that no one got lost on the way. Iluna wondered if he would notice if she or Aunty went missing.

"Tamatu," Ulof shouted and Iluna's heart sank the way it did whenever she heard the word. Usually she only heard it from Yuli. His hatred was as obvious as the summer sky. No clouds of mercy dotted the endless colour of his contempt for her. Still, at least no one seemed to call her Frog Face anymore. Ulof had hardly said two words to Iluna her whole life, but she'd always felt uneasy around him. And his father, Ugot, seemed to dislike her too.

"Aunty Zelda is poorly. She needs help with her burden. You're to go to her and carry her satchels until we stop for camp." Ulof pointed toward the front of the company.

Aunty Agath spoke, "Why does Iluna have to do it? There are plenty of young men who could easily carry such a burden."

Iluna thanked Agath silently. She had her own satchel to carry. Ordinarily it was light enough. Her meagre belongings – a clean tunic, wooden bowl and bone spoon, the light leather hide for the shelter she shared with Agath every night they made camp, and a little bone statue of the god Shephet carved by Izhur many summers past, all made a light cargo. But the extra weight of food had made it as heavy as a river rock and the heat made her weak. Another satchel would make the journey too exhausting today.

Ulof spat, the way his father always did. "I've been instructed to order our *tamatu* to do it." His eyes burned.

"Ha! Ugot still harboring that old wound is he?" Agath spat too. "The girl has never harmed us, not once in eight summers. Tell your bitter father to carry old fat Zelda's satchels himself."

Iluna's jaw dropped before she tried to hide a smile. Aunty was always saying what she thought and it hadn't done her any favours. Once she told Zodor that the bigger his muscles grew the more stupid he became, and she'd done it at the evenfire meal in front of the whole clan. It had brought sniggers from some, but this made it worse. Agath was punished for it and she had to clean Zodor's family tree-dwell and do all of their dawn-meal cooking for a full eightnight.

Ulof's nostrils flared and a scowl contorted his already ugly face. "Be sure to return to the back of the host, once you have the satchel," he said to Iluna between gritted teeth. Then he turned and ran to the front of the column.

Iluna shrugged at Agath and lent forward into the wind, marching to the front of the column to find Aunty Zelda. She had to do what she was told.

∞

Iluna stumbled, but the thick grass that carpeted the river-bank felt cool and soft on her feet. The climb down from the high plains had been rocky and, in places, quite steep. Zelda's satchel, stuffed full of carved bone statues and pots of rose hips for her daughter's family in the Otter clan had made Iluna's back hurt. Zelda now sat on the riverbank with her feet dangling in the clear running stream of water that gurgled its way over glossy rocks.

"Your satchel, Aunty." Iluna dropped the large leather bag next to Zelda who nodded, before returning to the attentions of her grandson playing in the shallows of the stream.

It felt better being free from Zelda's heavy burden. The clear air and beauty of the forest gave Iluna a new lease of life, and she jogged over the grassy flat to the trees that lined the flood plain; the soft grass, a welcomed cushion underfoot. The trees were old and gnarled and appeared to Iluna like the grandfathers and mothers of the clan, standing tall but crooked with wisdom and aged limbs. She ducked under a low branch and the air became cooler. Darker.

"Iluna!"

She stopped and turned. Izhur, framed by the tree branch, stood with squinted eyes.

"Where are you going?"

"Just to explore a little. I won't go far, dear Uncle."

Izhur nodded. "Be sure not to. I want you back before even-fire. You need nourishment and sleep. Tomorrow is another big day and you'll probably have to carry Zelda's satchel again, although I'll try to get one of the young men to do it."

Iluna nodded, frowning. Why couldn't the fat old woman carry her own satchel? But she said, "Yes Uncle", before turning to explore the forest.

It was still and dark. Dusk finally advanced, but the vast leafy canopy made the forest seem as though night had already descended. Iluna smiled as she breathed in the cool earthy smells, touching the trees' bark as she walked. Forests always energised her. Life buzzed within the trees. Water traveled up the trunks to the limbs and every leaf. Sap oozed its way around like thick, lazy blood. And something deeper – whispering. It sung through her fingertips. This forest was calm, content, friendly – and very, very old.

A presence lurked here. Or another was missing. It didn't come to her at first. The trees were louder than most trees she knew. But there was something very different about this forest. Then, like a slow moon rising, it came to her. She frowned slightly, cocking her ear. Listening. But there was nothing. No sound or vibration. No movement.

Where were the animals?

She took a deep breath and tried again. There was something there, right behind her. Watching. The hair on the back of her neck bristled and she shivered a little despite the moist heat of the forest. Iluna couldn't make out what it was, or if it was friendly or hostile. But something was there, and its intensity was growing. She swallowed a lump and took a calming breath.

With little steps she turned around until she faced the strange energy. Straight ahead stood an old oak, taller than any other tree she'd seen here, with large deep green leaves. Moonberry shrubs surrounded its wide trunk – their shiny blue fruits, almost purple, contrasted against the dark green of the under-growth. The humming of the creature's energy, whatever it was, grew stronger, but where?

A loud squawk sounded and echoed throughout the forest. Iluna looked up. There, on a thick branch of the oak, sat a bird similar to the crows of their summer lands, but different. Its feathers were so dark they seemed to shine with a blue gleam. It was much larger, too, and the feathers under its beak gathered, as though it wore a beard.

"Raven," she whispered, and the bird squawked.

She'd heard about them from the evenfire stories. Ravens

were birds of day and night. Their paths crossed through this world and the Other – and Malfiren. They were not to be trusted for they could be good, neutral or evil; whatever took their fancy at the time.

One evenfire tale, that Aunty Agath loved to recite, told the story of Magut – a Soragan prentice who had been tricked by a raven back in the dream days when the world was still very young. Magut had a yearning to do great deeds for his clan. He used his gifts to help the hunters find their prey and to lead the gatherers to the most bountiful harvests. He would give energy to the tool makers so that their laborious task of knapping was more easily achieved. He would give strength when the clan found themselves under threat of a lion or pack of wolves.

Eventually he used his gifts to alter the natural circle of life – casting love spells and healing the ailing when death was the natural course. His teacher and the clan's Soragan, Pata, tried to rein in her young novice's zest for control. For such interference in daily life was unnecessary, and unnatural. But Pata, old and tired, could do little to curtail her prentice's fervor.

One night, on dusk, a raven appeared to Magut and offered him a gift – the raven would steal the collective power of all the Soragans and their prentices and give it to Magut. All the raven wanted in return was the promise that he would sacrifice one child every Ilun to the Malfir.

Magut was wary. But the desire to have all that power proved too tempting. He imagined all the good he could do for his clan, indeed for all of Ona's people, if only he had such power. He took the raven's offer. Greed and corruption quickly soured his soul and Magut became an abomination – a wizard of evil.

Iluna blinked. There was a lesson in the tale. Would this bird offer her a pact?

The raven cocked its head and squawked again.

"Leave," Iluna said, for she did not want to trust it. The bird obeyed, flapping large glossy wings and flying off through the canopy to the darkening sky.

A twig snapped and Iluna jolted, turning her ear toward the sound. Anton stood close, his eyes wide. Iluna held her breath.

"You control them, don't you?" he asked.

Iluna didn't move. The last time Anton spoke to her was three summers past, when he'd accused her of being a witch. Izhur and Belwas had given her a punishment for using her gift on him. She still smiled sometimes, when she remembered the way he had run from the forest. But she didn't deserve that punishment.

She'd had to stand in front of the evenfire for a full day and night, on two feet, no food or water. She wasn't allowed to sleep, or to cry out. And she was forbidden to speak. It was a cleansing – proof that she was protected by the Benevolent Ones for she survived the night and no evil claimed her. Yuli had spat on her and called her names when he thought no one was looking. But his brother, Anton, had seen it and done nothing to stop him. He'd just watched with those blank eyes – the eyes of a hunter. Those same eyes that watched her now as he repeated his question.

"I said you can control them, the animals. Can't you?"

She didn't want to be punished again. To be set up by this mean hunter-boy. So she ran, fast through the forest. She ran until her legs ached and her chest burned with hard breathing. When she reached the soft grass of the floodplain she collapsed onto her back and watched the stars in the darkening sky until she got her breath back. When she sat up she could see the evenfire had been lit and there was already an aroma of charred meat that made her mouth water. She looked back over her shoulder toward the forest. But Anton hadn't pursued her. She bent her head in relief.

∞

ILUNA SAT on her reed mat under the hide lean-to she shared with Aunty. The Wolf had not long arrived in Ona's Valley – a land abundant with forest where the Agria was always celebrated. After their arrival each member of the clan had been given an orange fruit by members of the Bear who had arrived first. Agath laughed when Iluna examined the round fruit with a quizzical look.

"Like this." Agath stuck her thumbnail into the fruit, peeling back its skin. Juice squirted everywhere and ran down her fingers before Agath pulled off a section and popped it in her mouth, munching with a smile on her wrinkled face.

Iluna did the same. The fruit awoke a tingly taste sensation that she never knew existed; so sweet. Juice ran down her chin and she tried to catch it, licking her fingers so that none of the sugary substance was wasted.

Aunty laughed, her chin glistening with juice. "It's good, Iluna. Yes?"

"Yes, Aunty. Will we get more?"

"There's more than enough here for all our clans and the squirrels in the mountains."

Iluna lifted her eyes to follow the line of the summit that surrounded the valley. The very tops remained capped with remnants of winter snow. But it was warm down in the basin, hot even.

The festival grounds sat in a large bowl. Clans were still arriving, making their camp on the grassy flat of the valley floor. The surrounding forests were abundant with root vegetables, bulbs, herbs, and many different fruits and nuts. There was lots of game, too – deer, rabbit, squirrels, pigeon. Trout leapt from the river waters. It was a land of paradise.

Izhur and Agath had told Iluna all about the festival to come. Agria lasted eight days and nights. There would be a ceremony to mark the official beginning and one to end it. Some clans would arrive days or weeks earlier, or leave well after, to enjoy the spoils this land offered. It was a communal place. Owned by no clan, but all. All would leave it eventually and not return until their meeting in eight summers' time. The clan of the Wolf had arrived two days early. Agria marked the solstice of the longest and warmest summer – the Summer of the Sky. It was a magical and festive time in which all three night bodies – Goda's night-sun, Imbrit's moon and Atoll's star – could be seen together in the night sky. The night was almost as bright as day. Izhur had told her that the world changed during Agria. People were just as active during the 'night' as they were during the day, often more so. The magical light caused by the three night bodies was beautiful and healing, and people wanted to experience every moment of it. Iluna couldn't wait to see the dancing and to taste more of the food that grew here.

Iluna and Aunty's lean-to stood at the outer ring of the Wolf encampment. They were to sleep next to the main path into the valley, as befitted their lowly status. A lot of people lined it just now as clans continued to arrive. Iluna watched as she wiped her face with the back of her hand, her lips sticky. Old friends and relatives raced to greet each other. Most hadn't seen one another since the last Agria.

Iluna's excitement continued to buzz as she watched various clans set up their camps, but a lump also caught in her throat. At the last festival her mother had been pregnant with her. She had never known her mother, or her father. They had both died, leaving her all alone. Except for Izhur and Agath. Ida cared for her sometimes. But it was difficult with Zodor and his sons. Iluna suspected something had happened the night she was born – something that caused a great rift between Izhur and Zodor. But Izhur wouldn't tell her when she had asked, saying only that she had been a great gift. But if that were true, why was she the clan's tamatu? She shook her head and banished further sadness from her mind. The sun was warm. The birds were singing. This was a time for happiness.

There was a lull in the amount of people arriving now and Iluna took the time to more carefully arrange their camp. She tied down the lean-to with the leather thongs until it held firm. They had some shade from a vine that grew up an old dead tree – probably more than they deserved as tamatu, but no one had said anything. She collected some rocks from the river to make a firepit where Agath and she would share the dawn-meal, and she wondered what dawn would look like. A slow transition from one light to another?

The evening meals were always a communal event around the evenfire and it would be no different for Agria. Iluna tried to imagine how big the fire would have to be to provide for the meals of eight clans. She shook her head trying to fathom all the new experiences. As it was, she'd never seen so many people, and clans were still arriving.

Iluna had made a perfect circle with the stones when she heard the voices and noise of another clan approaching along the path. A woman led them. She wore many colourful beads around her neck; beads similar to Izhur's. The beads that marked him as Soragan.

Iluna's mouth fell open and she shook Agath awake. "Aunty, that woman, she wears a Soragan's beads."

Aunty grunted and opened one eye. "Yes, little bird. Your eyes do not fail you." The old woman closed her eye again.

"But, Aunty. She's a girl."

Agath sniffed but her eyes remained closed. "The best Soragans are women in my opinion. Often they are both Soragan and medicine women. Powerful healers. Now let an old woman sleep!"

Iluna stared with an open mouth. She'd heard of women being Soragans in the evenfire tales. But they were always in the Dream Days, when the world was young. The only real Soragans she had known were Izhur and Belwas, and Tyvan of the Eagle. Izhur had sometimes spoken about the Grand Soragan who was from the Snake clan. He was famous because he had introduced the bronze magic to the clans after his hermitage. All the Soragans she knew of were men. Now that Iluna looked more closely, this Soragan wore more beads than Izhur. Iluna wasn't exactly sure what the beads meant as they were guarded with great secrecy by the Soragans, but Izhur had told her the most powerful Soragans had the most beads. This woman had at least as many as Belwas, maybe more. She was very old. Her silver hair had been chopped and clung close to her head. Her eyes burned with a sharp blue. Her stride was sure and strong. And she was very tall, for a woman. She even towered over some of the men in her clan.

Iluna watched her pass, and she continued watching until the entire tribe had gone by. It was a large clan, much bigger than the Wolf. Iluna guessed they were the Otter – a clan from the south. They all seemed a little taller than the people of the Wolf and Iluna noted more variance in hair colour. Most of them had dark brown hair like everyone else, but some had lighter hair the colour of sand, and others even had the colour of fire. Fine ornaments adorned their dress. The women had turquoise stones sewn into their tunics. All wore a sandal on their feet. Iluna couldn't take her eyes off them. They seemed somehow better than everyone else. Their clothes more fine, more decorative.

At the back of their host, where the dust swirled, she looked for any signs of tamatu, like she had with other clans. But she wasn't prepared for the sight that greeted her. There amongst the swirls of dust was a creature half human, half something else – tall and big. One of his legs was skinny and deformed and he had a club where he should have had a foot. He walked with a lumbering limp and Iluna thought of the twisted malfiren monsters that came at Ilun to feast on innocent spirits. Or so the evenfire stories told. The monster drew closer and Iluna swallowed as she studied his face. Broad lips seemed to gulp for air the way a fish does and thin strands of saliva fell from his lips.

Large bulbous eyes scanned the crowd before him, as though on alert. He was bald. Iluna couldn't stop staring as he limped past, but she wasn't the only one. People along the path had stopped. Children were pointing at the creature and asking parents what it was.

"Durg."

Iluna heard the word and her eyes widened again. Of course, he was a durg. Iluna had never seen one; she'd only heard of them. They were supposed to be exposed as babies or young children, but here was one grown up, a man, still alive. Iluna wondered how that had been allowed and realised it must have something to do with the female Soragan. She must have persuaded her Circle of Eight to allow the durg to live when he was a baby. Iluna blinked and shut her mouth.

She couldn't imagine Zodor or Ugot allowing a durg to live in their clan. She wasn't even sure if Izhur would allow it.

Iluna's mind was so focused on the revelations she had just learnt, wondering at distant possibilities, that she didn't notice the flutter of wings. Or the soft squark that sounded from the vine-tree next to her shelter. She felt it, before she heard it – its essence. Just like a few days ago in the forest by the flood plain.

She turned her head and there sat the raven, its dark feathers glossy in the midday sunshine.

"You again," she said.

YULI

"Anton! Anton!" Yuli ran through the Wolf camp, almost tripping on the ties of other tents.

"Watch where you're going!" someone shouted, but Yuli kept running until he saw the white tent. His father had hunted the white bear before Yuli was born. White bears were giants that lived in their winter lands. The skin and fat had provided more than enough leather and waterproofing to make a large family tent. They took it with them whenever they traveled to visit other clans. It was heavy, but could be divided into four sections and they each had to carry a part on the journey. Yuli's mother had painted it with images that represented their family; there were many fearsome creatures – lions, wolves, snakes. But there were softer images too. Red spring flowers dotted the entrance – his mother's favourite.

"Anton!" Yuli shouted again as he entered the tent.

Inside his mother was putting down reed mats. The daylight from the smoke hole at the top of the tent filtered through, but Yuli still blinked, trying to adjust his eyes.

"I've sent your brother to fill our water jugs. A job you should have done by rights." His mother gave him a frown. "He won't be happy with you."

Yuli shrugged. He shouldn't have to do all the jobs. Just because Anton now joined the men on their hunt and was betrothed, he thought he was better. Well, Yuli would be Soragan one day. Then no one could boss him around and other people would have to fetch water for him.

Just then Anton walked in carrying two clay jugs; water dripped onto the mat.

"Try not to spill it, son. I've just put these reeds down."

"Yes, Mother." Anton placed the jugs at the back of the tent next to the clay cups, bowls and oil pots.

"Anton!" Yuli still shouted a little. "Some of the others have started a game of Lion and Wolf down by the river. Let's go and join them."

Anton smiled briefly before frowning. "I am ten summers old now, Yuli, almost a man. I have no interest in these childish games."

"But you love Lion and Wolf. It's your favorite game, and you're good at it. You'd be sure to win."

"There is no shame in playing with the others, son," their mother spoke. "Your father used to love that game too when he was your age. I remember playing with him when we were at Agria. We had been betrothed, he and I, just as you are betrothed to Hennita."

Anton scratched his head, still frowning.

"I think Hennita is there. It will be a chance for you to spend some time with her. Come on, brother." Yuli reached up and clapped his brother's shoulder.

"No. Father and a group of hunters are going to survey the surrounding forest. There's a good chance we will bring back a deer, or boar. I will go with them." He left the tent.

"Strange," his mother whispered.

"I know," Yuli said. "He loves that game."

"I'm not so concerned about his lack of interest in the game."
She looked towards the entrance, folding her arms.

"I suppose I'll have to join in without him then," Yuli said.

"Go on, have fun," his mother said with a smile. "And Yuli—"

"Yes, Mother?"

"Don't be a sore loser."

∞

Yuli walked toward the river trying to work out what was
wrong with Anton. All the children of their clan had played a
game of Lion and Wolf not long before they had left for Agria.
That was not even a turn of the moon ago. It was all right for
Anton to play then; why not now? Oh, well, he'd play without his
brother. He'd already made some new friends. Smiling, he picked
up his pace.

"Yuli."

Yuli stopped, recognizing the voice of Soragan Izhur. He
pretended he couldn't hear. Izhur would want to give him a
boring job – or worse – make him sit through another boring
lesson. He started running again.

"Yuli, I know you can hear me. Come here, please."

Yuli stopped and, with shoulders slouched, walked to Izhur
who stood outside the large tent the Soragans shared during
Agria. It was coloured with various decorations. Each clan had
designed a section of the tent over the years. It was painted
with images that represented all eight tribes –Wolf, Bear, Lion,
Eagle, Snake, Ox, Otter and Deer. After every Agria, each clan
would take custody of their section of the Soragan's tent,
protecting it until the next Agria. Then, when all the clans met
again, they would put their sections together to make one very
large tent – large enough to house each Soragan.

It stood in the centre of the camp. Yuli had watched the tent being erected the day before. It had taken the strength of grown men, all hunters, to raise it on a tall pole and hitch the eight leather sections together. The huge shelter could be seen from any point in the large encampment.

Yuli walked toward it, wishing he had gone around rather than cutting through the middle of the campground.

"Yes, Izhur." He kicked a lump of dirt.

"What were you in such a hurry for, Yuli?"

Yuli kept his gaze on the ground. "I want to play with the other children."

"Have I taught you nothing? Are you so spoiled not to look at your Soragan when he talks to you?"

He looked up, forcing his eyes to meet Izhur's. "I am sorry, Soragan."

"That's better." Izhur's shoulders relaxed a little. "I want you to run and find Iluna. It has been many days since our last lesson. Just because we are at Agria doesn't mean we can be lax with our studies."

Yuli pouted. He could feel his bottom lip poke out like a fat slug. Izhur didn't like it when he pouted. But Yuli couldn't help it. Why should he have to fetch Iluna? She should be the one to run after him.

"What is it now?" Izhur asked, quietly.

"Why can't I have some fun with the other children? And why do I have to fetch Iluna? Why does she have to do lessons with me at all? I'm going to be the next Soragan. We're to have the promising ceremony tomorrow."

Izhur sighed, but when he spoke his voice was friendly and kind. "Yuli, let me tell you why we must include Iluna in our lessons." Izhur walked to a nearby cherry tree and sat beneath its shade. He patted the ground next to him. "Come sit with me for a moment."

Yuli's pout disappeared. This was unexpected. No lecture?

He skipped over and sat.

"You know Iluna has the gift, don't you?" Izhur asked.

Yuli nodded. Everyone knew that.

"If such clan members – and they are clan members no matter what rank they have, mark my word, Yuli." Izhur's face looked very serious. "If such members as Iluna are not taught how to manage their gift, they create a risk to the entire clan. The Malfir may find them and corrupt them, using their powers for evil. Or, they may even learn skills by themselves and leave the clan to wield undisciplined power as isolated nomads. Either scenario is dangerous for a clan. This is why we must include Iluna. And why you must understand, as our next Soragan, your responsibility in training such members if this happens in the future.

"The likelihood of having three gift-born in a clan again is very low. But you must keep this in mind, Yuli. Consider this an important lesson in a Soragan's responsibility."

Yuli nodded. He understood, but he still didn't like having to fetch her. He stood, nonetheless, and brushed off his short tunic. "I'll get her now."

∞

HER SHELTER WAS at the very edge of the wolf clan's camp, as it should be for the lowest member of the clan. The old woman sat by her breakfast fire, in front of their lean-to. The hide was very plain compared to the large elaborate white tent owned by his family. If they got heavy rain it would be difficult for the two of them to remain dry. That was also fitting.

Yuli stuck his nose up in the air and asked the old woman where Iluna was.

She pointed. "Our little bird has found a friend."

Yuli walked behind the lean-to. A heavy vine had grown over

itself as well as a long dead tree, but he heard Iluna talking; asking strange questions.

"Do you prefer moonberries? I can bring some for you next time," she was saying.

Yuli rounded the vine slowly, wondering who she was talking to. It couldn't be anyone important; he didn't like the thought of Iluna making a friend.

"I know just where to find them, too, up there in the mountain forest. You don't have to climb too far before you come across them. The biggest patch of moonberries I have ever seen. I brought some back for Aunty for our breakfast, but we ate them all." She laughed.

Yuli stepped closer.

"They're so delicious."

With another step he could see her, but no one else. Who was she talking to? He took a step and the sharp snap of a stick sounded.

Iluna turned her head and locked dark eyes with him. Yuli was just about to ask the question on his mind when a large bird, like a crow, squawked and flew off over his head. He ducked, covering his head with his arms. The flapping sound gradually disappeared, but Yuli stayed down; he didn't like birds. When he was small the birds used to dive and peck at his hair. He would cry and Anton would laugh at him.

"What do you want?"

He looked up. Iluna stared at him, a scowl on her face.

"Who were you talking to?"

She didn't answer, but her eyes flicked to where the bird had perched on the highest branch of the dead tree-vine.

"You were talking to that crow?"

"It's a raven."

"Raven?" Yuli had heard of ravens, in the stories about witches. They were evil birds and their powers were used by evil witches to hunt little boys down and eat them. He'd heard the stories around the evenfire when his mother thought he'd been asleep in her arms.

He slowly raised his finger, pointing to the branch. "You were talking to a raven? They are evil." He screwed up his face. "I knew you were a witch. I'm telling Izhur." He turned to march away but almost ran into the tallest woman he'd ever seen. He had to bend his neck back to look up at her. She had short hair. He'd never seen a woman with short hair before. All the women in his tribe had long dark hair, or grey. This woman had light hair, almost the colour of straw, but it was grey too. She was very old. Wrinkles lined her face like the crinkles in autumn leaves.

"You're quite mistaken, boy," she said.

Yuli gulped.

Her eyes were a sharp blue, speckled with ice, and they didn't shift from Yuli's. Something about her frightened him.

"Excuse me, Aunty." He circled her, stepping backward, trying to tear his gaze away. "I have to go." He turned to sprint away but ran into someone else – a monster with an oversized head and all the features of a person somehow strangely twisted and wrong. The monster had bulging eyes of different colours and a mouth that drooled thick saliva. One foot was not a foot at all, rather a club that made the cretin sway like a moon monster and lurch in front of him. Yuli felt his stomach drop.

"Boy," the monster groaned, repeating the woman's last word. Yuli yelped and ran.

∞

THE EVENFIRE WAS the biggest Yuli had ever seen. Its flames reached higher than a young tree. His eyes followed the path of the red glowing sparks that floated ever upwards. A handful of stars peeked through the blanket of sky, but they would remain dulled over the next eightnight – or so he had been told. Yuli looked to the west. The daysun had just gone down leaving remnants of pink and purple splashed across the horizon. Above, the nightsun shimmered, and toward the east the full moon reflected the daysun's setting glow, shining red in the purple sky. He shifted his gaze to the eastern horizon. When Atoll's Star showed its familiar blue face, Agria would begin.

All the clans had converged for the ceremony. The eight Soragans stood in a perfect circle around the evenfire while the few novices tended the flames, adding more light to the evening. Then, with a wave from the Grand Soragan, the novices sat on the ground behind their masters. There was a murmuring of excitement as he turned to the milling crowd.

"All, be seated now," the Grand Soragan said, limping forward.

And all eight clans sat with a hush.

Drum beats started a slow rhythm; a singular thrum that echoed in the evening air, followed by another. Cal, the Lion novice kept the tempo on the ceremonial drum, a great instrument larger than any man and very old. It had been used to mark the start of every Agria for more summers than anyone knew. Yuli wondered if it was the drum that had started the very first.

The Grand Soragan began the chant. "Ona, Great Mother, open your protective shield to us." He was very old. His face was lined with deep crevices and his shoulders bent forward. He leaned heavily on a twisted staff. Yuli's mother had told him the old Soragan could turn the staff into a slithering snake with a click of his fingers, but Yuli thought that must have been a story. Like the evenfire tales, not everything the elders told him was true. One thing was true though, the Grand Soragan was quick-witted despite his age. Everyone said so.

One by one the other Soragans joined in the chant, from oldest through to youngest. The old woman went second, her ice eyes clearly visible in the night's light. Yuli hadn't known any female Soragans until he'd run into her. Now he had to resist shivering every time he looked at her. And that monster who followed her around everywhere – the man who hadn't been exposed as he should have as a babe. Yuli would never allow that when he became Soragan. Abnormal babies would be given back, as was the natural way.

The eight Soragans were in full chant now. There was another female amongst the men, Jana, from the Deer. The women's voices added a strange harmony to the men's timbre and Yuli shivered again.

"Close the paths to the Malfir, and let us walk free in day and night. Let the light given by Goda, Imbrit and Atoll protect us. Bless us with holy spirits and ancestors past so that we may accept the wisdom of what has gone before and what is yet to come in the circle of time."

A cool breeze flowed and the Soragans' tent seemed to shimmer beyond the evenfire, its stones and gems glimmering. Then everyone looked to the east and there it was. The rise of Atoll's star was slow, as always, but the line of blue fiery light shone strong and true as it crested the horizon, slowly becoming larger, casting its azure radiance on the faces of the clan. There was a happy murmuring from the vast crowd until Cal stopped drumming and silence descended.

Xaroth's voice rose loud and clear. "Ona, with this Agria it is time to reward your Soragans, protectors of your people."

The Soragans stood and walked into their tent as Cal started the drum beat again. This was the most secretive, and Izhur told him, most important part of the celebration in which each Soragan would receive more strings of beads. Yuli hadn't learnt much about the beads yet, but he knew he was to receive the mark of the novice – a string of wooden beads that symbolised the power of trees. He couldn't wait; it would show the clan he was important.

During the Soragans' absence the novices started the chant of light known by all of Ona's people and the entire host took up the song that would give the Soragans energy and protection. The voices of more than ten one hundred people became one large beast, enough to frighten any dark lingering evil.

After the song the Soragans returned and the people cheered them, welcoming them back. Izhur now wore two more strings of beads and more colours reflected in the firelight as he strode back to his position in front of the evenfire.

Cal stopped the drumming and the Grand Soragan spoke to the crowd once more. "Ona, welcome into your light your new young apostles who will promise to accept the wisdom and guidance of your sacred name."

This was Yuli's cue. He pulled his ceremonial robe close, admiring the way the pale leather glowed in the evening light. He held his head high and walked toward the blaze. There were two others becoming novices tonight – Jethro and Kiar – and they also approached.

The fire was as hot as the burning heat of the midday summer daysun. Yuli turned to face the seated crowd. Izhur walked toward him carrying a bowl and a string of wooden beads.

"Novices —" the Grand Soragan's voice seemed to effortlessly reach every ear, "your sacred vow – to serve, to guide, to protect your clan will now be given. You will promise to follow the guidance of your master Soragans and learn, serve and protect. Do you swear to undertake this?"

"We humbly ask the great Mother Ona to take us into her service. We promise to learn and to protect." Yuli said the words Izhur had taught him, his voice matching that of the other two novices.

"Then accept the Mother's gifts."

Izhur stepped forward. First he extended the bowl.

"Drink so that the essence of your totem may give you power to defend your clan against the constant threat of malfir."

Yuli took the cup. It was the blood of his totem, the wolf; a lucky totem matching that of his clan. Only two people knew Yuli's totem – Izhur and his father. But it was Izhur's role to know the totems of all of his clan. Every father knew the totems of their sons, and every mother her daughters'. Unless you were tamatu; no one held the knowledge of a tamatu's totem.

Zodor had hunted the wolf himself. Izhur had mixed a substance with the blood to keep it fresh, but it did not ease the copper taste. The heat of the evening and the fire had warmed the viscous fluid and Yuli concentrated hard to get it down without bringing it back up, for that would be ill-omened; a sign that the totem had been rejected, and Yuli would have to walk away in disgrace. He had to drink it all, too. He took his last mouthful and licked his lips. The salty warmth stuck to his teeth.

Izhur turned the bowl upside down to show his fellow Soragans that Yuli had drunk all the blood, and that the totem had accepted Yuli.

"Now bend your heads, as you always will to our blessed Mother and accept the gift of one of her greatest treasures – the trees."

Yuli followed the Grand Soragan's instructions and stared at the ground as Izhur placed the wooden beads around his neck. This would be his first string of beads. They felt light on his chest. He glanced at Izhur's when he looked back up. Amongst the amber, azurite and jade he saw the light coloured wood. The beads Izhur would have received when he was noviced.

"It is done."

And the drum sounded eight times, to represent the eight years between each Agria, the eight nights of the festival, the eight spirits of Ona – sky, mountain, river, plains, oceans, forest, valley, lakes.

Yuli glimpsed his mother in the crowd. Tears streaked her cheeks and reflected in the firelight.

"Brothers, sisters," Xaroth intoned for a final time, "our prosperity is assured and Agria has begun."

The drum was followed by other drums now and the clans stood and danced becoming one seething celebration. All three night bodies shone high in the sky and a silvery-blue glow lit the evening. People sang and danced and laughed. Skins of alza were brought out and shared, and a whole deer was returned to the evenfire, the aroma of roasting venison filling the night.

Yuli laughed when his father embraced him and threw him in the air. "My son, you will make a fine Soragan, one that our clan will never forget."

He ran to his mother who kissed the top of his head.

Anton also embraced him. "You made us proud, brother."

Yuli beamed and held up his beads for his family to inspect. Then he went to get his bowl, his stomach was still queasy after drinking the blood and Amak had told him that she would make a fennel and clove tea after the ceremony to help with the digestion. Waves of nausea washed over him, but he was determined not to bring up the contents of his stomach. That would not please his father.

He raced to their white tent to retrieve a bowl and returned, looking for Amak and her promise of the tea, but he stopped when he saw Izhur in the distance. The Soragan spoke with Iluna. Yuli felt his stomach clench again and he swallowed hard to keep from vomiting. Izhur hadn't said one word to him after the ceremony, but there he was talking to Iluna. Sometimes he thought his master needed lessons, not him. He lifted his head. Well, one day he might just get some.

ANTON

"*Your* strength is good, son. It's your aim that needs practise, but it will come in time." Zodor coached Anton on his hunting skills as they trekked down the mountain. He'd missed the doe with his spear. The deer would have made a decent contribution to the summer feasting, and the praise he'd have received would have gone down just as well as the venison. Anton's disappointment bit deep, but his father buoyed his spirits.

"You remind me of myself at your age." Zodor smiled. A gleam of sweat made his muscles appear as defined and strong as the stone axehead he held.

Like all hunters' sons, the best compliment was that he was just like his father.

Anton smiled. "Well, at least I didn't come back empty handed." He held up the rabbits that he had caught with his traps, and his satchel, overbrimming with mushrooms.

His father stopped to pick up a mushroom and sniff it. He took a bite and munched. "These are very fine. You know they are your mother's favourite? I'll tell you something else, son. Knowing your wife's favourites is an important thing."

"So that's why you like to gather mushrooms and poppy flowers when you go hunting."

Zodor ruffled his hair. "I always bring back more than what she was expecting. It makes her faith in her husband stronger. You should seek out Hennita while we are here; find out some of her favourite things."

Anton froze. He didn't want to talk about Hennita.

"Have you seen her?"

"Yes, Father. She is well."

"At the next Agria you will be bonded. You will be eighteen summers then. I was bonded to your mother at sixteen. But I'm sure you can wait."

Anton had witnessed a number of couple-bonds the night before last. It was considered good luck to bond on the second night of Agria, and most couples did so.

"I will wait." He agreed. The truth was he didn't like Hennita. He wasn't sure when he'd decided that but the few times he had seen her and talked to her this Agria were enough to confirm it in his mind. She was pretty enough, with those curls and big eyes. But she lacked something; something vital.

"Zodor, greetings." The Grand Soragan had called out to his father as they made their way through the camp. He was a very powerful Soragan now, his mother had told him. Xaroth had performed the couple-bond ceremony for his parents. Anton's mother had reminisced about it many times. He liked hearing the story, too. It was customary for the Soragan of the woman's clan to perform the rite. That meant old Belwas would perform his couple-bond rite at the next Agria. If the old Soragan was still alive in eight summers. Eighteen summers was an old age to get married. But Zodor was determined to have the ceremony take place at an Agria, and ten summers was too young for a boy to marry. Anton had no choice but to wait. And he was not unhappy about it. He would have a long bachelorhood.

"Grand Soragan, it is a great pleasure to see you again." Zodor bowed his head.

The old Soragan limped toward them, bent over his staff, but he still seemed tall and powerful. "How is your wife? We of the Snake still miss her."

Zodor's head flung up with pride. "I do not doubt it. She is a jewel in any clan, my wife. Come, Grand Soragan, will you share a cup of broth with us?"

The Soragan nodded and Zodor turned to Anton. "Run and tell your mother that I am bringing the Grand Soragan. She will want to be warned."

Anton sprinted to the river. His mother spent time along the riverbank every morning with his grandmother, collecting sorrel leaves and other herbs.

"Good morning, Grandson."

"Good morning, Grandmother." Anton liked his grandmother. She was kind and warm and loved to tell him that she knew he would be a great hunter one day, just like his father. Anton loved Agria most for the hunting, but he also enjoyed spending time with grandparents, aunts, uncles and cousins, most of whom he'd not seen since he was just two summers old, and could barely remember.

His mother put her hands to her mouth when Anton told her of their coming guest, and then reached out to hold his hands. "Anton, this is a great privilege. Quickly, we must return to our tent." She dropped her basket of herbs and told her mother she would return later. Then she marched her son back to their tent.

"Help me sweep the mat. No! Here, run and fill these, and if you see your brother tell him to come home." She handed him their water jugs.

"Yes, Mother." Where was Yuli? He spent too much time with the other children and not enough time helping their mother. Whenever Izhur called to take him for a lesson, Anton had to go looking for him. The boy had no discipline. It was true what others said; Yuli was coddled, surly.

Back at the river he filled the jugs quickly, but was distracted by a sound – the flapping of wings. He turned to see a large black bird land on a boulder by the riverbank. Its squawk echoed off the river rocks. The morning sunlight reflected blue gleams on its feathers.

"Oh," someone said behind him and he turned.

There she was – Iluna. His stomach jumped the way it always did when he saw her now. Would she set the animals on him? Or tell that bird to pluck out his eyes with that huge beak? She was a witch, his father had told him. And looking at her, her hair as blue-black as the bird's feathers, her eyes darker, he believed she was. He tried to stare her down, but fear took over, the way it always did now.

"I have to go," he said, holding up the jugs of water, and he walked as fast as he could until he returned to the safety of the white tent.

He opened the flap of the tent and entered. His mother was serving his father and the Grand Soragan some of their breakfast broth. He walked through and set the water down in the corner.

His mother nodded and then gestured to the flap and he went outside. Clearly this was a conversation for the adults only.

He wondered what they were talking about. Probably his future couple-bond. His ears burned and his curiosity could not be restrained. He walked around to the back of their tent. The branches of a hazelnut provided enough cover to hide, and he made a comfortable spot beneath its heavy leaves, inclining his head so that his ear almost touched the tent's surface.

"She is evil, I tell you. Just as you had foreseen, Soragan." It was his father's voice. "And he is blinded by it. All he speaks of is her light. As if the rest of us know what that means."

"Husband," his mother whispered.

"Do not interrupt, Ida. More broth, Grand Soragan?"

Anton gulped, imagining his mother agreeably doing her husband's bidding.

"Go on, Zodor. Tell me more." The quiet voice, almost a hiss, was the Grand Soragan's.

"You know how she came into this world?"

"I've heard some wild statements from Izhur. Nothing from a rational mind. I'd appreciate hearing your view of things."

Anton swallowed. His father didn't like Izhur, even though he had entrusted his second son to him. But he'd had no choice there; Izhur was the clan's Soragan and Yuli had the gift. Anton had wondered, though, why Yuli had so many tantrums and pouted so often. The truly gifted were supposed to be calm and selfless, according to the evenfire tales; the opposite of his young brother.

"That night she came into the world. I will never forget it. The dark storms filled the sky. It was the first night of Ilun. We tried to tell him, our Circle, that it was ill-omened. There was evil in the air; we could all feel it. The Malfir – just as you predicted."

There was a pause. Anton steadied his breathing. They were talking of Iluna's birth. She must be a witch!

"So many ill-omened events had occurred. Her father, Osun – he was a great hunter, one of our best – he had been killed on our way back from Agria by a lion. How could that happen to a hunter such as he?"

"Yessss," the Soragan whispered. "Go on."

"Many other things happened, too. But Neria, dying as she gave birth, I tell you this girl was not meant to come into this world. She will only bring harm, great harm. And he teaches her with my son by his side."

"Husband, she has brought no ill-luck since—"

"You must forgive my wife, Grand Soragan," Zodor cut in. "She has also been blinded by the girl. She was forced to give her breast when the girl was a babe. She has a mother's soft view of the witch."

"Do not call her that." Anton's mother's voice was tight.

"So the Circle of Eight," the Soragan interrupted, "they tried to have her sacrificed?"

"We did. I swayed them, just as you told me to do. It was easy to get them on side," his father continued. "Izhur went off to do the task, but he returned, saying wild things about how she had a strong light, and that she was a gift, not a curse. He summoned some great magic and forced us to keep her. And now we are stuck with her."

Anton gasped. Iluna was supposed to die?

"Shhh."

"What is it?" Zodor asked.

"Are you sure we're quite alone?" the Grand Soragan whispered.

Anton stood and skipped under the hazelnut branches before sprinting away. He ran to the back of the wolf encampment and slowed, wandering along the path that had brought them to Ona's Valley. He calmed his breathing, trying to order his thoughts of Iluna – the witch. And then he saw her. She was peeling an orange fruit. Her black hair almost gleamed blue in the midday sunshine. She looked up and her dark eyes widened with fear.

Good, she was still afraid of him. That was something.

IZHUR

*B*lue light struck through the smoke hole at the very top of their tent. It was the fourth night of Agria and Izhur sat with the other Soragans as they did every night after the evenfire meal. He watched the spiraling smoke from the small fire as it wound its way slowly up.

"Hentyl, this is a delicious brew. I enjoy it almost as much as Izhur's honey drink." Belwas held his cup for a prentice to refill. Stains blemished his tunic.

"I think you come here for the food and drink alone, Belwas. If we had to fast during this festival, to be sure we wouldn't see you here," Hentyl replied, disapproval on his aged face.

Belwas scoffed, but he had a devious glint in his eye.

"Soragans, I'd like to discuss a serious matter," Grand Soragan Xaroth interrupted, darting a glance at Belwas from beneath troubled brows. His balding head, hook nose and small eyes always reminded Izhur of something cunning, predatory even. "As you all know, I still have no prentice."

"Yes, that is serious." Talso nodded his agreement as he always did whenever the Grand Soragan spoke.

Izhur raised an eyebrow. Xaroth was the oldest Soragan,

veritably ancient. He should have chosen a prentice years ago, but his stubbornness had affected this issue, as it did everything else. Xaroth wanted to choose a novice from his own clan, the Snake. The trouble was, every year with every new birth, no child had presented with the gift. It wasn't uncommon for clans to go through lengthy stretches in which a Soragan had to choose a novice from another clan rather than their own. It had happened with Izhur in fact. He had come from the Bear. Jakom had chosen him as there was no gift-born child in the Wolf at that stage. He had been young when he first left his family and clan to go with Jakom to the Wolf, just one and ten summers.

It had been a hard beginning. Zodor in particular made it difficult. He'd enjoyed playing his cruel boyish tricks at Izhur's expense – snakes in his bedroll, tadpoles in his morning broth. Izhur got his revenge sometimes by using his gift, filling Zodor's dreams with nightmares so that he went sniveling to his mother, like a baby. He and Zodor had hated each other from the very start.

But for a clan to go without a gift-born child for so long was very rare. Xaroth had become Soragan of the Snake at a young age, and he'd been waiting ever since for a novice to be born. It was past time he gave in and accepted a young one from a different clan.

Xaroth now looked at each of them as he spoke, his small dark eyes piercing. "I am asking you to tell me of your options. I intend to take a prentice with me when we return to our lands."

Izhur raised his eyebrow again. Usually the novice would be sent for after the clan and family had been consulted and a time agreed on. That way everyone had the opportunity to prepare and say goodbye. It would be a long time before the child would see family again.

"That's very soon," Jana said, her young voice wavering.

"I will not negotiate on that; the prentice will leave with me and my clan, two days after Agria."

Izhur looked to the floor, studying the reed mats. This was odd. After all these years Xaroth was now in a hurry to acquire a prentice. Did the old man have a premonition of what was to come? Did he believe his time to train a novice was diminishing? Jakom used to say that Xaroth was old when he was a boy. Izhur squinted at the Snake. His skin was papery thin and lined deep with a crisscross pattern of wrinkles. But his mind was sharp, and his quiet voice never wavered. How old was he?

"So I ask you again. Tell me your options," Xaroth said.

Jana spoke once more, her voice shaking. She was the youngest Soragan among them. "We have a boy with the gift, though he is only four summers."

Xaroth waved a hand. "That is no matter; I started my instruction at three."

"I was planning on taking him on myself—"

"I will have a look at him," Xaroth interrupted. "You are young, Jana, and too inexperienced to take on a novice just yet."

Jana nodded. A light blush reddened her cheeks.

Izhur bit his tongue. Xaroth had no right to take another's prentice, regardless of his Grand Soragan status. But Jana straightened and told Xaroth that the Deer clan would be honoured if he took on the young boy as his novice.

Xaroth nodded. "Anyone else?"

Silence.

Izhur caught Belwas's eye over the rim of his cup as he wiped his chin and sat up straight to listen. The old bear was ruminating on something.

"The gifted are not as prominent as they once were," Cypra spoke. As the second eldest, she was more the Grand Soragan's equal than any other, and she held her stare level with Xaroth, seated beside her. "We have known this for many summers. Things have changed since the time of our ancestors; indeed since my own youth. As you know, it is a subject I have broached for discussion on more than one occasion." Her eyes moved to each of them in turn.

Izhur remembered past Agrias. She had indeed brought up the topic of the diminishing numbers of those gift-born. And she'd been shut down for it.

"We're not going to discuss that now, Cypra. The subject at hand is my new prentice." Xaroth's authority filled the space with the quiet hiss of his voice. "Now, does anyone else have a likely candidate to offer me?"

More silence.

The woman spoke again. "It seems to me that my topic is a most relevant one after all, Xaroth."

The Grand Soragan licked his lips, his thin tongue just visible between slender lips as he shot her a poisonous look before quickly drawing a mask.

Izhur had attended four Agrias, two as a Soragan, and two as Jakom's prentice. In that time he'd seen discussions and passionate debates but he'd never seen a violent disagreement among Soragans. The tension in the tent was as thick as a valley frost, and as cold. To have the two most senior Soragans argue would destabilize the entire Agria. With so many people, there were always disagreements among the clans, sometimes there were fights. People looked to the Soragans to guide them and provide stability in such matters. Izhur felt he should speak, or someone ought to.

"And what of binding? Very few of us have that gift now. Once, every Soragan had the ability, now we can count the bonded on one hand. And no child in two score summers has been born with that particular gift. When we die," she nodded to Belwas and the other older Soragans around her, "that gift will die with us. If we do not start discussing it here…"

"Enough," Xaroth's quiet voice cut through. He stood, thin eyebrows furrowed. He pointed his staff at Cypra, an offensive gesture. "I said no more of that. This discussion is about my future novice, no more!"

Cypra also sprung to her feet, as quick as a doe, and while she was nearly of an age with Xaroth, her posture stood tall, as tall as Xaroth's if he didn't bend over. The amplitude of their many beads was on display and they glimmered and shimmered in the mixture of light from moon, sun, star and fire. All those strings of beads lay heavy round the bearers' necks. It seemed to Izhur they were equal in number. Curious. He had assumed Xaroth would have earned more than Cypra over the years. That was the natural order. The oldest Soragans wore the most beads.

"And I said," Cypra's voice was a harsh whisper between curled lips, "it is time to discuss this matter."

"You dare to affront the Grand Soragan …"

Izhur rubbed his temple. The tension was rising. It was not his place to interfere. One of the older Soragans should step in – Hentyl or Belwas. This problem of binding had never been acknowledged openly. Izhur looked desperately at Belwas, who now finished off his drink and nodded at Izhur. The old Soragan stood, or tried to. The combination of his ample stomach and the drink made him look like a fat summer bear trying to stand on its hind legs after gorging on honey.

"All right let's remember who we are," Belwas said from his cushion, and the tension calmed a notch. "Lentyl, help me up for Ona's sake!"

Belwas's prentice came running and put his hand out, but the boy's skinny body was no match for the large weight of Belwas, and rather than helping Belwas stand, he was flung onto his master's obliging belly.

Izhur heard a few hushed giggles and the tension lowered all the more. He allowed himself a smile and stood. "Come Lentyl, let's try it together, and then I might propose a subject of my own. That Soragans shouldn't grow too fat."

More laughter. Better.

Izhur and the prentice pulled Belwas to his feet and the old Soragan stood between Xaroth and Cypra. He was much shorter, and wider than the pair of them. He reached up and put his hand on each of their shoulders.

"We are the Soragans of our clans. Our people look to us for guidance. We must remain calm."

The tension had eased considerably, but Xaroth's eyes remained tight slits. Cypra just stared with a look of ice.

"Now, Cypra," Belwas tapped the Soragan's shoulder. "I agree. These topics are worthy of our attention and it is well past time we brought them up. I suggest we do so tomorrow evening."

"That is all I ask, Belwas." She gave a curt nod and returned to her cushion.

Belwas then tapped Xaroth's shoulder. "And there is another gift-born child you may like to look on, Grand Soragan. A girl with the strongest light I've ever seen. Izhur? Tell him of Iluna."

Izhur stopped smiling. No, not Iluna. He'd rather give up Yuli. Xaroth couldn't have Iluna. Izhur would never allow it.

Jana spoke, her voice more confident now. "Iluna? Isn't she your clan's tamatu? Wasn't she cursed at birth? I don't think this would be a good match for you, Grand Soragan."

Izhur swallowed. "Yes, you're right, she is our tamatu. She wouldn't make a suitable prentice for our Grand Soragan." The words tasted like betrayal. He hated calling her that. "Perhaps I could offer Yuli?"

There were gasps.

"But Yuli has already been bound to you, Izhur. We cannot undo what is done," Xaroth said, eyes squinting further. "No, bring me this girl tomorrow, and Jana, you bring me the boy. We will make a decision after the evenfire."

Izhur looked at Belwas. What had the fool done!

93

ILUNA

*I*luna took the last scoop of venison stew and held it in her mouth for just a moment. It had been the Lion's turn to cook and the mix of strange spices was tantalizing. The venison had simmered in large clay pots for most of the day and everyone had complained about the delicious aroma and being made to wait. The meat melted with every bite and the fresh root vegetables had absorbed the flavours of the spices. If it had just been her and Aunty around their small fire in their home-land Iluna would have licked the bowl. But she daren't do that here.

The drum sounded eight beats, as it did every evening after the communal meal. There was a hush, for the evenfire tale was about to begin. One of the Lion elders walked toward the fire, a woman almost as old as Aunty Agath. She wore a lioness's pelt around her slim shoulders.

"After the Dream Days, when the world was still young, there was much fighting between clans." The old woman's voice carried well, even to her and Aunty, and Iluna understood why she had been chosen to tell the tale.

"In those days there were nine great tribes, all Ona's children, but all vastly different – the Lion, the Wolf, the Bear, the Deer, the Eagle, the Ox, the Snake, the Otter, and one more – the Dragon."

Muffled gasps spread through the camp. Tales about the fabled Dragon clan were always a favourite.

"At one time two clans outshone all others in their rivalry and hatred – the Lion and the Dragon. The Battle of the River was a bloody and terrible war that lasted more than eighty-eight summers. Both great clans laid claim to the bountiful banks of the Mittha River, and neither was willing to compromise."

Iluna gently put down her bowl and cocked her good ear toward the speaker. There was nothing better than a good even-fire tale, and Iluna thought she hadn't heard this one before. Even Aunty paused her dinner to listen.

Iluna closed her eyes. It was the tale of the traitor, Tilda, the Lion's Soragan who had met in secret with Borun the Strong. He was a famed Dragon hunter. Iluna had heard many a tale about his heroism, but she'd never heard this particular part of his story.

"Tilda had fallen in love with Borun, as he had ensorcelled her with his charms." The old woman told a good story. "She, a Soragan, betrayed her own clan, telling them that the River was safe to hunt, but Borun and his fellow Dragons lay in wait. The Lion hunters were ambushed and slain. Skulls were cracked on the river rocks, hearts torn out and smashed, men flayed and burned alive. And for a time the Mittha River's waters ran red."

Iluna's imagination took over as the old woman's voice and the gasps of the clans faded. Images of fires and panic came to her, and the water, a river of blood.

The circle of time has cast a traitor once more.

Iluna blinked. Was it a voice in her head or a premonition?

The great drum started its slow beat once more and Iluna shook her head to ward off the sense of foreboding the tale had sparked in her. The Lion elder walked back to her mat. Soon the space around the evenfire would be a throbbing mass of dancers. Iluna stood, still trying to shake off the ominous feeling from the tale. She had other things to do.

She bid goodnight to Aunty Agath, still chewing beside her. Eating was slow work for Aunty on account of missing so many teeth. Iluna then wove her way through the mass of people. Some still sitting in family or friendship groups; clans intermingled, still talking about Tilda the Traitor, or old times; others folded up mats, getting ready for the dancing. She went to the river and washed her bowl and spoon before returning to the lean-to where she grabbed her satchel and headed for the mountain.

Iluna meandered along the now familiar trail through the mountain forest. Aunty had told her moonberries tasted sweetest in the evening, and every night after the evenfire meal she wandered up to get some for their breakfast. And for Raven.

Star, moon and nightsun sat high in the night sky, casting a gentle blue light that transformed the world into something magical. Rays of bluish silver struck through the canopy of the oaks, birches and elms that flanked the path. Little toadstools on the forest floor glowed with iridescence when the sliver-blue beams touched their skins. Iluna smiled. This place was special now. She already knew it the way she knew their summer lands.

She'd kept to herself as she always did. There were tamatus from other clans, but they were all mostly old, like Aunty Agath. There were no other girls her age to befriend. So she'd spent most of the Agria so far exploring the mountains. She could have easily traversed the forest blindfolded. Closing her eyes she tried, and other senses were awakened as she walked. Warm air filled the forest, but a slight breeze lifted her hair every so often, cooling the hot night air. The crickets sang in unison. There was an owl over there in the distance. A bat chirruped to her left. And on the other side, down the mountain path, the beat of the dancing drum throbbed. Many now danced by the evenfire. The dance drum rarely ceased during Agria.

And there was something else.

The thud of wings rushed overhead.

"Raven," she whispered and smiled, opening her eyes.

The bird perched on a low branch of an elm, its dark feathers reflecting the blue silver of the light. She stepped closer. The raven ruffled his feathers, shaking his head.

"You want some moonberries, too?" Her hand went to her satchel; she had stuffed it full of the little blue fruits.

The bird cocked its head.

She held out her hand with a few berries and the raven took them and swallowed.

"Good." She breathed. "Let me try something." Her voice was gentle and soothing and the raven blinked.

Iluna had always had a great affinity with animals. Her gift helped her to connect with them easily, allowing her to influence, control them even. But this raven was different. It seemed in control of its own destiny and no one else could get a grip of it.

She held her arm up, elbow bent, so that her forearm was in front of her chest.

"Come, fly to me," she whispered.

The raven cocked its head.

"All is well, Raven. Come." She raised her arm a little higher. "I will give you more berries."

The bird squawked and flapped its wings and in a blink flew in the air. It landed on her arm and Iluna was not prepared for the weight of the bird. He was heavy, but she steadied her arm.

"There, that was easy."

The bird's eyes were dark. Darker than anything Iluna had seen before. Everyone spoke of Ilun, the time of darkness that came after Agria as being the darkest thing in the world, with no light for eight full days. No nightsun or daysun, no moon, no stars; just thick inky blackness. But surely even that couldn't be as dark as the raven's eyes. She swayed, suddenly feeling giddy, and the bird flew off, squawking again.

She called out as she made her way back down the mountain path but the raven did not seem to be willing to return to her that night and his presence – that mysterious wave of energy – remained out of reach. Perhaps he wasn't happy that she hadn't given him more berries. He loved the moonberries. Next time she'd give him some straight away.

As she drew close to the camp the music of the drums and singing pulsed in louder wafts with the gentle gusts of breeze. The aroma of roasting meat still filled the air like it did every night. Another sound came to her, too – laughter, children's laughter. And something else.

The path took her down to a ford that crossed the river. It was a popular place for swimming and fishing. And just now she could see that Golldo stood, still as a river boulder, with his fishing spear in hand. Iluna had learnt his name not long after the arrival of the Otter clan and their Soragan – her name was Cypra, she'd learnt that too. And she was one of the oldest Soragans, nearly as old as the Grand Soragan himself. Iluna would never forget the day she first saw her; the way she walked so tall, with some strong and determined will in her expression, and Golldo, with all his imperfections, limping along behind.

In any other clan a baby born with such abnormalities would have been exposed almost immediately after birth, releasing his soul from the anguish of his physical imperfections. But Golldo was now a man. There were whispers about him throughout the entire camp. Izhur told her that Cypra had taken pity on him and allowed him to live and to stop asking questions about it or she'd be just like all the other gossips with nothing better to occupy her mind. Iluna didn't want to gossip. Who would she gossip with? Aunty slept most of the time or just chuckled quietly to herself whenever Iluna mentioned anything about Golldo or Cypra. But she was curious. She wanted to know more.

She took a step closer and peered down at the giant. He hadn't moved. He seemed to be waiting. Agria was a good time to catch fish as the insects were just as active during the night as they were in the day, more so possibly. She'd eaten more trout and eels here than she'd had in her entire life. Their rich oily taste was fast becoming her favourite. Aunty liked them too, they were easy for an old woman to eat, she'd said.

Blue light reflected on the water and Golldo still hadn't moved. Just then something hit the giant on his leg making him swat and lose his balance a little. The giggling returned, closer. She could feel them, and a familiar essence among them – Yuli.

A rock flew out of the undergrowth and Golldo completely lost his footing. He yelped and fell into the river. A mighty splash echoed off the rocks. Laughter flowed out with the children. There were many of them – nine or ten perhaps. Yuli was foremost among them, laughing and pointing at Golldo as the big man's arms circled in the water.

"In the river where you belong, fish-boy," he yelled and the other children laughed all the more.

Golldo came up and his mouth opened just the way a fish did when it tested the air. His arms still flailed, making foamy waves in the blue water.

"See, he even breathes as a fish does." A boy, a little taller than Yuli, mimicked Golldo, gulping in air like a creature of the deep.

"More like an eel," Yuli said, laughing.

Golldo's eyes showed more white than she'd ever seen in a person and his arms thrashed wildly. His head tried desperately to stay above the water but he was tiring and he was beginning to breathe the water, coughing, his panic making it worse.

The other children were still laughing and name-calling, oblivious to what was happening. Why was Yuli so stupid?

Iluna stepped out. "He's drowning, you fools." She paused long enough to see a change in their faces before diving from the top of a large boulder into the river. Under the water the laughter of the children muted and darkness billowed before her. Her skin prickled in the cool depths of the river. Above, rays of silver penetrated and danced in the dark blue. Golldo still thrashed, but he was tiring fast.

She kicked her legs and reached for him. With one arm around his jaw she found the surface and breathed.

The children's laughter had been replaced by panic. "What will we do?" one said.

"We're in so much trouble. Cypra's going to punish us!" said another.

Iluna spoke quietly to Golldo. "Breathe, let me take you. Just breathe."

Gradually they came to the shore and she dragged him up along the rocky riverbed, the smooth round surface of the river rocks felt warm underfoot.

"Let's run!"

Iluna looked up. It was Yuli who'd said it. The children followed his order in an instant. She watched them go, scrambling over the boulders that lined the river. None of them looked back. She frowned. They wouldn't receive a punishment now. Who'd believe the tale of a tamatu?

She turned back to Golldo. He was sitting to the side, coughing up water.

"That's right, keep coughing. It's a good sign that your body is getting rid of all the water. You'll be safe now," she soothed.

He glanced at her as he coughed. His large eyes and oversized lips really did give him the appearance of a fish. What a cruelty that he couldn't swim like one.

"What happened here?"

Iluna jumped and turned to see the woman standing in a beam of nightlight that penetrated the canopy. She gulped. Would she blame her?

"Your – friend. He fell in the river – he was fishing. There was – an accident."

"Accident? I doubt your words, child." The Soragan's eyes were sharp, their ice blue almost seemed to glow in the night. "Golldo is the best fisherman I know. He has not once fallen in the water. No. I think some trouble has befallen him tonight."

Iluna nodded, slowly. There was no use denying it. This woman would know a lie, she was sure. She licked her lips. "Some of the children, they were teasing him. He lost his footing and slipped." She pointed to the spot where he had fallen. "He couldn't swim."

The woman's eyes changed subtly as she looked Iluna over. Iluna glanced down at her tunic. It was wet and dripped on the rocks. Her hair hung in dark limp tendrils over her shoulders. She must have looked like a water nymph.

"I see what has happened here … Iluna."

Iluna's heart jumped. "You know my name?"

The woman bent her head. "You are Izhur's charge. You must go to the Soragans' tent. But you cannot go like that. Do you have a ceremonial robe?"

Iluna nodded. "Yes, but it wasn't …"

"Run, put it on, and brush your hair."

Iluna's breath shuddered a little. She sniffed and blinked. It had been many years since she had cried, but this was too much. She was the one who had saved Golldo. She stepped forward.

"Hurry, child, we will be expecting you before midnight. I will help Golldo now."

Iluna nodded and ran as best she could with blurred vision. She remembered the last time she was punished by Izhur and Belwas. Now she had to front all of the Soragans together. It wasn't fair! Yuli and Anton, they were never punished.

YULI

"*W*ill you keep up, Yuli!"

Yuli pouted but quickened his pace. Izhur hadn't said anything about Iluna, or what happened to the fish-man, but he'd found Yuli not long after and was now dragging him to the Soragans' tent. The little witch must have told him, and now Yuli was to be punished by Xaroth himself. He should have told Izhur about the raven, but the woman had scared him out of it. He prayed to Atoll that he wouldn't be punished. He didn't want to displease the Grand Soragan. He was the most powerful Soragan around; more so than Izhur. Yuli wished he was Xaroth's prentice rather than Izhur's, but then he'd have to leave his mother, and he wouldn't like that.

"For Ona's sake, hurry, Yuli." Izhur had stopped to urge him on again. "And ready yourself for the sight of your young life. Finally, they will all know of what I speak."

Yuli pouted again. Izhur had been murmuring to himself as they walked through the camps. He always did that when he was excited. Yuli had wondered if Izhur was happy that Yuli was going to get a punishment. He'd always favoured Iluna.

"What am I going to see?" he asked half-heartedly.

"Oh, her light, her bright light!"

"Whose light?" Yuli's father was always saying that Izhur was half mad; perhaps he was right.

Izhur stopped. "Iluna's light." Then he doubled his step.

Yuli stared. Iluna? "What do you mean?" He ran to catch up, trying to stop his voice from sounding whiney.

Izhur didn't slow down as he answered. "She is a gift, from Ona herself, our Iluna. Now, finally they will all see what I have seen."

Yuli didn't really know what Izhur was rambling on about, and he didn't like the sound of Iluna getting all the attention. She didn't deserve such a privilege. But at least he wasn't in trouble; it didn't sound like it anyway.

They came to the Soragans' tent and finally Izhur stopped. He put a hand on Yuli's shoulder, looking down his slender nose as he spoke. "You are to sit right behind me. When it is time, use the sight as I have been teaching you." He hesitated. "Or at least try to use it. If nothing happens then just sit still and be quiet, and don't fidget until it is over."

Yuli nodded and followed Izhur into the tent. The other Soragans were all seated and those with prentices had them sit directly behind them as Izhur had instructed him to do. Yuli took a cushion and sat. Then he saw her, Iluna.

She stood in the middle of the space wearing a ceremonial robe, the one she'd worn for the opening ceremony. It was a plain leather cloak, brown and beaten, with no engraving or decoration. At least it showed everyone her status as tamatu. Iluna looked wide-eyed around her. Belwas was whispering in her ear and she nodded, but fear stirred in her eyes. Yuli smirked. She didn't belong here.

A boy stood next to her. Yuli had seen him around camp but did not know his name. Soragan Jana was talking to him. The boy was young, perhaps four. He looked just as scared as Iluna.

Xaroth struck his staff eight times and silence followed. "It is time."

Belwas and Jana took their cushioned seats, and everyone looked to the Grand Soragan.

"Tonight we will find my new prentice and he, or she, shall return with me when my clan leaves Agria." His voice, its usual raspy hiss, made him sound more powerful. "I will hear what you have to say. The boy, Ityl, who will speak for him?"

Jana stood. "I will."

Xaroth nodded. "I'm listening."

The young Soragan walked into the centre of the circle so that she stood next to Ityl. After his scary experience with the old woman Soragan, Yuli decided he didn't like girls to be Soragans. Her voice wavered a lot. "Ityl has shown much promise. He has a strong light and there are early signs of divination abilities."

Jana spoke about Ityl's family, and his other skills. He was a promising goat herder, too. Yuli realized this same process would have been done for him when he was a baby. He wondered what Izhur would have said about him then. No doubt he would have spoken about his father's great hunting skills.

Finally Jana finished.

"I thank you," Xaroth said, before gesturing to the boy. "Come closer. Let me look upon you."

Jana put a hand on the boy's shoulder and nudged him forward. The boy walked reluctantly to Xaroth, tripping on a reed mat.

"Good, now look at me." Xaroth gestured toward his own eyes. "Soragans, prentices, open your eyes and see his light."

Yuli recognized the cue. "Please let this work, Ona," he whispered, and stilled his breathing, opening his sight as Izhur had instructed him scores of times. Sometimes it worked, sometimes it didn't, and Yuli had no idea why. But this time it worked. His sight opened and he saw through the filter of the Otherworld, where spirits good and evil lurked. Each Soragan and prentice was connected. A fine silver thread ran through each of them, making something akin to a spider's web in the starlight. It was breathtaking.

"Ona, show us his light," Xaroth intoned.

And a small blue glow radiated deep within the boy's essence. It pulsed, like a beat, and whispy tendrils wove out from the centre.

Yuli's eyes widened. He'd never seen anyone's light before. It was beautiful. And it was the mark of the gifted. He wondered what *his* light would look like.

"Thank you, child," Xaroth said, and Yuli lost the vision. "You may sit." The Grand Soragan gestured with his hand and the boy returned to the centre of the tent, eyes wider than before.

Yuli's gaze then turned to Iluna and he remembered what Izhur had been muttering. *"They will all see what I have seen."* Was her gift really so great?

"Who will speak for the girl?" Xaroth's voice rasped again.

"I will." Izhur stepped forward and placed a hand on Iluna's shoulder.

"I was present at Iluna's birth. As many of you know it was a difficult time, one that required my presence as Soragan, for it was the first night of Ilun."

There was an audible intake of breath. Yuli heard his own, too. Izhur had never spoken about the details of Iluna's birth, but he'd heard whisperings about it from his father, and others in the clan. He'd always known there was something strange about the girl.

"It was during the birth that I first saw her light. I had to help her in the Otherworld. And it was then the brightest light I had ever seen. But she was just a babe, her light has grown since and continues to." Izhur's voice had taken on the fast pace it always did when he was excited. "Soragans, prentices. I suggest you brace yourselves."

There was a buzz of excitement.

ADERYN WOOD

"Wait." Xaroth's whispery voice seemed to cut through the din. "I need to hear of her skills, her abilities, her usefulness to the clan."

Izhur's head snapped up and he peered down his long nose at Xaroth "Everything. Healing, dream-guiding, spirit-warding, Otherworld traveling, visioning, path-finding, soul-seeking, daydreaming, animism, imagining, and divining." Izhur paused.

Yuli pouted. This couldn't be true. He'd never seen Iluna do any of these things. And Izhur hadn't taught him any of it either.

"And one thing more," Izhur continued. "I believe she holds the gift of binding."

At this there was an outbreak of voices as Soragans turned to each other, speaking at once. The old hag, Cypra seemed to be smirking.

Xaroth raised a hand for quiet and the voices hushed. "What makes you think so?"

Izhur shook his head. "I have no clear evidence. It is but a feeling. Her animism is strong."

Xaroth's eyes seemed to smile.

"I would agree with Izhur," Belwas spoke. "I met with him at our northern gathering a few summers past. I saw her light. But she has something else. A deep ability, I felt it."

Iluna's black hair hung in messy strands. Her eyes were dark and wide, and watched everyone at once as though looking for an escape. She was a witch. Couldn't they see that?

"Is her totem known?" Xaroth asked, his eyes squinting.

"No. I have been training her in the rudiments only," Izhur said.

It was a lie. She'd received just as many lessons as Yuli had, probably more by the list of talents Izhur had just rattled off.

"I am happy to speak to her other strengths." A woman's voice cut through the silence – Cypra. Yuli remembered the way she'd looked at him that day he saw Iluna talking to the raven. He wished he could speak now, to tell them the proof that she was a

106

witch. Only witches consorted with ravens despite what the old woman had tried to tell him. Maybe she was a witch, too.

Xaroth frowned. "Go on."

"I can tell you that she is brave and righteous. She is exactly the type of prentice we all look for. Tonight I happened across a group of insolents teasing Golldo. The poor soul had almost drowned after being forced into the river."

Yuli gulped.

"All of the cowards ran when he started to flail," she continued. "But Iluna, she dove straight into the dark waters of the river, fearless, and saved his life." Cypra's icy eyes met Yuli's, and he froze. Did she know?

The mood had changed. The Soragans and prentices were all looking at her with admiration, hope even. Yuli felt his lips start to pout again but he forced them to relax.

"Enough," Xaroth said. "Come here, child."

Izhur whispered to her and Iluna stepped forward.

Xaroth gestured toward his eyes again. "Ona, show us …"

Suddenly there was only light. Yuli wanted to turn, to squint even, there was no respite! It radiated out from her in golden beams. Like trying to look at the daysun, it hurt his eyes.

"Stop her! Get her away!"

Yuli snapped back from the Otherworld to see Xaroth cowering behind his cushions and holding his hands in front of his face. Izhur grabbed Iluna's hand and guided her back to the centre of the circle.

Izhur turned as he spoke, eyeing every Soragan. "Now you understand? She is a gift, a great gift from Ona. She, more than any other, needs to be prenticed."

Xaroth seemed to recover and dabbed his forehead with his robe. He sat back on his cushions and resumed some semblance of authority.

"Thank you, Izhur. That will be all." He gestured towards Izhur's place in front of Yuli.

Izhur frowned. "But this is worthy of discussion. You would all agree there is no other possible candidate. Iluna must be fully prenticed! If not to Xaroth then to one of you. At first I was loath to give her up." Izhur looked to the ground, his stiff shoulders slumping a little. "I was being selfish. Her gift is so great it would benefit all of us – all clans! Someone must take her on."

"I said that will be all!" Xaroth's hiss cut the air.

Izhur stood for a moment, glaring at the Grand Soragan. Then he turned and stalked toward his cushion.

"Thank you. I have made my decision." Xaroth looked at the circle. "I will take the boy."

There was uproar as all the Soragans spoke at once, Izhur the loudest among them. "How can you do that?"

Xaroth put his hand in the air again. "I have made my decision. The circle is closed for tonight."

"But there is another matter we agreed to discuss. Surely you had not forgotten, Xaroth." Cypra stood in front of him, blocking his way out of the tent.

Xaroth's lips turned to a snarl and he shook his head. "I said the circle has closed. We will meet tomorrow night. Jana!"

The young Soragan got to her feet. "Yes, Grand Soragan?"

"Tell Ityl's people the decision has been made. He will be leaving with me two days after Agria."

The young Soragan nodded.

Xaroth stepped around Cypra, and limped out of the tent.

PART IV
WINTER OF THE VALLEY

IZHUR

*I*zhur sat in his tree-dwell with two wolfskins tied tight around him. His small fire blazed, offering light and warmth. Outside the daysun danced along the horizon, while the thin crescent of the moon slid higher in the black sky. Both the nightsun and Atoll's Star had gone to their wintry rest five days past. The seasons were growing colder and darker. Ilun would return the winter after next.

An icy breeze shivered the back of his neck and Izhur inched closer to the fire to continue his task – grinding cinnamon bark. Yuli didn't do enough to help with such menial tasks as restocking their stores, and winter was the time to do it. Still, the boy had shown much improvement since – since ...

Izhur grimaced. He focused on his stone and bowl, and the rhythm of grinding. Yes, Yuli. He had improved. The young man now took their lessons more seriously, and his gift had grown in power. He had aspirations, he'd told Izhur, to be a great Soragan, one so powerful he could fend off attacking tribes.

Izhur had to smile. No clan had been attacked by another for an age. The oldest evenfire tales were filled with the great battles between Wolf and Bear; Bear and Snake; Lion and Dragon.

Particularly the Dragons. But the Dragon clan no longer existed. Their former lands were far away; the memory of how to find them had been lost. Some even doubted the Dragon had existed at all. But images of the legendary battles came to Izhur now that he thought of those tales. Blood spilled from spears and axes, battle fires raged, screams pierced the air as mothers and fathers ran to protect their children, and great beasts had flown through the sky, breathing fire. Soragans hurled lightning from their very hands, just as Izhur had that night Iluna was born. A static energy passed through the tree-dwell, causing Izhur's skin to prickle. He blinked and realised he was looking at his hand. Strange, he'd never been able to do the lightning trick again, not since that night.

The creak of the steps made him turn to see Talith at the tree-dwell's entrance carrying an oil pot. Talith was the clan's messenger boy now, and Izhur wondered what ominous news would be sent at this time.

"Talith, come in out of the cold. What troubles you?"

The boy stepped toward the fire, holding a hand to the flames, shivering.

"I have come to fetch you, Soragan. We have a visitor."

Izhur frowned. A visitor – in the middle of winter? It was rare and smelled of trouble, but he nodded and pulled another wolf-skin around his shoulders. "I will come."

Izhur's tree-dwell was set apart from the others, as befit his status as the clan's Soragan. Now that Yuli was his prentice, the boy shared the shelter, but returned to his family's tree-dwell frequently. More often than he should, although Izhur didn't reprimand him. The boy was fast becoming a man at nearly four-teen summers, and was now capable of more mature conversa-tion. He pouted less and threw fewer tantrums. Sometimes, Yuli's company was almost pleasant. But Izhur valued his privacy and delighted in the nights of solitude his prentice's absence granted him.

It was dark now. Just the thin sliver of the moon filled the sky. Whispy puffs of clouds concealed it every now and again. They'd probably see snow soon.

Talith's oil pot lit their way, revealing spakling icicles on the rocky ground, until they came to the evenfire. The entire clan was there, as was their custom, trying to gather warmth.

"He's here," Ugot said.

Izhur saw the visitor and his mouth fell open. Her height and short cropped hair made her instantly recognizable.

"Cypra," he said.

"Izhur." Her eyes burned their ice-blue. "I would talk to you alone."

"If you have news we would prefer it shared among the Circle." Zodor stepped forward.

Cypra nodded. "And I will share it. But first I will talk to your Soragan. Alone."

∞

IN HIS TREE-DWELL Izhur added another log to the fire before offering Cypra a cushion and a warm fur.

"Some honeywine?"

Cypra nodded. "Please. It will help take the chill off. Your winters are much colder than ours."

He poured a small cup for both of them and joined her by the fire. "Why are you here, Cypra? Something is amiss, is it not? A visitor in winter is a rare thing."

Cypra sipped her wine and closed her eyes. She was thinner, drawn. The wrinkles at her eyes seemed deeper. She had aged these last six years. "Yes." Her eyes, when she opened them were red and teary. "Izhur! My clan, they're all gone! Killed!"

Izhur gasped. The Otter Clan? All gone? It must be a mistake.

He reached out and touched her arm. Eventually her sobbing calmed and she took another sip of the honey drink, hands shaking.

"How?" Izhur whispered.

"Strangers. People. Monsters. Not from any clan. They were strong. So many." She wiped her nose and caught her breath. "The men, they attacked us and there were too many of them for our hunters to resist. Their hunting tools; they were made of stuff stronger than stone and when they hit rock they caused sparks to fly. They sliced right through our men. And they, they – assaulted our women.

"I tried to use my gifts. To help in some way. But there were so many of them, and they had their own Soragans. So powerful. Izhur, I saw fire come from their hands and worse. Their magic." She shook. "I couldn't compete with it."

"How did you get away?"

"Golldo." Cypra shook her head. Her tears ran thick and fat drops of them fell on the wolf pelt on the floor. "He took my hand and forced me to move, to leave. I followed him blindly through the forest. Abandoning my clan."

"He wanted to save you."

Cypra wore a sad smile. "But one of them, the enemy, he followed us. He tried to swing at me with his knife. But Golldo, he – he ..." Cypra put a palm to her eyes as more sobs took her voice away.

"He stood in the attacker's way?" Izhur suggested gently.

Cypra nodded.

"And he died for it." Izhur closed his eyes. Golldo was always considered a monster, a durg. But few would be as heroic.

"So I took what little power I had left and disguised myself as best I could, and fled. To warn you."

"Cypra ..." Izhur hesitated, the shock stalling his tongue. "To see such horrific things befall our clan, it is our worst nightmare."

Cypra closed her eyes, sniffing.

"I was only tonight reflecting on the old evenfire tales our children enjoy to hear." Words finally came to Izhur and he let them spill out. "The Dream-Day tales of Doom that tell of the ancient wars and battles. We've all thought those days were in our distant past. But I see they have come around again, as all things do. Perhaps it was not a mistake that I thought on that tonight. Divination is not my strength, as you know, but those thoughts and images, they were vivid. And I have a feeling just now; your clan will not be the last to suffer."

Premonitions always left a sickness in him, and Izhur's stomach roiled with foreboding. Ona's people had a dark and unknown enemy.

Cypra nodded, wiping her cheek. "We must send warning to the other clans and summon a meeting of elders and Soragans. We must prepare."

"Yes." Izhur gazed into the fire. "Let us go and speak with our Circle. We will put things in motion tonight."

"Wait." Cypra reached out and touched his hand, her fingers light and cool. "Before we go, I want to talk to you of the girl."

Izhur swallowed.

"Have you continued training her?"

"You know it was forbidden." They'd made the decision last Agria. The Grand Soragan had stacked the votes, that was certain. Only three people voted against it – himself, Cypra and Belwas. There was nothing he could do. He was to cease Iluna's lessons at once and treat her like the tamatu they all deemed her to be. At the next festival, the Grand Soragan had said they would take her gift.

"Yes, we all forbade it. But why has that stopped you? You're far enough away from Xaroth. A little training on the side, he wouldn't know about it."

Izhur clenched his teeth. "I thought about it. But Zodor was in league with Xaroth. I know it. How else did he know so much about what happened at her birth and everything else in our clan? If I trained her, Yuli would know. And he would tell his father who would send word to the Snakes. It could be that I would lose my gift. My hands were tied, Cypra. I had to stop training her, for her own safety as much as mine. Better that she is not trained and alive than trained and burned as a witch."

"Well, it may come to that. But I fear, after what I have seen, she may be our only chance. We all know how strong her gift is, Izhur. You more than any know this."

He nodded.

"She may be the only one who can save us if these savages move north."

"It is likely, isn't it? They may come for all of us."

"I think your premonition may be right. I heard them speak amongst each other, but it was a different language. They were so intent on killing and thieving. They took everything we had – our clothes, our gems, our gold. They were particularly fond of our gold. And they took us. Some of our children they did not kill but took them. I hope they will treat them decently. I worry about them every day. Perhaps the ones that died are the lucky ones. But this killing – this taking. They were hungry for it and they will want more."

Izhur tapped his temple. "Xaroth's clan, the Snake, their country is closer to you. Why not go to him first?"

"Because, as I have told you, the only way we can stand against them is to train Iluna. Izhur, I've spent a lot of time meditating on this as I walked the long distance to your clan. This is why she has been given to us. Only her power will give us a chance. You know Xaroth will not allow that. The man's pride stands in the way of making sensible decisions. We must do this without his permission. We must turn against our fellow Soragans."

Izhur didn't like it, but Cypra was a powerful Soragan and if she was unable to defend her clan they were all at risk. Perhaps Iluna was the answer. Perhaps this was her purpose.

"And Belwas," he said. "He has a strong power of foresight. Perhaps he has seen something?" Izhur blinked, something tugged at his memories. "Yes, in fact I think I remember Belwas telling me of nightmares he'd had. He was sure they were a premonition, but we thought they were some sort of warning for the Bear clan. At last Agria, he told me he'd had no more dreams, but perhaps he knows more now."

"And their lands are close."

"We could be with the Bear in less than ten nights." Izhur scratched his cheek. "Come, let's tell the others. We will talk more of Iluna later."

ILUNA

*I*luna collected the last of the carroots in the dying light. Her hands were cold and muddy from digging in the icy soil. She rubbed them together before picking up her satchel and heading back to her shelter. It had been Aunty's tree-dwell, and it stood away from the others here in their winter lands. Iluna had liked that when Aunty was around. It meant they could hide away from their clan members. But Aunty Agath had passed over to the Otherworld last winter, and Iluna lived alone now. Her loneliness wrapped around her every day, more tightly than the wolf skins she wore. It had been six winters since Izhur had stopped teaching her, and she missed his lessons desperately. Not for the teachings, although she loved to learn. No, it was the company she missed. She even missed Yuli's tantrums.

Izhur was still her friend. Every full moon they would share the moon meal. It was the custom for families to share a private meal during the full moon. Iluna and Izhur had no family – they only had each other. She looked forward to the full moon constantly.

Now, the moon, a sliver as thin as a strand of hair, was covered by dark clouds most of the time. The stars remained hidden and as the daysun sank even further, darkness billowed. She shivered, tasting ice in the air. There would be snow tonight.

She paused at Izhur's shelter, took a handful of carroots from her satchel and climbed up to put them in his tree-dwell. Last night she'd dreamt he'd return tonight, and if that was true she wanted him to have something to eat.

He'd left over two eightnights ago with Cypra and the others. Izhur had told them of Cypra's clan, the Otter, how they had all been attacked and killed and worse.

The woman stood tall and proud, but tears had streaked her cheeks. A foreign tribe with a strange language had raided the Otter as they slept, stealing their possessions and their children. The men were killed protecting their tribe and the women were defiled and murdered. It was worse than any evenfire horror story, but they had to hear it. Many had cried, especially the children, and now they were frightened – now that Zodor and the other strong hunters had left with Izhur and Cypra to meet with the Bear clan. There were hunters who'd remained to protect them – but not of the strength and leadership of Zodor. Iluna felt the tension in the clan – a constant buzz of anguish. There had been tears, and even arguments. Amak and the other elders had done their best to quell the clan's fears in Izhur's abence, but the medicine woman was panicked herself. Everyone awaited their return.

Iluna wasn't scared. Not now. She had been before, when she'd had the dreams. Hearing the story of the foreign tribe attacking the Otter clan had matched the images she recalled from her dreams. She'd seen it happen in her sleep. The realisation had made her stomach drop when it came to her. Then she was hit by another truth. It was early autumn when she'd had those dreams. She'd wake to morning sunshine streaming through the golden leaves of her oak. But the massacre had happened in the winter.

She'd foreseen it.

It was more proof of her gift, the power she had. But this knowledge she kept hidden, deep. She would not tell Izhur or Cypra. She would not tell anyone. For if she practised her gift the Grand Soragan would take her powers, and if she resisted they would burn her as a witch. She knew this; she'd overheard Yuli talking to his brother and father about it. And Izhur had ceased their lessons. He wouldn't speak of why. He simply told her he had to focus on teaching Yuli now that he was his recognised prentice. But Iluna knew the truth. So she didn't tell anyone she could see the future in her dreams. She didn't tell the clan Izhur, and Cypra and Zodor, and the others would be returning to them tonight. And she didn't tell them Zodor had been injured. She didn't tell them either of her secret lessons she administered herself in the forest when the clan thought she was looking for berries or roots. She would practise everything Izhur had taught her and more. Ideas and thoughts would come to her as though nature itself had become her teacher and she felt her power growing.

But Izhur had taught her one last thing.

"A vital lesson, Iluna. It will keep you safe," he'd said. He'd showed her how to disguise her light and hide her gift deep within. She had practiced this every day so that now her light looked dull and sometimes blank, and anyone searching for her essence would see a normal girl, or one with a weak gift. She kept herself disguised at all times around others. It had drained her energy at the beginning, and made her sleepy; now it was as easy as wearing a cloak. In the forest, when just the trees and the animals were witnesses, she revealed her gift and knew it would be as bright as the daysun if anyone spied her.

She smiled at her little secret as she stepped down out of Izhur's shelter and walked to her own tree-dwell. The old oak was bare now. The last leaf had fallen over two moons ago. But her hut, Aunty's hut, was warm and cosy. She had double packed the walls with mud to keep Agath warm in her old age. Aunty had appreciated it. "You're such a treasure, little bird," she'd said everyday. She'd slept more than ever in her final days, but she still managed to tell her stories, and Iluna had loved them.

Iluna shook her head and swallowed the lump in her throat as she squatted to unpack the carroots from her satchel.

That was when she heard the shouts. Out there, by the even-fire, there was shouting, and Iluna knew by the sound of desperation in their voices that Izhur and the others had returned. Zodor's injuries had become known. The sense of panic grew as she knew it would. A woman's screaming pierced through the shouting – Ida. Zodor was the great hunter of the Wolf clan; he was a rock upon which their security was founded. "Let them try to attack us." She'd heard Ugot say one day, "they haven't met the likes of our Zodor." But now he was injured, their faith would be injured, too. Their strength faltered.

The shouting continued as Iluna stoked her little fire. She would not attend the evenfire tonight. There would be nothing she could do anyway. She fetched a bone pot and filled it with water from her stone jug, tiny icicles floated on the surface. She'd make a mash with her carroots that would warm and fill her stomach.

Then the wailing started – a high piteous sound that carried to her easily through the trees. Ida again. Mourning and grief spread thickly in that wail. Iluna hesitated with the bone pot in one hand. Ida had cared for her despite the cruelty of her husband and sons. She'd fed her and bathed her as a babe. And she'd clothed her, always handing her old robes and smocks, and wolf skins. She'd done as much as she could for her, more, considering her husband. Iluna sniffed as she poured the icy water into the pot. Everyone else in the Wolf had treated her like a burden; something to be tolerated at best. Well she had done her best to ease their burden, withdrawing more and more from the clan. She rarely attended evenfire now. It worried Izhur; he wanted her to go every night to the communal meal. But he didn't know what it was like to sit amongst people who despised him so. It was more lonely than being alone.

Ida's grief-stricken cry came to her again and Iluna could feel pain and grief through her very limbs. Ida had always been kind. Iluna swallowed and put the pot down. Perhaps she could do something.

She wrapped her wolfskin around her and descended into the night.

The shouting had ceased now, but Ida still wailed. As Iluna drew closer the shadows of the clan danced in the flames of the evenfire. Some were moving around, still in a panic, not knowing what to do.

She came into the circle of light and saw him. Zodor lay by the fire on a bed made from two tree limbs and a skin. They must have carried him on it. He had just the one wound, but it was deep and fatal. Something had cut open his abdomen and slow blood gushed.

Amak and Lili bent over him, together holding a poultice pressed down on his belly, but the blood still flowed.

Izhur crouched beside Amak whispering in her ear. Cypra stood by his feet, her head bent. Her stance told Iluna all she needed to know – Zodor was as good as dead. Yuli and Anton stood by their mother, wide eyed. Yuli was crying. Anton was trying to stall tears, but they escaped despite him blinking them back. Ida held Zodor's head in her lap and wept loud sobs, repeating the word, "Husband, husband, my husband."

The whole clan was in mourning. Ugot and his wife and sons were rocking where they sat. Gwend walked in circles murmuring to herself. "We're doomed, we're doomed."

Mothers tried to comfort their crying children while they cried themselves. A group of young hunters spoke rapidly about finding the beast that did this. A mountain cat had attacked the group and injured Zodor when he'd tried to protect them.

Mountain cats get hungry in winter. Iluna knew this, as did everyone. It was why they didn't travel during the winter moons.

Izhur had finished talking to Amak and now he looked at Cypra. There was a subtle nod between them, and Izhur held up his hand. The clan quieted. Only the gentle sobs of Ida could be heard.

"Amak can do no more for our great hunter." His eyes looked more grim than Iluna had ever seen them. "And there is nothing I or Cypra can do either. The beast that did this to him went too far."

Ugot spat, the way he always did before he spoke. "If only Jakom was still with us. He'd be able to save him. He was worth ten of you."

Izhur bent his head, as though agreeing. Iluna breathed hard, flaring her nostrils. She restrained the urge to send a fat winter buzz fly over to bite Ugot's thick hide.

"Please, Soragan. Is there nothing you can do?" It was Anton who spoke. He was almost sixteen summers now, and was truly a man. His muscles gleamed as powerfully as his father's had. But the look on his face was more boy than man. His eyes, tear-filled and swollen, looked at Izhur with desperate hope.

Izhur sighed. "I am sorry, Anton."

Yuli sobbed then, with his arms around his mother, they rocked together gently. Iluna felt for him for the first time in her life.

"What about her?"

Iluna's head snapped up. Anton was pointing to her. His head danced above the flames of the evenfire and she could see his eyes, burning.

"She has powerful magic. She can do it." He shouted now.

Iluna shook her head as panic rose in her heart. She shouldn't have come!

"NO!" Yuli was on his feet again wrenching his brother's pointed arm down. "She is a witch. She probably did this to him."

"Don't be a fool, brother. She has much power; we all know this. He's been saying it since she was born." Anton gestured at Izhur, who now held his face in his palms. "She is our last chance; we must try it."

"No!" Yuli stomped his foot the way he used to as a child.

"Anton, Iluna does have much power it is true, but she has no training in this. She wouldn't know what to do," Izhur spoke quietly and Iluna breathed a little more easily.

"And Yuli could be right. What if she did curse him?" Ugot added.

Iluna thought about the buzz fly again.

"She wouldn't have, Ugot." There was a hush. It was Ida who spoke. She looked up at Iluna. Her eyes and nose were red, her cheeks wet with tears. "Iluna, can you do it?"

Everyone turned to her, even Ugot.

Iluna swallowed. She'd healed animals before, in the forest. A squirrel only two nights past laid panting and dying on the forest floor; Iluna had touched it with her hands and gone over to the Otherworld to mend his wounds with her essence. It took a lot of energy to heal small animals. She'd slept a full day and night, and was as hungry as a bear in spring afterwards. She wasn't sure if she had the stamina to help Zodor, but her fingers itched to touch his wound.

"I can try, if you like?" she whispered.

Ida smiled then. "Please, I would like that."

Iluna nodded and stepped forward, just as the snow started to fall.

ANTON

$\mathcal{T}$he fire crackled in the pit. The circle members, amongst others, sat crammed in Zodor's tree-dwell, foregoing the Tree of Knowledge on account of the hunter's injuries. They had to sit close together on the furs. The smell of sweat and fear mingled in the tight space, and Anton longed to be out in the forest where he belonged. His father lay on a wooly skin. On his wound lay a poultice of dried comfrey, which Amak had applied when Iluna had finished her—Anton took a deep breath. Whatever it was she had done, she had saved his father's life.

"How are you, Zodor?" It was Ugot who spoke.

Zodor nodded. "I am well. I will recover." He smiled. "Amak has done good work, as usual. We are fortunate to have her in our clan."

Anton studied the others. Izhur was looking down, rubbing his temples. The elders and hunters all watched Zodor, clearly relieved he had survived.

No one had told Zodor the girl had saved him. Indeed, no one had spoken two words about it that morning, or afternoon.

Anton started to ask his mother about it, but she had tutted him. "Let's not talk of it in front of your father," she'd whispered.

It was spectacular. She'd walked up to his father, who was dying, placed her hands on his wound, and by midnight he had healed. Or healed enough for Amak to take over and do her work. Iluna had been exhausted and couldn't even walk afterwards. Izhur and Cypra had put her to bed.

"Yes." Ugot spat. "Amak is a fine medicine woman, thank Ona we have her." He popped a tulu nut in his mouth and started chewing.

"What happened at the Bear clan, Zodor? What did you discuss?" Hogath asked.

Izhur answered. "They were just as shocked and frightened as we had been, and they agree that we must act. The Bear will send runners to the Lion and Eagle Clans. We are to go to the others. Every clan is to send their Soragan, if they can, and their senior Circle members. We shall all converge here on the final moon of winter. That should give them enough time for the journey."

"Winter is a dangerous time to be traveling," Ugot said. "The hinterbeasts and mountain cats are notorious; we all know this. And recent years have been ill-omened for us. We know this, too."

Anton read the unsaid meaning in the old hunter's words. Ugot sat with his hands held loosely in the sign of warding on his lap, fingertips just touching. He remained distrustful of Iluna, and still believed her to be a witch. He now spoke of her as the Malfirena, the demon who was foretold to bring about the ultimate downfall of all Ona's people in the Dream Day tales of Doom. But she had saved Anton's father. That counted for a lot.

"That is why we must send our best hunters as messengers. Men who can protect themselves," Zodor said, wincing slightly with pain.

"We sent our best hunter to the Bear. Even the great Zodor

could not protect himself from a mountain cat." Ugot stirred the fire.

"That was different, my friend. I was wounded because I was protecting the others. A hunter alone, unencumbered, will outwit any beast, even in the very dark of winter."

"Who do you have in mind?" Wogul asked.

"Gandro can go to the Ox. He will be glad of the chance to spend a night with his wife's clan, to tell her mother of her grandchildren."

Ugot nodded. "My son, Ulath, will go to the Deer. He will see his betrothed while he is there."

Zodor looked to his son expectantly, and Anton breathed deep, grateful that the Bear already knew of the news and he did not have to spend a night talking to his betrothed. "As the Bear knows of this, I will go to the Snake to see my mother's people." His father nodded approval and Anton exhaled.

Izhur spoke, "It is decided then. I suggest we break circle now and that our messengers are fed well at tonight's evenfire. I will give you each a blessing at first light, an amulet for good travel and protection." Izhur's eyes bore their usual intensity. "I thank you all for your efforts. It will be a difficult journey for you. Remember your message. We will all converge here with the last moon of winter. And stay safe."

∞

SNOWFLAKES DANCED as slow as lazy winter insects. They created a soft translucent blanket on the forest floor, but didn't hinder his tracking. Someone had gone before him, perhaps before dawn, but he was gaining on them. Anton tightened his satchel and lengthened his stride. They were traveling in the same direction as he, and he was curious to catch up and see who it was.

They had to be a clan member for he'd first noticed the tracks near the tree-dwells.

He walked past an artyroot that looked too good to leave. He dug it out quickly and put it in his satchel. Food was scarce in winter. Every bit of it would count and he'd have to hunt on the way. It was at least three eightnight's walk to the Snake clan; that was with the whole tribe. Such a journey wasn't made often. Mostly they visited other clans to witness funeral rites. A large portion of the clan had made the trip last summer, when they'd had a runner inform them his grandfather had died.

Anton remembered the way the women had wailed, his mother included, and they smacked their heads with their hands to show the distress of grief that he had died. Anton spent his time hunting the rabbits and hares that populated the Snake's dry lands. He remembered his grandfather as very old, and not too friendly, and if he was to be honest, he had trouble feeling anything for his passing. But it did distress him to see his mother beating her own head that way.

He remembered the discussion between his father and the Grand Soragan. Yuli and Ugot had been there, too. They'd spoken about their distrust of Iluna. Anton hadn't said anything, but he'd agreed with them. Of course he had. He'd been told all his life she was a witch. Why should he have thought any different? His father spoke openly again about the night she was born and the way Izhur had "defied him". It seemed to be an incident his father could neither forgive nor forget. The Grand Soragan had nodded his head and spoke of next Agria when he would take her power and if she refused she would burn. "I swear it on Ona's light."

But now Anton wondered. His mother had always spoken quiet words of dissent. "She is a good girl," she'd say. His father dismissed it as a woman's folly, especially as she had given Iluna mother's milk as a babe. His brother seemed to despise Iluna most because of that fact. Was he jealous of the attention their mother had given Iluna? His mother had never had a daughter. They all knew of the little kindnesses she had done for the girl over the years. She'd even brushed all her knots out once.

But Iluna had healed his father. He'd seen it with his own eyes. Izhur and Cypra were very powerful, but even they couldn't do what this girl could. And she hadn't even all the training Yuli had. Izhur used to say how the girl was a gift from the Great Mother. That she would make the most powerful Soragan Ona's people had seen. His father had told him this with scorn. But perhaps Izhur was right. Perhaps a powerful Soragan was all that they needed to defend themselves against the marauding foreign tribes.

Perhaps he should speak with Soragan Izhur. But most clan members still distrusted Iluna. All he could do was focus on his task. Anton planned to make the trip in half the time it had taken them to get to the Snake lands the previous summer. He was young, strong and unencumbered. He had good eyes too and could travel in the night; particularly in their own lands.

He paused again to collect a parsroot. He bit the end and put it back in the satchel. The bitter-sweet root crunched in his mouth as he eyed the tracks. The snow had grown heavier and the tracks were a little clearer now. He was close. He swallowed his mouthful and ran on.

He soon came to a clearing in the forest. One he knew well. It was a lookout that he and other hunters in the tribe used often to scout for prey in the valley below. Trees flanked it on one side and a sheer cliff face on the other. The tracks in the snow led to it. They were fresh. He slowed his pace and his breathing, and stepped as quiet as a snow leopard.

And that's when he saw her.

Iluna.

She sat on a boulder cross-legged, her back to him. It looked as though she watched the valley below. Or the world. Her black messy hair stood out in strong contrast with the white snow that surrounded them.

He moved silently. But she turned when he was not five paces near. Her eyes large with some emotion – fear? She sprang to her feet and ran back toward the forest.

"Don't run. I won't hurt you!" He said it quickly. He didn't want her to leave. Not yet.

But she kept running.

"Please. Stay. I won't hurt you."

But on she ran, almost out of sight now.

"Iluna!"

She stopped.

It was the first time he'd ever said her name. Growing up he'd always called her tamatu or witch, or frog face.

"Iluna," he said it again. It seemed to roll off the tongue, like an evenfire song.

She turned; her eyes wary. Her hair, so black, had caught the soft snow. Her lips were tinged with blue.

"You're cold," he said.

She didn't reply, but remained still, blinking occasionally, looking as though she could run again at any moment.

He breathed. "I never thanked you, for what you did."

Silence.

"You saved my father's life. I know no one has spoken of it since. And everyone is pretending it didn't happen. But I saw it. And I know you healed him. And I thank you, Iluna. I thank you."

Her eyes flicked to the snow on the ground. She didn't look as though she'd take flight as much now.

"And—" He wanted to tell her more. "I'm sorry."

A fleeting frown rippled across her brow.

"I'm sorry about when we were younger." Anton remembered the way he had treated her. Many times he had called her names and thrown rocks when the adults weren't around. And there was the time he had chased her down and accused her of witchery in front of the circle.

Her eyes looked frightened again. She didn't know whether to trust him.

"I am truly sorry, Iluna. I was young and foolish. I wish it had never happened."

She looked down at the snow again. Icy flakes fell thickly now. Her lips had turned a darker shade of blue. She wore only one wolfskin wrapped around her small body.

"You're cold, Iluna. You should return. See my mother and tell her you saw me and ask her to make you her ginger tea. She has much of the stuff dried from our last visit with the Snake. That will take the chill off." He nodded and turned to leave, exhaling slowly and watching the steam that flowed from his mouth. It reminded him of the fire dragons in the evenfire stories.

He strode back toward the clearing, hoping she would take heed of his words. Grey clouds moved closer above, pregnant with snow. The day grew colder.

"We're all safe." Her voice sung like a wooden pipe.

He stopped and turned and she stood right there in front of him. He hadn't heard her steps in the snow. She'd make a fine hunter herself. "What do you mean?"

"We're safe. All of us. For now. They won't attack again before the next Agria." Her eyes shifted to the snow and she bounded off, almost as though she flew.

Now it was Anton's turn to blink. They were safe she had said. And he believed her. But what would come after Agria?

"She will bring our downfall if we don't do anything." The old Grand Soragan's words came back to him, and Anton shook them off as he shook off the snow and moved on.

YULI

"Thank you, Mother. The pigeon was delicious." Anton wiped the grease from his chin and gulped down the last of his ginger tea.

"Yes, Mother, thank you," Yuli added, irritated his brother was always the first to compliment their mother's cooking.

"You are very lucky, sons, to have such a mother. And I am a fortunate husband."

Yuli studied his father. Zodor's wounds were healing. He could move more freely now, and was able to hunt the pigeons they had enjoyed for the moon meal. But there was something different about him. He seemed soft and gentle. His father had always been hard as rock. Yuli frowned as he wiped his hands on the reed mat.

"Grandmother is well. She kept telling me if I didn't stop growing she'd have to shout for me to hear her. She said to tell you that Aunt Kira looks after her, and not to worry," Anton said to their mother.

She smiled with glistening eyes.

Anton had told them all about his visit to the Snake clan when he'd returned the previous night. The Grand Soragan would be arriving, along with all the other Soragans and clan elders, at the next full moon.

"Did Xaroth have any other news?" Zodor asked. "For our ears alone?"

Anton wiped his hands on his wolfskin as he answered. "Not as such. But I spent only a little time with him, and his circle members were present. He did ask after Yuli. How your lessons were progressing."

"And what did you tell him?" Yuli asked.

"That you don't do enough to help our mother and that you still pout too much."

Yuli scowled and Anton laughed.

"I also told him you take your lessons more seriously now, and that Soragan Izhur is pleased with your practice."

Yuli squinted. "How do you know that?"

"I have a hunter's ears and eyes. I observe much, brother." Anton stood.

"Where are you going, son? There's dried figs yet." Their mother loved the moon meal; she had her men all to herself.

"Thank you, Mother," Anton replied. "But I want to catch Ulath. He has fashioned a new slingshot, it is whispered, and I want to have a look at it before we go hunting at first light."

Anton's eyes seemed to dart around the tree-dwell. He was such a poor liar, and he was certainly lying now for Yuli had overheard him speaking quietly to Izhur that afternoon, just after Anton had addressed the Circle.

"I need to speak with you – alone," he'd told Izhur.

Yuli intended to find out what he had to say, so a few heart-beats after Anton had climbed down the tree-dwell, Yuli made his own excuses to his mother, and followed his brother quietly behind.

Anton moved swiftly, and took an odd path that circled through the forest. It must be very secretive what he had to talk about if he was this careful. Yuli lost him, but he wasn't concerned. He knew exactly where he was meeting Izhur – in the Soragan's tree-dwell. Yuli laughed before covering his mouth. It wasn't a clever meeting place.

He made his way out from the forest and took his own careful path underneath the tree-dwells of fellow clan members. He could hear their various activities as he moved. Almost everyone still enjoyed their moon meal with family members. Although Charal and Bentha had evidently finished theirs early, and were now taking the opportunity to do what newly bound young couples did best. Yuli felt a stirring in his groin as he heard the pleasure groans of Charal. He was tempted to stop and listen some more, but his curiosity to learn what his brother was up to proved stronger. He picked up his pace, ignoring the squeals of ecstasy that still sounded behind.

In the light of the moon he could see Izhur's tree come into view. It was supposed to be his shelter, too, now, but Yuli continued to think of it as the Soragan's. He didn't feel like it was home the way his family's tree-dwell did. He crept to a nearby holly bush and waited, keeping his breathing shallow and quiet. A moment later a shadow crept out from the tree – the crouch and demeanor typical of a hunter. Anton. His brother ascended the tree-dwell in silence.

Yuli held his breath and drew closer. He crouched down, leaning on the trunk of the big old oak, hoping no one would see him. The brightness of the moon made the snow glisten. But if anyone cared to walk out, seeking Izhur for help on translating a dream or to receive a moon blessing, Yuli would be seen. He swallowed a lump; he would have to deal with that if it happened. For now he cocked his ear and listened intently to the hushed voices above.

"... Anything she says is worthy of attention." It was the old woman, Cypra, who spoke. She had been sharing Izhur's hut since she arrived. Izhur trusted her implicitly and would have told Anton to trust her, too.

"I know that now," Anton's voice trembled. "The way she saved my father. No one speaks of it. But I will never forget the way she did that. I'll be forever thankful."

Yuli scowled. Of course everyone knew of it. The whole clan bore witness that night. But it proved another thing. She was dangerous. If she had the power to undertake such a healing, then what destruction could she also bring? Questions were being asked about her activities. She spent a lot of time away from the clan. Ugot had spoken quietly to his father about the possibility that she had cursed the journey Zodor undertook to notify the Bear. The sooner she was dealt with at Agria the better.

"It is – refreshing to hear you speak like this about Iluna, Anton," Izhur spoke. "But I fear it is also dangerous – for her. I think we all need to carry on the pretense that we have forgotten what happened that night, like everyone else."

"But it is wrong. She healed him, we all saw it."

"Shhh, mind your voice," the woman spoke again. "You were careful, weren't you?"

Yuli quickly dulled his essence, pulling the blackness around him like a cloak so that neither Izhur nor the woman could feel his presence in the Otherworld.

"I don't sense anyone close," Izhur said.

Yuli closed his eyes and allowed himself a breath.

"I was careful. I came here through the forest."

"Good," Izhur answered.

Yuli heard the clink of clay cups.

"Some tea?"

Yuli's teeth started to chatter. He wished they would hurry up and get on with it.

"Now, tell us," Izhur said, his voice nearly a whisper. "What did she say?"

"It was the day I left. She was south of here, at the lookout we use for scouting. She told me we were safe, all of us. We are safe until next Agria, she told me."

There was silence and Yuli moved carefully onto his other foot, wriggling toes in an attempt to stop the numbness. His fur-lined moccasins only kept the cold out for so long. He was glad he wasn't a hunter. Staying still, tolerating such discomfort was not for him.

"She has the power of foresight," the old woman spoke again. "Izhur, we have to train her—"

"Shhhh. We will speak of this later," Izhur spoke rapidly, the characteristic euphoria was in his voice and Yuli sensed his excitement through the Otherworld. It tinged the air with static. He could taste it on his tongue, like the air of lighting.

"Thank you, Anton," the Soragan continued. "You have been most helpful. Be sure that you do not speak of this to anyone."

"Do you think what she speaks is true? That we are not at risk from further attack?" Anton asked.

More silence. Yuli kept wiggling his toes but the numbness was winning. To top it off the snow began to fall again, and his nose froze in response.

"We cannot be sure," Izhur spoke finally. "But she is probably right. We will let you know more – later. I think for now you had better leave. Go through the forest, just the way you came."

"I will. I'll be quick. I need to go to Ulath's tree-dwell."

"And remember," Izhur's voice was a whisper. "Mention nothing."

Soft footfalls sounded above, followed by the creak of the steps. Yuli crept a little to the right and craned his neck to see a shadow stalk swiftly back through the trees – his brother. No doubt eager to look at that new hunting tool he spoke of.

"We have to start teaching her, Izhur." The woman spoke a little louder now, the urgency in her voice clear. "She has the power of foresight and healing. And her animism is so strong. You yourself have advocated her light. Izhur, can you be in any doubt that she can also bind?"

Yuli should have left after Anton did. His feet and hands

needed a fire, and he didn't want to be discovered. But this information, it was too good to forego. Binding was still a mystery to
him, the Soragans all seemed reluctant to speak of it in any detail.
Yuli stilled his breathing and stretched his ear, eager to learn
more.

"Binding requires an initiation ceremony. How are we to
convince the others to participate and contribute their power?"
Izhur's voice was tinged with desperation. "In any case, the more
powerful she appears, the more they will want to take it all away
from her. Or worse."

"Izhur, for Ona's sake! That is why we need to be careful. We
need to plan it. But let's agree that she must continue her
training."

"Yes, I will agree to that. But we cannot let her enemies
know. We cannot slip up, not once. To do so will see her surely
burn."

Her enemies. Did Izhur know Yuli was among them? Yuli
smiled despite the burning pain of cold.

"Do you know her totem?" the woman asked and Yuli's ears
pricked all the more.

"I haven't performed the rite. It seems – disrespectful. She is
not my prentice." Izhur's voice was now tinged with sadness and
Yuli grimaced. Izhur had always favoured Iluna and no doubt
wished she was his prentice, too.

"I think I can tell you her totem without having to perform
the ceremony." The woman's voice was light, cheerful – almost.

"How so?"

"I observed her, a lot, last Agria. She spent most of her time
with a creature we don't see much in our lands of the south, but
can be found in Ona's Valley. Although they are not as common
as some other birds there."

"So it's a bird you think?"

"Yes, an oft maligned bird at that. With wings so black they
shine blue."

The raven. Yuli's eyelids widened so much that he could feel the icy air in the corners of his eyes.

"You think that is her totem?"

"I'd be willing to stake my life on it."

Yuli stood and covered his mouth when he almost cried out. The pain in his feet shot up through his legs when they tried to take his weight. But he had to leave.

He crunched through the light blanket of snow as quietly as he could. They were going to train her; to make her powerful. A deep pang of jealousy welled in the darker layers of his heart. How dare she be more powerful than any of them. She was nothing more than a tamatu.

∞

THERE IS MORE than one path to power.

Yuli dreamt.

But now his eyes fluttered open and he sat up, panting, cold sweat trickling down his back. Dark coals cast a glow throughout his family's tree-dwell, like the colour of blood in his dreaming. His family members slept soundly, their breath deep and slow.

Yuli shook his head. The dreaming was clear and vivid, and it left him hot and cold, energised and spent, all at once. The images replayed in his mind. Dark granite. Iridescent patterns. A blue moon. Blood. So much blood. And the sound, that voice – so familiar.

There is more than one path to power.

It was a dreaming. One he must heed.

Quietly he stood, dressed, and slipped down the steps into the snowy night.

Anger, dark and brooding, simmered deep within and it warmed him. He clutched it with his heart, embracing it like a desperate lover. He stalked to the rough path that began on the outer circle of trees, beyond the comfort of tree-dwells. A cloudy moon lit the way and snow softened the hard edges of the stony track, glistening in the blue light of night.

He walked quickly. Ruminating on all that was shown in the dreaming. Yes, it was the way; the only way.

There is more than one path to power.

His head bent and his legs marched. Anger and promise bubbled and boiled, and he barely felt the cold.

Soon the path came to its inevitable end. There it stood, as it always had, in the center of the large rock chasm – the winter altar. The light covering of snow did little to hide the iridescence of blue that was triggered by the moonlight, etched in the intricate carvings created scores and scores of uncountable winters past.

Moonlight appeared intermittently between snow clouds and the iridescence in the patterns would shine bright before blinking out, only to shine again when clouds passed. So beautiful. Yuli walked to it, his concentration never wavering. He would risk anything to stop her. But to do that, he, too, needed power. Yuli knew the truth of it, deep down, and the dreaming had shown him. He had but a fraction of the gift she had. His disinterest in his lessons and lack of discipline in practise had not helped him to improve in his younger years. But that had changed since the last Agria. He had refocused his energy, his concentration. He now took his lessons very seriously. Even Izhur had complimented him on his improvement. But he needed much more if he was to best her.

There is more than one path to power.

He reached the altar and bent to kiss it. The icy snow stuck to his lips and burned. Then he looked up. Imbrit's moon shone directly above the altar. Snow flakes fell in circles and whirls. It was midnight.

He raised his left hand and with his right he removed the little ceremonial knife from his belt. The knife made of bronze magic that all Soragans and prentices carried.

He struck both hands in the sky and at the top of his lungs he shouted into the night. "Malfir! Spirits of Malfir, hear me. For I have need of you and will make this promise in your sight. I, Yuli, son of Zodor, son of Ida, future Soragan of the Wolf, I give myself to you. Teach me, give me your great power and I will be your ever faithful servant."

With that Yuli brought his hands together and the knife slashed at his left palm. Blood dripped down onto the altar and made a pattern in the snow. Yuli counted eight breaths and put his hands down to study the pattern of blood. At first it looked like nothing but splotches of dark red. But soon he saw the symbol – and it was vivid. The head of a wolf, looking for all the world like it had swallowed a raven.

IZHUR

*T*he blue light of Imbrit's moon shone over the camp and mixed with the orange glow of the fire to illuminate the grim faces of the assembled company. Soragans, hunters and circle elders from all Ona's clans had arrived over the last two days. The Wolf had done their best to make room in the comfort of their tree-dwells, but a few tents had to be lashed together with thick skins and furs to keep the winter cold at bay.

They met under the Tree of Knowledge rather than in it. Fitting everyone into the tree's shelter would be impossible. Izhur had looked to each of them in turn as he spoke, summarising again the tragic events that had resulted in the extermination of an entire clan. He turned to Cypra often, measuring his accuracy in the detail of his telling by the sadness in her eyes. It still seemed like an ancient evenfire tale the way he told it. But it was a living threat.

"Sister Cypra, we of the Eagle were very sorry to hear of this tragedy. You know that our kin have strong connections. Only last Agria we had two couple bonds between our clans. We grieve for you, and your great loss is also felt by us." The elder, Janae, had tears in her eyes as she spoke.

Cypra nodded. "Thank you, sister. Your words are a comfort."

"We also grieve, sister. Know that you are welcome in the Bear," Belwas said.

More words of condolence and comfort followed, and Cypra breathed deep, her eyes glistening.

Izhur's heart lay heavy in his chest as it often did now. Such words of comfort were a poor replacement for one's homeland. And Cypra was homeless. It was warming that so many offered her a place in their clan. But he knew the truth of it – she would never again be Soragan, for she had no one left to guide and protect. Xaroth had already questioned her presence in this new temporary Circle. But Izhur had put a quick stop to that. "Of course she will be present, Grand Soragan. She is the only witness to this unknown enemy." He'd been as blunt as he could, but Xaroth had only stared with those black beads for eyes, his expression speaking his dissent.

"Is there any detail that I have left out, Cypra? Anything we have perhaps looked over or not seen? It is important we consider all information so that we know what to do next." Izhur was keen to keep her opinion relevant. She was, after all, one of the more powerful Soragans among them. Or at least had been.

Cypra shook her head. "Izhur, we've been over this many times. I have thought of little else since arriving here. I've searched the dark recesses of my memory for anything I may have overlooked, but I cannot add to the account you have relayed to us tonight."

Izhur nodded.

"Why would this happen?" Lacyl of the Lion clan spoke. He looked into the fire, his young hunter eyes searching for meaning.

"We cannot know for certain. But the way they looted and stole from the clan, filling their satchels with every possession they could find, perhaps they are thieves?" Izhur responded.

"It could be more than our possessions they want. They took people, too. Yes?" Belwas asked.

Cypra nodded. "The children."

"Perhaps it's the land itself they covet. Our lands." Hentyl was the third eldest among the Soragans. He was known for sending runners to the Agria lands once a year to make sure no other clan was claiming its gifts when they weren't supposed to.

Izhur grimaced. Such disputes were a common theme in the Dream Day tales of Doom. It was not unrealistic to believe that battles over land would cloud their future too.

"Has anyone returned to the Otter's lands since Cypra arrived here?" It was Yuli who spoke.

Izhur frowned. The boy knew prentices were supposed to remain silent at such meetings, to learn from their elders so they would come to the role of Soragan with wisdom, rather than always favouring their own opinions. Soragans who lacked the skill of listening were no Soragans at all. Izhur was about to remonstrate the boy, but the Grand Soragan interrupted.

"An excellent question. And what is the answer, Izhur?"

Izhur breathed deep and opened his mouth to speak.

"No, not as yet," Zodor intercepted. "It has simply been too dangerous, Grand Soragan." He rubbed his belly where his wound still healed.

Izhur blinked. It was not the first time the hunter had surprised him lately. Zodor seemed to have gained some wisdom since his brush with death.

"Nevertheless, I did suggest it, Grand Soragan, not long after Cypra came to us. It seemed to me that gathering such information was important. But our wise Soragan disagreed." Yuli gave Izhur a smile that revealed strong white teeth. Like a wolf.

Izhur pursed his lips. The boy was becoming bold, and too confident, and was now even happy to contest his own father. "Our Circle of Eight deemed it best to make a decision once all of us were together. That way we wouldn't be at such a risk of losing more lives. This group destroyed an entire clan. They are dangerous. That much is certain."

"A wise decision," Belwas said.

"But perhaps it is time to send a group back to the Otter lands. We must know if these new enemies now reside there. They may plan on moving north next. We don't want them to do the same to the Wolf, now do we?" Xaroth's voice was almost a whisper.

"I agree," Zodor replied. "With more of us it will be safer. Although I would prefer that we wait until spring. I suggest that each clan provides one or two of their best hunters. We meet at the Snake's lands, as they are closest to the lands of the Otter, in the first full moon of the spring. Together we will investigate and bring back the information we need to make a further decision."

"Yes, we need to gather more information. But to send our best hunters will leave the rest of us vulnerable," Ugot said.

Zodor shook his head. "One or two hunters from each clan will not make a big difference. We will leave behind capable men who'll be more than able to protect everyone. And we'll be quick. Without the women and children we will move like wolves on a summer's night."

"Women?" Hilda interjected, the glow of her long spear reflecting in the fire. She'd made the weapon herself using bronze magic at the last Agria. It had a long sharp spike, and she honed the edge every day with a flat piece of rock so that even the slightest touch would draw blood. "I'll remind you that the Ox's best hunter is a woman, Zodor." Hilda smiled as she spoke and there was a murmur of laughter. She was almost the tallest person there, and her hunting strategies were renowned.

"I stand corrected," Zodor replied with a respectful nod.

Izhur believed Iluna's premonition – they were all safe for now. But he couldn't let the others know such thoughts. "I would also suggest that we carry on our daily scoutings to check for any activity around the immediate country of our clans. At least until our hunters return," he added. "With enough notice there is a chance we could fight back, or escape if we have to."

"Agreed," Xaroth replied, and Izhur's eyebrows rose in surprise. How refreshing it was to have him agree for a change.

"And the Soragans should conduct daily protection rituals. The spirits are likely to warn us of hostile activity," Cypra added.

"Excellent idea," the Grand Soragan said.

Izhur squinted. Why was he agreeing all of a sudden?

"So we have a plan." Cypra summarized the decision and they all consented to meet the following night to discuss ideas that may come to them in their dreams.

Izhur stood to leave. He wanted to check on Iluna. She'd been particularly withdrawn and elusive since the arrival of the other clan members. It was full moon, usually the time for their moon meal that he looked forward to sharing with her every cycle, although tonight this would not be possible. He had to maintain a distance.

"Izhur."

He turned to see the Grand Soragan waiting for him. The flames of the fire caused a strange red glow to emanate from his bald head giving Xaroth an almost ominous appearance. Izhur blinked. "Yes?"

"Walk with me a little." Xaroth put a hand on Izhur's shoulder and led them away from the fire, leaning heavily on his staff as he limped. Izhur shivered. The snow had stopped falling a few days ago but the air remained icy.

"How're your dealings with the girl?"

"The girl?" Izhur asked between tight teeth. He knew who the Grand Soragan meant, but he wasn't going to make it easy for him.

"The witch."

Izhur grimaced and his knuckles clenched, but he took a deep breath and forced a smile. He and Cypra had plans for her now, and it would be better to play this little game rather than give it away.

"Iluna? The poor little thing. She is quite harmless now. I have stopped all training as was asked of me. I check in on her to make sure she is – safe, if you take my meaning." He gave Xaroth a knowing look, hoping his feigned collusion would pass as genuine.

Xaroth flicked a tongue. "Good. Safe is good, for all of us, Izhur. One does wonder how such evil has come to pass. I'm sure you take my meaning." Then he left, clutching his staff as he walked.

Izhur let his breath out and turned on his heel to go in the opposite direction. *Such evil? Old fool!* Why couldn't he see that her power could be the greatest asset for all of them? That she could keep them safe? What did he have against her anyway? Izhur stopped walking. *What does he have against her?*

He turned to look back. Xaroth was just visible in the light of the moon. He was talking to someone else now – a young man in pale robes. A prentice. Izhur squinted, and swallowed. He was talking to Yuli.

YULI

"**W**ould you like some tea, Yuli? Sethra makes a delightful blend."

Yuli sat in the large indigo tent that the Wolf had erected for the Grand Soragan. It was the most elaborate tent they had, with two sections – an area for the Grand Soragan's companions and a private space, separated by a wall of thick bear hide, for the Soragan to sleep and mediatate in solitude. Thick fur cushions and rugs lay strewn on the floor, and the hide of a wooly mountain yak lined the interior, keeping warmth in. It was just as comfortable as the most mud-packed tree-dwell.

Xaroth's companions from the Snake – Jesama, the elder, and Verit, the hunter, had found space in the tree-dwells amongst their kin of the Wolf to sleep. Only Sethra shared the tent with the Grand Soragan, and the tongues had been wagging ever since their arrival.

Sethra now approached with a steaming cup. She was a beautiful woman with dark hair that came to her waist. She had large eyes and full lips and Yuli couldn't help but notice the curve of her ample bosom. His eyes kept returning to the outline of her nipples that stood out through the sheer snakeskin vest. She must have been very cold. That vest was almost see-through and her bare arms had only the heat of the fire to warm them.

Yuli took the cup, still trying not to stare at the woman's breasts, or wonder why she was here at all. The gossip about Sethra hadn't ceased since the first night she slept in the Grand Soragan's tent.

Soragans weren't supposed to take wives. Yuli had asked Izhur about it, but he knew little. "He calls her his ward," Izhur had told him as he massaged a temple. Ward. That is what Izhur had called Iluna. No one seemed to get any closer to solving the mystery of Sethra and why the Grand Soragan allowed her to sleep in his tent. But then, Izhur had also spent a lot of time with Iluna. It was common knowledge they shared the moon meal together. Perhaps this was similar. Iluna wasn't as beautiful as Sethra, and she never wore vests like that. Even if she had, Iluna's skinny hips and small bust would fail to take a man's breath the way Sethra did.

"So tell me, what information do you have to share?" Xaroth asked in his whispery fashion.

Sethra slipped away to the other section of the tent, leaving behind the scent of jasmine and almond milk, and Yuli turned to face the Grand Soragan, clearing his throat. "I overheard something – last full moon – just after Soragan Cypra arrived."

Xaroth nodded, slowly. "Cypra is no longer a Soragan, of course. But please, go on."

"Well I overheard two things, actually." Yuli took a sip of tea and gulped it down; the spices warmed him.

"How fortunate." Xaroth's eyes burned.

"The first thing was about Anton, my brother. When he started out on his journey to your lands, to tell you about the Otter, he found the girl at the border of our lands here. She told him something – like a premonition."

The fire cracked and Yuli jumped.

"What did she tell him?" His voice a whispering hiss.

"She told him there would not be another attack before the next Agria."

The flames of the fire danced, giving Xaroth's shadows a life of their own. Yuli frowned. They seemed wrong somehow; beastly.

"And what did your brother do with this information?"

Yuli swallowed – hard. He didn't want to bring his brother into this at all. He wanted to keep the focus on Izhur and Iluna. "Anton did what any young man would do; he told his clan's Soragan."

"And this is the conversation you overheard?"

Yuli nodded. His face flushed with warmth. The spice of the tea was in his blood, and he relaxed a little.

"Go on."

"Afterwards, I heard Izhur talk with the Sorag—, the woman, about Iluna."

"Cypra?"

"Yes. They said Iluna had some great power and it should not be wasted. That she might be able to do something about this foreign group and—"

"They agreed to train the witch secretly?"

Yuli's eyes widened. "You knew?"

"I surmised where your story was leading."

Yuli nodded.

"You have done the right thing in informing me, Yuli."

Yuli allowed himself a smile.

The Grand Soragan reclined on a cushion as though making himself more comfortable. His shadows danced again, swirling and striking like an angry beast, such a contrast to his quiet voice. "The witch lies."

Yuli's eyes widened. "So we are not safe?"

"We are never safe, Yuli. That is why Ona has blessed her people with us, the gifted. It is the role of the Soragan to protect his people from the evils that are ever present. To be sure, a great evil will befall us next Agria."

Yuli's breath shuddered and he bit his lip, suddenly wanting to return to the safety of his tree-dwell and his mother, as he often had as a child. But he couldn't do that. He was a young man now. He had to control his fear. "Will we all die?"

"I am the most powerful Soragan of all Ona's clans. My gift for foresight is unsurpassed. Yes, I have seen the evils that befall us, but I have also seen a path to our survival."

Yuli nodded. "So we can save ourselves. We can stand up to the enemy?"

The Grand Soragan took a deep breath and studied Yuli again with his little black eyes. "How goes your training? Are you happy with it?"

Yuli frowned slightly at the sudden change of topic, but straightened his shoulders. "I am improving, Grand Soragan. Izhur is pleased with my progress. I've memorized all the spells and blends for healing. And my dreaming is advancing more than any other skill."

"Yesss." Xaroth hissed.

Yuli squirmed. There was an uncomfortable pause in their conversation in which the Grand Soragan simply watched him. The fire hissed and crackled, and the shadows whirled.

"The girl's evil power will continue to grow if they train her. It is possible that she is the danger that will provoke our fall. I have foreseen it." Xaroth finally spoke.

"Can't you stop them? Order Izhur not to do it?"

Xaroth's tongue flicked at his thin lips as he considered his next words. "We will let them continue their little scheme."

"But—"

Xaroth held up a hand. "Have you heard the Doom-tale prophecy of Malfirena?"

He had. Ugot had told it more than once of late, in the depth of night when most had gone to their furs. "I know a little of it.

Malfirena is the witch foretold to bring about our end; the end to Ona's people."

"Very good, Yuli. And do you believe this tale of Doom?"

"I – I don't know. Should I?"

"No. Don't believe any of those barbaric tales."

Yuli frowned. "Then why are you talking about it?"

Xaroth smiled. "It could serve usss. It is a little fire that might just help our cause – with the right sort of fanning."

"You want me to start telling the tale?"

"No, not exactly. But when it is mentioned just make a few comments, little seeds planted in the wilds of your clan member's minds. Perhaps this witch, Malfirena, reminds you of the nature of a fellow clan member; a subtle link to your tamatu. Then, when Izhur and Cypra retrain her, your clan will start to fear her all the more."

"Making it that much easier to burn her next Agria." Yuli smiled. *Yes, this plan could work.* "But if she becomes more power-ful, then isn't there a danger she will overcome us?"

"That is why we must work together. We must defend our people when the time comes."

Yuli pushed a hand through his long hair, wishing momen-tarily that he'd tied it back. "I'll never have the power she has, Grand Soragan."

Xaroth squinted and his eyes looked even smaller. "There is more than one path to power."

Yuli froze. Those words evoked vivid images – the altar on a moonlit night; blood in the shape of a wolf. He turned his hand and stroked the raw scar on his palm.

There is more than one path to power.

That voice – almost a whisper.

"It was you. You came to me in my dreaming that night."

Xaroth smiled. "Has Izhur spoken to you of your hermitage as yet?"

Yuli frowned. "Only a little. He says I am not yet ready." In truth the idea of going off into the wilderness, seeking solitude, for one full summer and one full winter frightened him. All Soragan prentices went through with it, and usually before their twentieth summer. But he certainly didn't feel ready.

"I think we might try to convince Izhur to let you go next winter."

Yuli swallowed. "Next winter. But that will be the Winter of the Lake."

"Yessss. One of our coldest. But the timing will be ripe and I know just the place for your solitude. Less than a day's walk from the lands of the Snake."

The meaning dawned on Yuli and his heart quickened. "So you can train me."

"Quite so." The Grand Soragan clapped his hands and Sethra returned, as silent as a hunter. She now wore nothing but a strip of leather around her neck with a topaz pendant that sat nestled between her breasts. Her nakedness was more than Yuli could take. The stirring in his groin pulsed the way it did when he secretly watched the young women of his clan bathe in Mittha's River.

Sethra eyed his stiffness and smiled, and took another step closer, as though inciting him to have a better look.

"Tell me, Yuli," Xaroth whispered. "Can I offer you a reward for your loyalty?"

Yuli licked his lips. The spice of the tea now ran hot through his blood. The scent of almond and jasmine filled the space and his head swirled. His eyes couldn't stay away from the woman and her lips, her breasts, her ...

"I would like to discuss this further. I think we could come to a mutually pleasing agreement if you continue to be my eyes and ears here in the Wolf, until the winter, of course."

Sethra began dancing, swaying her breasts and hips to an imagined rhthym. Yuli tried to concentrate on what the Grand Soragan was saying. Were the shadows more frenzied now?

"You see, Yuli, my gifts are many and my power is stronger than any other – including the witch. I have a number of treasures at my leisure." He waved a hand toward the woman. "Name what you want and I will grant it – in return for your loyalty."

Sethra stepped closer again and placed her hands on her hips. Yuli's manhood throbbed hard. He swallowed. He wanted the woman, but there was another desire, much stronger, that came from somewhere deep within.

"I want …"

The woman went to her knees and her hand touched his thigh stroking up.

"I want – I want – to learn – I want …"

Her hand touched him there, and his explosion was quick and hot under his robe. "Power …" he groaned, lifting his desire-drenched eyes to the Soragan. "I want power."

The Grand Soragan smiled. "Don't we all."

PART V
SUMMER OF THE SKY

ILUNA

The mountains in the distance were vivid in the crisp morning air. Iluna's pulse quickened the closer they got.

"We must be getting near," Cypra said, puffing.

Iluna nodded. "Yes, those mountains. That is where I first laid eyes on him."

"Good. We'll be there by noon. It is not so far, and I am looking forward to the rest. These old bones are starting to wear."

Iluna looked at Cypra. The old woman still stood tall and proud, but her wrinkles were deeper now, and she was thinner.

The last time Iluna had walked this path it was with Aunty Agath, eight summers past. She had been a girl then. Now she was sixteen summers old and a woman. She had not grown tall – not like Jenta or Mycal – but she was full grown. And the world was new.

People treated her differently. She remained the clan's tamatu, but they were less likely to order her around as much. In fact, people were less likely to interact with her at all.

It was that night that had caused the change – when she'd

healed Zodor. Izhur explained that her extraordinary power had intimidated the clan.

But she suspected Zodor and Yuli and Anton still spread rumors about her, although, it had been a long time since she'd seen Yuli. He'd been gone since the end of last summer, to seek his hermitage. And Anton didn't call her names anymore. He didn't say anything to her now. But often she would catch him looking at her – across the evenfire, usually. At those times, when she would meet his gaze, he'd flinch and look away.

The air in the forest was cool – a welcome relief from the hot summer winds of the last few days. The clan had descended from the high plains the previous morning. Their march to Agria would be cooler now as they followed Mittha's river. The forest grew tall and thick, and the scent of pine lingered in the air. Iluna breathed it in.

"Do you – feel him?" Cypra asked.

Iluna paused her step and cocked her head so that her good ear could hear the hum of the forest. Izhur had told her the story of her birth and how a bolt of lightning had struck his arm, dislodging his knife, the knife meant for her sacrifice. He believed it was the thunder so close to her young ear that had caused her deafness. He'd told her everything about the night she was born, and so many mysteries were suddenly solved. She could understand why the clan had distrusted her. Not that it had made it easier to bear.

Her arms extended forward and she felt with every inch of her being, reaching out to the forest. The trees were so old here. They had lived more summers than anyone could count. But unlike the first time she came here, now there was an abundance of life. She closed her eyes to focus. A squirrel sat still on a branch high above, watching Iluna and Cypra. A pair of wrens were busy feeding their young in a small nest in the birch right in front of them. Iluna smiled. Chicks were so demanding of their parents. She sent her essence further. A doe nibbled on berries.

Iluna whipped her essence to snap a branch, urging her on. If the hunters found her, the doe would be roasting on their evenfire that night. The deer sprang away and sprinted, deeper into the forest. Behind, Iluna felt another presence – something more predatory – a human – a man.

She spun, scanning the forest.

"What is it?" Cypra whispered.

Iluna frowned. "Someone is following us." She squinted, but their pursuer remained hidden.

"We know you are there. Please show your face," Cypra said.

A moment of silence stalled them before the branches moved and the agile and muscled form of the young hunter came forward – Anton.

"I'm sorry, Soragan." He bent his head in a sign of respect.

Highly respectful. Few called Cypra 'Soragan' now. They had in the beginning, when Cypra had first come to them two winters' past. They had respected her and called her Soragan for a time. But now Cypra had no people, no status. Iluna had not heard them call her 'tamatu' yet, but it would't be long now. And she knew the reason. Cypra had shared her tree-dwell once the clan moved to their summer lands. It was convenient as it allowed Cypra to continue Iluna's training, in secret. But Iluna's tamatu status had rubbed off on Cypra and she no longer enjoyed the respect she once had. Iluna felt bad about it. She didn't mind being a tamatu; she'd known nothing else all her life – but not Cypra.

"No need to apologise, Anton," Cypra said. "But what, may I ask, are you doing?"

"I was tracking a doe. She came this way not long ago. Have you seen her?" Anton glanced at Iluna briefly, his eyes lingering for a second before returning to Cypra.

The Soragan shook her head. "No, we have not seen a deer, Anton." She narrowed her eyes. "Was that all you were tracking?" A smile danced on her mouth.

Anton blushed and glimpsed at Iluna again. "I am sorry to disturb you." He bounded off ahead of them, and in another heartbeat he was gone.

"That's the third time he has snuck up on us since we left the plains," Cypra said.

"There was a doe; I sensed her just now."

Cypra raised one eyebrow. "How convenient."

Iluna wasn't sure what she meant by that but she had a feeling it had to do with talking more about Anton, and she didn't want to talk about Anton or his family. "We should move back with the group."

"Soon enough. We can sense when we are too far away, and we're in no danger with our young hunter keeping an eye on us."

Iluna ignored that and kept walking, trying instead to focus on the whispering trees and the essence of the forest animals, searching still.

"Did you feel him?" Cypra asked again.

Iluna sighed. She'd been reaching out since they left the high plains, trying as hard as she could to find the raven. But there was no answer – no hint of his essence.

"No, I cannot feel him." She couldn't help the tone of disappointment in her voice. She'd thought she would have found him straight away.

"Keep faith, Iluna. He will find you."

Iluna hoped so. Izhur had performed the rite last summer. She'd witnessed the process, all part of her lessons. A drop of her blood was mixed with the root of Goda's Eye – a powerful plant, and a gift from Goda herself, the goddess of night, stars and spirits. Izhur had shredded the soft root and placed it in a bubbling broth with her blood, letting it simmer for a day and a night. When he had finally drank he lasped into a trance that had lasted a full day, and had come out smiling. "Yes, the raven is your totem, Iluna. And he awaits you."

She'd seen a few ravens on their travels to Agria. They were elusive and shy, and mostly stayed out of view of humans. She'd smiled when she spotted them knowing that she had a special connection with the dark creatures. But that raven, the one she'd seen last Agria, he was special and she wanted to find him. It was as though she needed to find another aspect of herself. She was complete when she was with him. Perhaps he held some answers for her; answers to her troubled dreams. Agria was nigh, and with it would come danger.

"Come, let us use this time for study. The group is far below, following the river. It will be safe."

Cypra and Izhur had begun retraining her two winters ago, after the meeting of clans to decide how to deal with the attack on the Otter. They were constantly surprised by how much her power had grown and her aptitude for the lessons. She never told them that she had continued to practise on her own. Izhur and Cypra's teachings were valuable, but, more than this, she appreciated their love and companionship.

She knew what they expected of her, and she was nervous about being some kind of saviour. She had saved Zodor's life that winter, and it had not made her any friends. If anything, people were more wary of her now. They seemed to forget that she had saved his life. Well, except for Anton. He had thanked her for it.

"Yes, I suppose we should," she replied to Cypra. She needed to keep up her lessons if she was to help protect them from the enemy. They were all safe for now. Iluna had seen that much in her dreams. But something was about to happen at Agria. The trouble was she couldn't see if it was a blessing or a curse, peace or war, good or evil. If only she could find the raven; perhaps she'd get some answers.

ANTON

"*There'll* be almost two-score couples altogether. You and I, and ..."

Anton's betrothed prattled on about the couple-bond ceremony that was to take place the following evening – too soon. She'd latched on to him as soon as Agria's opening formalities had finished and demanded they go for a walk, as she had every evening since their arrival. Every now and then her big eyes would turn to look up at him, shining in the full light of the sky. They were beautiful, her eyes, and her hair, as were her small nose and rose bud lips. She had round, child-bearing hips and a soft nature; she'd make a good mother – a dream wife for any young man. He should be happy.

They walked the bank, along a river path. It was acceptable for betrothed couples to spend time together before they were bonded – encouraged even. But Anton had always avoided Hennita. Last Agria he'd made quite an art of it, although his mother had given him a lengthy talk about the importance of spending time with Hennita this Agria, lest he offend her clan. He grimaced as he guided her over a fallen log, and she continued to prattle. There was to be a large hunt tonight and he was missing it for this.

"Botha and I have sewn new robes with the lapis lazuli of our lands; we collected it last summer. She's dyed her robe with tulu nut, but I washed mine with limestone and the salt of the sea, and now it is as white as your winter snow. I do love white, it's so pure, don't you think? I wonder if that's why Soragan prentices wear it. What do you think?"

"Ah, I wouldn't know. You could ask my brother." Yuli had arrived at Ona's Valley only the night before, with the Snake clan. He'd spent the summer and the previous winter at his hermitage. His mother had broken down when she'd seen him, crying the way she had when she'd mourned her father. Anton expected her to start hitting her head again, but thankfully she didn't go that far.

Yuli had changed. He was taller, and thinner. It was almost shocking to see him. He'd always been a chubby child. He lost his pup fat by his tenth year, but Yuli had never been slender, like this. Their mother had cooked all his favourite dishes at the evenfire that night. Anton was instructed to hunt and gather the ingredients earlier – a satchel of mushrooms, trout, rabbit, beet leaves and everything else. It took him all day, but those dishes were delicious. Everyone had commented. His mother was one of the best cooks in the Wolf, but Yuli hardly touched his food. He sipped only a little of the ox broth. And Anton wasn't the only one who'd noticed; their mother was instantly worried about her youngest son and told him not to go back to his hermitage after Agria.

"You know I must complete the summer, Mother. By rights I shouldn't even be here now; a hermitage is supposed to be unbroken. I must return to it as soon as Agria has finished. I shall come to our lands of the Wolf before the first snows – before Ilun." Yuli had said. He even spoke differently now.

"Anton, are you listening?"

Anton blinked.

Hennita was standing ahead with her hands on her hips and a frown on her face.

"Ah, I'm sorry, what was that?"

"I said, these enemies, the ones who attacked the Otter. Do you think they have gone away? I hope so. My father has tried to get it out of Belwas, but all he kept saying was that we'd know more this Agria, and to keep up our offerings to the Mother. But we're at Agria now, and nothing's happened. I do hope they don't interrupt our ceremony. And Belwas had better not embarrass me during our vows ..."

Anton let her prattle as he remembered the visit to the Otter's lands the spring before last. A company of eight hunters along with the Soragans Izhur and Tyvan had traveled swiftly to the river lands of the Otter. They found the grounds of the attack. Blood had stained some of the walls of their cave-dwells, and decomposed corpses lined the banks of the river. But there was no physical sign of the enemy clan that had wrought such terror. Izhur had tried to sense them through the Otherworld, but no evidence lingered there either. The enemy had not returned to the Otter lands. They had come, killed, stolen, and left. The mystery remained unsolved. So they gave the corpses to the river, on a bed of fire, as was the way of the Otter. Izhur asked Mittha to take their brothers and sisters back to the Otherworld and to Ona. Then they had returned to their own lands, with few answers to impart.

Iluna had told him they were safe until Agria. Well, Agria had started. Were they safe still?

"You remember Botha, don't you?" Hennita's question cut through his thoughts like a knife.

"Ah, Botha?"

"She helped me catch your witch when we were children. Remember that? I thought you were quite the brave hunter."

Anton halted. Yes, he remembered. A warm rush of shame caressed his cheeks.

"Is Iluna really a witch, do you think? I mean I know she is your clan's tamatu, but do you think she does possess dark power? Perhaps she will leave your clan and run off, like Tysha in the evenfire tale. I do love that tale; it never fails to scare me half to death, even though I've heard it scores of times. The way she feeds on the blood of babies always makes me shudder. You know, I've heard some call Iluna the Malfirena."

"Don't call her that," Anton said.

Hennita turned and tilted her head. "Anton, what did you say? You better keep up. I don't want a mountain cat attacking me. I need your protection, husband." She giggled.

"I'm not your husband yet."

"But you will be tomorrow evening."

Anton grimaced and turned to go in the opposite direction.

"Wait, where are you going?"

"I'll meet you back at camp."

"But, Anton, what about our nice walk?"

He ignored her and ran up the mountain path where he knew she wouldn't follow. His muscled legs carried him swiftly so that Hennita's protests faded quickly. They had been just a stone's throw from the outskirts of the encampment. The beat of the evenfire drum would scare off any mountain cat, or any other creature. She was safe. He continued moving up into the thickening forest. He had to get away. To think. Or not to think. He needed to do something to stop thinking – *of her*.

His hands rested on a large boulder and he pulled his body over it and sprinted. He concentrated on the sound of the fruit bats – their little chirrups and calls. His breath was coming out fast now and made a kind of rhythm with the chant of the insects. It drove him on.

His thoughts kept returning no matter how often he tried to divert them. He couldn't get her out of his mind – her dark messy hair; her small bust; her legs; the way she cocked her head on account of her deaf ear; the way she moved. Her serenity. She always seemed at peace. He wanted to talk to her, but it was impossible. She was either with Izhur and Cypra, or off in her own secrecy, in places he could never find her.

He'd been able to track her on their way here, and he delighted in the glimpses he stole. But the old woman, she seemed to know what he was doing and he had to give that up, too. If only he could talk to her.

He reached a plateau and bent over with hands on knees to catch his breath. The night was warm and now he was thirsty. He had no skin of water, and the river was a long way down. He would have to wait. Stumbling along and breathing hard, he noticed little blue berries shining under the trees. He laughed and grabbed a handful, crunching out their sweet juice. Further along more berries sprung up and he ate them, quenching his thirst. He would have to return to this place with a satchel for his mother. He bent to take a third handful and noticed the blue flesh left over on a branch. Just beneath it, a footprint dented the soil. He put his own foot beside it. Someone, smaller than him had been here only moments before.

He paused. Could it be her? He walked on – slowly – bending every so often to pick another berry, thinking all the while. She was known for her secrecy. She spoke to no one aside from Izhur and Cypra. She was rarely seen in the camp. Each evening he would glance at her for a brief time at the evenfire. She would stay only long enough to eat her meal.

As he moved, he noticed more footprints. He bent to smell, and the earthy aroma of broken leaves and freshly turned soil greeted his nostrils. He was close. Whoever it was had only just been here.

Holding his breath he walked on, listening for a sign. He came to a small clearing surrounded with more berries than he had ever seen in one spot. Ahead a low branch of a shrub moved. It had to be her.

"Iluna? All is well. You can come out. I am here alone."

There was a hoot in the distance. No, surely she hadn't moved so quietly. The branch moved again. His hunter's eyes spotted it. She was still there.

"Iluna, please, I just want to talk to you."

He held his breath again – listening.

"Talk about what?"

The sound of moving branches came from behind. Anton turned, and Yuli stepped into the clearing.

"Yuli?" Anton whispered.

"What are you doing here, brother?" Yuli's amber eyes held a burning fire. He was breathing hard, too. There was something different about him. Anton looked him over. He held something in his hand.

"I was – walking."

Yuli squinted. "You were asking for her. I heard you. What did you want to talk to her about?"

Anton focussed on Yuli's hand. Something fell from it. A dark trail lined the back of his hand and came from somewhere further up, under the pale embroidered sleeve of his robe. In the light it glimmered, dark red. "Yuli, what have you done? Are you bleeding?"

Yuli hid his hand fast behind his back. "Mind your business, brother." Then he stalked off through the bushes.

Anton frowned. He had a mind to chase after his brother. Whatever he was up to it was strange.

Yuli was sixteen summers now, and a man. He should trust him to know what he was doing, but what did the blood mean? Last winter, just before he'd left for his hermitage, Anton found him at the quarry; at the altar. Anton rarely went there but it was a good hunting spot for quail that basked in the warmth of the sunshine.

Yuli was at the chasm whispering strange words, and blood covered the surface of the altar from the crow he had killed. He was furious with Anton for disturbing him, told him he had no business spying on him.

Izhur had never acted like that. The Soragan only sacrificed animals during Ilun, and it was known how he hated the task. Yuli had appeared to be enjoying – whatever it was he had done to the crow.

It had bothered Anton for days after. He went to Izhur to ask him about it and the Soragan didn't even know that Yuli was doing this. Izhur asked him to keep an eye on Yuli. There had been plenty of things Anton had noticed – Yuli going off by himself for great chunks of the day without telling anyone where he was, or what he was doing. And he was less whiney, more aloof and standoffish. He rarely seemed to speak to him anymore. It seemed his hermitage had made him more of a stranger. That blood was unnerving.

"I must tell Izhur," he muttered and he turned to go down the mountain.

"He was searching for me."

Anton looked to his left and there she stood. Her dark hair shone a deep blue in the night's light. It was untangled for a change. Perhaps Cypra had brushed it for her.

"Iluna," he whispered.

"He uses some dark magic now, and he looks for me often. He spies on me."

Anton frowned. "Dark magic?" He shivered with the thought and touched his fingertips together in the sign of warding. "Why? Why would he do that?"

Iluna stared at him. "You were looking for me, too."

Anton's cheeks warmed and he shifted his gaze to the berries. "Why would *you* do that?"

"I – just wanted to talk to you." His embarrassment burned through him.

She frowned, then nodded. "Go on."

Anton laughed. A nervous laugh. Now that he had his wish he didn't know what to say. "Ah. What are you doing here?" He scratched the back of his head.

"Looking for moonberries."

He nodded. "Well, I think you've found them. They're all around here."

She continued staring.

He bit his lip. She wasn't making this easier for him, not that he could blame her. "Do you like those berries?" Ona, he needed help.

"Yes."

"Ah. The ah – well, ahh." Anton scratched his chin, feeling the stubble of his beard.

"Is that all you want to say?" she asked and turned a shoulder as though she was about to walk off. He had to think – quick!

"The thing!" he sputtered. "The thing you told me – about us being safe, until this Agria."

Her eyes returned to his and their darkness looked troubled.

"Well, so, do you know any more? Will we be safe after the festival?"

Her eyes flicked away and the shadow of a frown crossed her face.

"I'm sorry." He put his hands up. "I don't mean to make you feel sad or worried. I'm just curious."

She nodded behind him. "You weren't expecting to see your brother here? You didn't know he was looking for me?"

Anton's eyebrows arched. "No, I had no idea. I rarely see, or talk to my brother any more. He's – different since his hermitage."

"Will you tell Izhur what you saw? The blood?"

Anton squinted. "You saw that, too?"

Iluna nodded. "Yes, I was watching. He uses blood to help with his gift – sometimes his own, sometimes an animal's blood."

"Blood? Are you sure?"

"Yes."

"What is he doing?"

"Something evil." Iluna's eyes were so dark Anton had difficulty reading them.

"Should I tell Izhur?"

She looked away briefly, as though considering this.

"Yes," she said, finally. "Tell him."

Anton cocked his head, considering her again. "What were you really doing up here tonight?"

Iluna shifted her gaze down. Her eyes held all the world's sadness. "I was looking for a friend."

Before Anton could ask who, she was gone – as quick and as silent as a night hawk.

ILUNA

"*W*here are you going?"

Iluna turned to find Cypra behind her, a look of concern on her face. Both Cypra and Izhur had been worried since their arrival at Agria. Not that Iluna had spoken to Izhur much, not openly in any case.

"Just up to the mountain forest," Iluna responded. "I want to look for him again."

Cypra nodded. "Be careful."

She shared her tent with Cypra, who was no longer permitted to stay in the Soragan's tent. It had infuriated Izhur when that decision was made. He had paced back and forth along the river, fuming.

But Cypra accepted it. "I'm more than happy to camp with Iluna, Izhur. No matter what the gossips might have to say about it."

"I'm always careful, Cypra." Iluna turned and walked through the encampment, avoiding people as best she could, but near the Soragans' tent she almost ran into the Grand Soragan who was just coming out.

"Excuse me, Grand Soragan," she whispered.

His small eyes squinted, and Iluna bent her head and moved swiftly on.

She'd had little to do with the Grand Soragan, spotting him only a handful of times over her life. Her encounter with him last Agria was intense. He had looked on her light and she had tried to do the same with him. But unlike with Belwas, she didn't see his totem. She didn't see his light either. All she saw was darkness.

He had taken a dislike to her after, and Iluna didn't know why. Perhaps he knew what she had seen and didn't want her to spread the knowledge. The last time she had seen him was at their winter lands, two winters past when the Soragans met with her clan. He was just as cold and hostile toward her then. She should do her best to avoid him completely.

Once in the forest she slowed her pace and breathed more easily. It was cool and sweet, and, as always, it calmed her. She stepped over the stones of the river to the other side, and began the ascent.

It was the third day of the festival. That night the evenfire storytellers would be performing their favorite tales to the delighted awe of their audience. The previous night had been the couple-bond ceremony. Agria was flying by and she still hadn't found the raven. She focused her mind as she walked, trying not to let worry disturb her flow. She had to find him.

But when she sent out her essence she sensed someone else, following behind – Anton. He was different now. Iluna knew he wanted to be her friend, but she didn't know why. Why, after all those years of hostility did he want to spend time with her? It was very strange. And now he was bonded to Hennita of the Bear. She'd witnessed their oaths the previous night. Hennita had worn the whitest robe she'd ever seen, and her many stones and gems had glimmered in the Agrian night.

Iluna stopped to wait for Anton to catch up.

It didn't take him long but he remained hidden behind a nightshade bush.

"You can come out, Anton. I know you're there."

He crept through the branches, eyes darting around. "I was – I was just on my way to get more of those berries for my mother." He held up a satchel as if giving proof.

"And for your wife?"

Anton blinked. "Ah, no. She doesn't like them. But my mother does."

Iluna couldn't help but smile. "That's where I'm going."

She turned to continue her trek up the mountain path. He ran to catch up and walk by her side.

"Do you mind if I walk with you?"

Iluna shook her head. "But when we are up there I need to do something in the clearing. And I need to be alone."

"Yes, of course." He grinned. "Are you going to get more berries, too?"

Iluna stopped. This was ridiculous. "Anton."

"Yes?" His eyes held something. Was it hope?

"Why are you here?"

"To get some—"

"Berries. Yes, you said that. But you know what I mean. Why? Why after all the years of teasing and then ignoring me. Why now do you want to talk with the clan's tamatu?"

Anton looked at the ground – his eyes searching for words. "I – I just …"

Iluna squinted. His essence pulsed. Something was igniting his emotions. He was excited; happy even.

She reached out and put a hand on his shoulder. His energy ran through her fingertips, a tactile force. "I think I understand."

"You do?" His eyes grew even more hopeful.

Iluna understood alright. He was attracted to her. It happened a lot in the clan when boys turned into men, and girls into women. Often they would become attracted to fellow clan members – members they weren't promised to. It wasn't openly accepted by the clan when it happened, but such couples who met in secret were not stopped – as long as it wasn't done openly.

But Iluna knew this was dangerous. She was the clan's tamatu, and people were frightened of her. She couldn't allow him to develop such feelings. She had to stop it now. Hennita would be returning with them after Agria to live with her husband and his people.

"You need to stop this. You have your wife now. If your family found out it would be bad for me." She thought of Zodor and Yuli. They would want something done; maybe convince the Eight to punish her, or worse – cast her out.

Anton looked down to the ground, disappointment and embarrassment mingling on his face. She walked on, but he grabbed her hand. A hot flush of energy bolted from him.

"Iluna, please, I can't stop thinking about you." His eyes burned with passion. "Have you bewitched me?"

She snatched her arm away. His comment hurt like a sharp sting. "I don't do that," she said between gritted teeth. "I thought you had changed. Clearly you have not."

She walked on.

"Iluna."

"Don't follow me."

"Iluna, I'm sorry. That was a foolish thing to say." His voice croaked.

Iluna kept walking. She couldn't deny his comment hurt; which was curious. She had built a thick hide so that the harsh words of others no longer scarred her. So why had his? She stopped to gather her breath as she realized what it meant.

"Don't be stupid, Iluna," she said to herself with gritted teeth. "You have no future with him. Get him out of your mind." She took a deep breath and in the next moment her focus returned to her task. Her mind was as disciplined as any hunter's – more so. She would not think of Anton again that day.

As the berries came into sight it was late afternoon, and sweat beaded on her upper lip. She bent to pick a handful of the treasures and popped them in her mouth. Their sweet juice refreshed her. She took another handful and munched on them as she walked to the clearing, thinking about the raven.

In the clearing she brushed her hands together and swallowed the last mouthful of berries. It was time to reach out for him. She had a good feeling today. Last night she'd had a dream. The raven had spoken to her, asking her to meet him at dusk. She looked up and to the west. It was difficult to see the daysun on account of the thick canopy above, but the pink of the sky told her that dusk was at hand. Imbrit's moon already floated high above, and Atoll's star would rise soon.

She stilled her breathing and closed her eyes, focusing on reaching out to him. As usual she sensed all the life of the forest – the ancient trees, the insects, the life of the moonberry bushes nearby – all pulsed with light and vibrations.

She knew how to alter them now – even the rocks in the mountain. If she wanted she could cause an avalanche by strengthening her essence at just the right place. She smiled, and then stopped herself. She must never be pleased with herself about this gift, Izhur had told her. That was the path to evil. The gift was a heavy responsibility to bear and she must treat it carefully, respectfully. He was right. Izhur was always right. And she owed him her life.

But Izhur and Cypra, while their lessons were useful, they had little understanding of the real extent of her power and knowledge. She had continued her solitary lessons with nature. The force of Ona alone was her greatest teacher, and she guessed she now had more power than any other Soragan in all eight clans.

Maybe even more than the Grand Soragan. Had he sensed

that? Perhaps that was why he was so hostile toward her. Was she a threat to him?

Izhur and Cypra also did not know why she sought the raven so desperately. They knew the raven was her totem – a dangerous secret. Ravens were known for evil more than good and if word got out to the other Soragans, or Yuli – especially Yuli – then it could mean Iluna would be cast out. She didn't want to be cast out. Her life was lonely enough as it was, even if she had Izhur and Cypra to spend time with now. Wandering the wilds all alone would be unbearable.

She put the thoughts aside and focused. Soon she would hear his wings. He had news for her – important news about the future attack on their clans. She had seen it in her dreams. That was why the raven was important.

There was a tug on her consciousness and she knew at once it was him. She stilled her heart and called to him through the Otherworld. He flew toward her now. Her excitement caused her to lose her connection. That's when she heard the sound of wings flapping and then he came into sight – blue black wings shining in the dusk light.

He squawked and landed on a low branch, eyeing Iluna.

"Hello, my friend." Iluna smiled. It was good to see him again. As always, something felt complete when he was near.

She approached him with her hand held out, her palm filled with the blue moonberries. The bird picked at them delicately and swallowed. Drops of juice sprayed out and Iluna laughed.

"You still like them, don't you?"

The raven squawked, then stopped eating. He became still and his eyes met Iluna's directly.

A wave of nauseating dizziness overcame her before she entered the Otherworld and a series of images befell her all at once.

A foretelling.

She saw the future. No, a future – one that could come to

pass. She flew behind the raven, and watched the beat of his wings. Slowly, but powerfully, they flew over the mountain peak. The snow at the very top glistened in Imbrit's light. They swept over at a great height so that the mountains became small, like anthills.

Why must we climb so high? she asked.

Because they have strong magics, the raven replied.

Iluna focused, wondering if their magics were stronger than her gift.

They flew south of the mountains and Iluna recognized the shapes and essences of the landscape they had traversed on their way to Agria. They were now about a day's walk from Ona's Valley and the raven spoke into her mind again.

Look close.

And she did, focusing her vision on the land below. They swept a little lower to allow a better look, and Iluna wanted to escape. But she held her mind tight. There beneath them was a camp so large it was at least thrice as big as all their clans put together. More than a hundred fires dotted the landscape, and people moved about everywhere. A strange energy pulsed, one that Iluna didn't recognize. It came from their hunting tools.

They call them weapons, the Raven told her. *And they are made of a substance called ironstone. They melt it out of the earth and shape it to their liking.*

These weapons. They are to be used against us?

Yes.

Iluna fought a sense of panic, fought the need to race back to herself and fly down the mountain to tell Izhur. She had to learn all that she could while she was here.

Look, the raven bade her, flying lower still.

Iluna focussed again and she sensed what he meant – a group of people, men, perhaps ten. Their light wasn't light at all – rather, a shadow. The same darkness she'd seen in the Grand Soragan – a deep, dangerous void.

They are the ones with the magics, the raven said. *They want to destroy you and yours.*

The panic rose and Iluna worked hard to control her focus. How was she to defend her people against so many?

Come, there is more I must show. The raven glided up into the starry, moonlit night and Iluna followed. They came into cloud and the vision changed here to a scene, suspended above a camp. People were below her, but they weren't her people. Their hair was light, like gold, and their skin was pale like the white sand of the river. Their clothing was different too. They wore shorter robes, tied together with straps of leather, and made from a material that was neither hide nor grass. Their legs were covered in the same material, somehow stitched together to allow free movement. All had sandals on their feet. They were a skilled people to craft such clothes. Everything was different – their clothing, tents, cooking equipment, their hunting tools – all similar but different.

You're looking through my eyes, the raven told her. *This is what I saw not two days past.*

A remembering.

In the vision the raven took flight and Iluna watched as the ground disappeared below and the tops of trees came into view. She circled and came down again within the forest, and landed on a low branch. Her view was obstructed by leafy branches but in the distance she could see a group of the magic people talking in a circle. She also saw the distinct sleeve of a Soragan's robe. No, a prentice's robe. The white sleeve embroidered with a circular pattern, moved as the arm gestured toward the north. She could hear their voices, but not their words; too far away. The prentice moved to the side. She could almost see his face.

Danger! I must take you back! The raven's voice was almost a squawk and she sped through the Otherworld, slamming back to her physical form. Her eyes opened. She lay on the ground in the clearing. The raven took flight, circling up, heading toward the

178

moon. Her body ached, exhausted from the visioning. Fatigue made her eyelids heavy. A dry twig snapped behind her and she slowly turned her head, her neck aching with pain. Yuli stood there, his eyes burning. Then he, too, turned to go and as he did she noted the circular pattern on his white sleeve and a chill went through her spine.

IZHUR

*I*zhur flung open the flap to the Soragans' tent and welcomed the fresh night air. He needed to cool his head. The dimwitted discussions of his fellow Soragans were becoming tedious. He ground his teeth as he made his way to the evenfire for a cup of chamael. They should have been talking about the attack on the Otter two winters past, but every time he raised it the Grand Soragan had guided conversation to other matters. Even Belwas believed there was no longer much danger. It was as though something had a hold over them. They all went along with the Grand Soragan's wishes. Izhur got the distinct feeling that if Xaroth told them all to jump off the mountain they would. He frowned. Why did he have such an influence?

Izhur found the chamael bubbling in a large clay pot, its sweet earthy aroma rose with the steam. But he had second thoughts when he saw the skins of alza that swung on a large tree branch beyond the evenfire, and his footsteps carried him to the tree. He took a nearly empty skin and popped the top off, not bothering to use a cup, and downed a mouthful of the sticky substance. The fire of it ran through his veins. He took another swig before stalking to Cypra's tent, his hand gripping the alza-skin.

"How was it tonight?" she asked as he entered. Five oil pots sat bunched in a corner, providing enough light for Cypra to sew a tear in a robe – Iluna's, no doubt. He pursed his lips. She should have done such tasks outside under the light of Goda's nightsun, but Cypra had become more and more withdrawn, avoiding contact with others as much as she could. Her eyes looked up at him, the robe put to one side. She missed being a Soragan. And he missed her support.

He sat on a reed mat and took another swig of the drink.

"It must have been bad if you're drinking, Izhur."

"It was." He swallowed the last mouthful.

"I have some pomegranate wine here." She pointed to a clay jug in the corner of the tent. "Would you care for another?"

Izhur nodded. For some reason he wanted to get senseless. Having things not make any sense in a sober state of mind was becoming too much to bear.

Cypra took a cup and filled it. "What did they talk of tonight?" she repeated her question as she handed him the cup.

"The usual ox dung about how we should release Iluna of her gifts. Who should do what, how the ceremony should take place." He frowned.

"We've put too much into that girl to allow this to happen." Cypra poured a cup of wine for herself and sat opposite Izhur.

"I know. But what can we do about it? Every time I try to protest or even question their reasons, the Grand Soragan takes control of the others. I've tried suggesting that we simply continue the way we have, since Iluna hasn't done anything wrong, not ever. But Yuli…" Izhur took another sip. It was too infuriating to consider what his little upstart of a prentice had said.

"What did Yuli say?" Her voice was calmly encouraging.

Izhur stood and refilled his cup, the oil pots danced with his movement. "Yuli told them about the way she had healed Zodor. Inventing a far fetched story of how she forced the medicine woman out of the way for the chance to perform her 'demon magic', he called it. And how he believes his father has never been the same since."

Cypra coughed on her cup. "That's one strange interpretation of what happened. Zodor has changed, but for the better I'd say."

Izhur shook his head. "Yuli – he's always had this deep hostility – no – anger toward her. He hates her. I can't help thinking it's my fault. There is no doubt I favoured her during our lessons. Yuli irritated me. He was a weak, spoiled child who always wanted to run back to his mother, rather than undertake his lessons as he was supposed to. No doubt I let that irritation show."

"You think he was jealous of her?"

Izhur nodded. "And that's why the Grand Soragan has taken Yuli under his wing." Izhur paused to take another mouthful of wine. "Xaroth is now talking about a special ceremony for Yuli."

Cypra frowned. "A ceremony for Yuli? What is it?"

"It came as a shock to me, and it will shock you to the core."

Cypra opened her mouth to speak, but the flap of the tent opened and she fell silent as Iluna stepped in, breathing hard. Something was wrong.

"Iluna, what is it?" Izhur's voice, a whisper.

The girl stepped forward taking a momentary glance back toward the flap.

"I found the raven," she said.

"Iluna, that's wonderful," Cypra replied.

Iluna raised her hand. "He showed me many things." Her breath was quick, like she'd been running.

"Have some water, child." Izhur passed her the water skin and watched as she took a large gulp.

She wiped her mouth and her breathing slowed.

"Tell us what he showed you, Iluna."

Her large dark eyes found his. "That clan – the ones who killed the Otter – they will attack in less than two days."

"What?" Fear was written all over Cypra's face. "No."

"There's more," Iluna said before taking another sip of water.

"Go on." An ice cold warning crept along Izhur's spine.

"Yuli and the Grand Soragan," Iluna looked at them with a face beyond her sixteen years, "they are in league with them."

ILUNA

The raven quorked and landed on her shoulder. Iluna smiled as she held up a palm full of moonberries.

"Hello, my friend. Won't be long now."

The Agrian sky grew purple above with Atoll's star now at its zenith. It was well past midnight. The raven squawked again and she tickled his beard the way he liked it. His feathers were soft, and his warmth calming. Her breath shuddered as she exhaled; there was much to do.

"Iluna?" a voice whispered and the raven took flight.

Iluna stepped out of the shadow of a large cypress and into the full light of the Agrian night. Two familiar shapes in long robes stood before her – one with strings of beads around the neck, the other without.

"I am here."

Izhur exhaled a grateful sigh and Cypra returned her smile. The raven circled above them before landing once more on her shoulder. She'd grown used to his weight now.

"You have trained him?" Izhur's wide eyes relayed his wonder.

"No, I've not, but he sits on my shoulder all the same." She turned to go.

"Can we not talk here? We are far enough from the camp, surely." Izhur looked back over his shoulder.

They were quite a way out, but it was not yet safe to speak of plans and such. "Not yet, Uncle. Follow me, and stay close." The raven flew off again, up the mountain, and the three of them followed.

Iluna set a swift pace, her steps almost a jog, but she had to stop often and wait for Izhur and Cypra the closer they got to the peak. Near the summit, the trees thinned and she waited again. Cypra was puffing heavily. Iluna squinted and sent out her essence to the old woman; a knot in her ribs caused a stitch of pain that slowed her. Iluna released some of her light and wrapped it around Cypra's torso the way Amak would apply a poultice of herbs. She could feel the pull, the drain of her energy, but Cypra needed the support. They had limited time and much to prepare for. It worked, and Cypra moved faster. Iluna readjusted the satchel that hung over her shoulder, and moved on.

"How much farther?" Izhur asked, a little out of breath himself.

"Just on the other side there is a cave; it is safe."

"How do you know this?" Izhur asked.

Iluna looked at him. "The raven told me."

She ignored the questioning look in his eyes and moved on. There would be time for questions after. The energy she fed to Cypra pulled her back somewhat, but soon they reached the peak, and just over the other side, the cave.

Strange line drawings and prints decorated the cave's walls: pictures of people and animals. There were scenes depicting a hunt, one of a birth, and another of death. Iluna reached out and touched one, her fingers tingled. The drawings were from another time, another people, from scores of summers past.

Cypra sat on a boulder and Izhur gave her his skin of water. Iluna kept feeding her energy through the Otherworld. Cypra would need it to recover.

Izhur drank from the skin before offering it to Iluna. A bead of sweat dropped from his slender nose and his hair hung in damp tendrils on his shoulders. The climb had taken a lot from them, but this was the only safe place to talk. To plan. To prepare.

"Perhaps we ought to have brought Belwas. We'll need allies if we're to stop these killers, and to convince the other Soragans that we need to act," Izhur said.

Iluna piled the sticks she'd collected in the centre of the cave. "There'd be no use, Uncle. They are all under his spell, even Belwas." The raven had shown her in a visioning. Xaroth had linked himself to almost every clan member – a weave of black thread touching them all.

"The Grand Soragan?"

"It must be true, Izhur," Cypra said. "You've wondered yourself why they all follow him blindly. This must be the reason."

Izhur looked to the sticks and dead branches that Iluna had collected while the two of them had rested. "Are you sure a fire is wise? What if we're seen?"

"The cave faces to the west. No one will see us from the valley." She gestured with a hand. Outside, Atoll's star was making its descent, and Goda's nightsun hovered above the canopy of trees below.

"What about Xaroth? He might search with his mind."

"The cave is protected, Uncle. Old magic. Open your sight and see for yourself. No one can sense us through the Otherworld here. The raven has told me."

Izhur frowned, but exhaled a long breath. "If you say so."

Iluna held her hand above the sticks and whispered a word, "Fire." At once the bundle of wood came to light.

Izhur sucked his breath. "How did you do that?"

Iluna looked at her elders. They wore an identical expression, mouths open, eyes wide – half shock, half wonder. "There is much you don't yet know about my gift."

Cypra and Izhur glanced at each other, a flicker of doubt now crossing their brows.

"Please, Uncle, Aunty, you need to trust me. Listen to my plan."

Izhur swallowed; the apple in his throat moving as he did so. "Tell us then, Iluna. How do you intend to stop them?" He took a seat on a rock next to Cypra. The new bronze and silver beads he'd received at Agria's opening glistened in the firelight.

Iluna took a small bone pot from her satchel and filled it with water from the skin. A handful of pine needles went in next, she swirled the pot and placed it on the fire. "The enemy clan is near; less than half a day's walk from this very spot."

"What?" Fear wrinkled Cypra's brow.

"They plan to attack us – all of Ona's people – the day after tomorrow. Xaroth and Yuli schemed long and hard for this day."

Izhur blinked. "How can you know this?"

"The raven, Uncle, he has shown me all."

Izhur looked to the cave's entrance. "Where is your raven now?"

"He keeps watch and will warn us of danger. The cave protects us but we are unable to sense danger out there. He is our eyes and ears, both in this world and the Other."

Izhur swallowed again. "So how can we stop them? Stop this attack?"

Iluna took a breath, and stirred the water with a stick. Small bubbles sprung up. "I will go to them, this enemy clan."

"No." Izhur shook his head. "It's too dangerous."

"Listen, Uncle. Hear my plan in full."

Izhur rubbed a temple as he looked into the fire, his eyes brimming with anger and frustration, but then he gave a curt nod, and Iluna continued.

"One among them speaks our tongue; the raven has shown me. I believe it was the Grand Soragan who first taught him."

"That snake," Cypra snarled.

"Quite right, Aunty. The snake is Xaroth's totem and as you know he can bind."

"And slither wheresoever he pleases," Cypra replied, anger in her snarl.

"It is the reason he was saved, all those years ago, when he first met this enemy clan on his hermitage."

Cypra frowned. "What do you mean? He's known them all these summers?"

"Scores of summer and winters, both. It all stemmed from his hermitage. He tried to escape them by binding and slithering off, but they caught him with a spear to his tail. It is why the Grand Soragan limps to this day."

"Go on," Izhur muttered.

"They were in awe of his gift of binding, and struck a bargain. Xaroth would teach them how to bind with an animal, and he would lead them to our wealth."

"Wealth?" Cypra asked.

"It is one of their words. I think it means to have many precious things, such as gold or jade." Iluna pointed to the beads around Izhur's neck. "They desired this wealth and also our land."

"And what would Xaroth get in return?" Cypra asked.

"An unnaturally long life. They would teach him their secrets. It is where he learnt the bronze magic that he brought back to our people. He also learnt of their dark magics which keeps him alive. He has risen among them, and plans to become a wealthy leader in the new world they hope to create on our lands." Iluna looked at the two Soragans before her. "I believe it is possible they had foreseen my birth, and that is why Xaroth has worked against me all my life – whispering in Zodor's ear that I would be an evil force, so that Zodor convinced the circle that I should be sacrificed as a babe."

Izhur looked to the fire, eyes wide. "Yes, it would explain everything. And why he is so adamant to take your power. And now with Yuli ..." Izhur mumbled his frown deep and furrowed.

"Uncle?"

Izhur looked at Cypra. "That ceremony I mentioned, for Yuli."

"Yes, back at the tent," Cypra said, nodding.

"It is a binding ceremony. Xaroth wants to perform the ceremony to bind Yuli to his totem."

Cypra's nostrils flared. "After all my efforts, he just up and decides to do it? Why Yuli? Why now? How will they get the energy required? I doubt Yuli has a strong enough gift in any case. It could kill him."

Izhur was rubbing his temples. "It must be related somehow to this enemy clan." He looked up, suddenly. "Yuli must have been associating with them on his hermitage!"

Iluna took the bone pot off the fire, and let it sit to cool. The scent of pine filled the cave and she took a cleansing breath.

The raven had not foretold of any binding, and she wasn't sure she believed the ceremony for Yuli would take place. She focused on the two Soragans in front of her. They were both angry, understandably so, but she needed them to pay attention to her. She needed them to listen so that the enchantment she would eventually weave took hold. She sent a pulse of calming blue light and waited a moment for their breathing to slow, their fires to wane.

"We must deal with Xaroth and Yuli after. First comes this enemy clan. As I was saying, I want to meet with them, to try and reason, to reach out to them and show them how their hostility has caused us such pain, such grief. To persuade them to turn back."

"Iluna dear, it is an honorable thought, but these monsters – I have seen them." Cypra was shaking her head, eyes glistening. "They are not capable of such sensitivity."

"No, Aunty. I believe that is true, but I must try. It is what Ona would expect of us." Iluna could feel their heart beats slowing; they were calmer now.

"I expect my attempt at negotiating will fail. So, I will enact the second part of my plan." Iluna wasn't going to tell them this part. She was simply going to go through with the enchantment, and then prepare for her journey, but perhaps they would give her further insight. She may as well tell them. They would only forget once they fell under the enchantment anyway.

"When my negotiations fail, I will send them away."

"How?" Izhur asked.

Iluna lifted her chin. "I will frighten them so they will be too afraid to enter one foot into Ona's Valley."

Izhur blinked. "You can do it?"

"Yes, Uncle."

Suddenly it seemed to Iluna that Izhur and Cypra were more like children, in their innocence, their awe.

"Come. Drink this. It shall refresh us." She held the bone pot out for them and they each took a slow sip. Cypra's hands were shaking.

Iluna stilled herself. It was time to weave the enchantment. To undo everything she had told them, and send them back down the mountain. She took a breath and held up a hand. They held palms to their eyes to obscure her blinding light, but Iluna ignored their discomfort, and her white light filled the cave, like a star.

190

ANTON

A loud squawk woke him and Anton sat up, blinking. On a large rock perched a crow. It cocked its head to one side, as though it watched him. Anton blinked some more, and the crow squawked again before taking flight, wings beating up a cool breeze. The sky had turned a dusky pink – dawn. Anton yawned before a sharp breath of panic woke him fully. He had fallen asleep!

"Fool!" he whispered.

On hands and knees he peered through the needles of the juniper tree. The cave's entrance stood a few steps away. Would they still be in there? His eyes scanned the terrain. No fresh prints. Perhaps he should risk a closer look.

Anton tried to remember the last thing he'd heard. They had talked about Yuli and the Grand Soragan. Both traitors, if Iluna was to be believed. And though he didn't want to, he did believe her. The enemy clan was close. She wanted to go to them. And do what? Anton shook his head, trying to remember. But a fuzzy cloud filled his mind and all he could recall was that bright whiteness that had come from the cave.

"What a beautiful day!"

Anton shrunk down. Cypra stood at the cave's entrance, a smile on her face.

"Yes, a good day for fishing, Cypra, or gathering orange fruit." Izhur followed her out, appearing just as jovial as Cypra's smile.

Something was at odds. Did they know he was there? Were they pretending their entire people were safe?

"Well, goodbye, Uncle, Aunty. I will see you soon." Iluna appeared at the cave's entrance, her black hair its usual mess. Dark rings lined her eyes. Clearly, she hadn't slept.

"Yes, dear. We'll see you soon." Cypra grinned and walked back the way they had come.

"Enjoy your time, Iluna. We'll see you back at camp." Izhur caught up with Cypra, and Anton could just hear their conversation about whether to pick some orange fruit on their way down.

He frowned again. What was going on? Had he dreamed their secret talk last night?

Iluna stepped out of the cave's entrance. The daysun had just breached the horizon and the first golden rays of dawn touched her hair, highlighting the blue. She still had her broad nose, her wide mouth; she was still a frog face. But he liked that face more than his new wife's. He liked it a lot.

She walked a few steps to peer at the path that Cypra and Izhur had just taken. Perhaps she was looking to see if they were truly gone. She reached out with her fingers, but otherwise remained still, and after just a few heartbeats she seemed satisfied.

Then she turned and looked his way.

"I know you are there, Anton. You can come out now."

He swallowed. How had she known? But he knew better than to remain hidden. Not that he wanted to.

"What do you think you're doing?" She was angry.

"I'm sorry, Iluna."

"You're to stop this foolishness. You've a wife now."

Anton knew it, though he'd give her away tomorrow if he could. Hennita had proved as uninteresting to him as she always had. "I wanted to talk to you again." He had much to tell her, and this time he wouldn't stumble.

Iluna's eyes softened before they scanned the sky and trees. She was looking for something, the way a hunter looks for clues when tracking.

"You followed us?" she asked.

'No. I tracked you.'

A look of irritation crossed her face. "I was careful."

Anton smiled. "Not careful enough."

Iluna raised an eyebrow. "Say what you have to say; and then you had best be gone."

"I will tell you what I want to say to you," Anton paused, his smile broadening, "when we return from this enemy clan."

Her eyes widened ever so slightly before resuming their search. What was she looking for?

"You overheard us?"

"Yes."

"Anton, I must do this alone. I won't have the energy to protect you. I'll need all my strength for what I have to do."

"I am coming with you. I'll help you fight them. You can't stop me."

"I can." She held her hands up.

"Iluna. Please. Let me help you. I'll do exactly as you say. Just let me help. I want to do this – for you, for our people, and for my mother."

Iluna put her hand down. "Your mother?"

"She suffers. She has seen the difference in Yuli, and she has fallen into a great despondency. If she knew Yuli was behind this, it would ruin her. I want to set things to right, as much as I can."

Iluna stalled, her eyes softening all the more. Anton could almost see affection in them. Was it possible she had feelings for him, too?

She shook her head. "Your mother is kind, Anton, and you are honorable to want to help her, but I cannot allow it."

"Please, Iluna. I don't care so much for my life, but if anything was to happen to you, or my mother, there would be nothing more in this world I would want to live for. Please let me help you."

Iluna took a deep breath and closed her eyes. "I'll do it on one condition."

"Name it."

"When we return – if we return – you forget about me. You stop following me about. You go back to treating me as the tamatu I am." She held her head high.

"Why would you want such a thing?"

"It would be better for me if you did."

"I'll do it. After I tell you that thing; the thing I need to tell you."

Iluna nodded. "Done then. Although – I must sleep now. I need my energy. We leave when Atoll's star rises this evening, but if I dream of what's to come, I may change my mind about you accompanying me, and you will find yourself sitting in front of the evenfire tonight, everything forgotten. Just as Izhur and Cypra will be."

A squawk came from the sky and Anton almost ducked when the crow flapped its wings and landed on his shoulder.

"Great Mother," Iluna whispered, her dark eyes like new moons.

Anton laughed. "Is this some trick of yours? Some magic?"

The crow preened a wing and squawked once more, but remained on his shoulder as though it belonged there.

"No," Iluna whispered. "No magic." Her eyes shifted to his. "It seems you will be coming with me after all."

The bird batted its wings and flew off.

"What a strange crow."

"Raven," Iluna said as she watched it circle high into the sky. "Come, let us gather some food. Then I must rest."

∞

ANTON WATCHED as Iluna took her first mouthful of rabbit meat. He'd hunted while she slept. Her eyes closed and she nodded as she chewed.

He smiled. "It's good, isn't it?"

She looked at him, grease shining on her chin. "It's delicious, but the fruits and nuts would have sufficed." She took another bite.

"You said you needed energy for what you have to do. Hunting rabbits is as easy for me as picking those moonberries you love so much." He held up a rabbit leg, juices dripping. "I pasted crushed moonberries over the skin. My mother cooked it like this not two nights past. It's good."

Iluna smiled. Her eyes twinkled and Anton relished it. Was there any better feeling in the world than making her smile?

They finished their meal and kicked dirt on the small fire. Then it was time to leave. Iluna stood outside the cave, her eyes searching the view of the forest to the south, down the mountain. A light blue haze had sprung up to the east. Atoll's star was about to join the moon and the nightsun in the Agrian sky. The raven squawked and landed on Iluna's shoulder. She fed him a handful of berries and the bird gulped them down before taking off again, heading south.

"It is time," Iluna said, and she followed the bird.

She kept a swift pace.

"You will not sleep before we get there?" Anton followed her over a boulder.

"No, that is why I slept today. We'll travel through the night and should arrive at their camp by dawn. As long as you can keep up and that spear doesn't get in your way."

Anton smiled. He'd made the spear out of willow wood. It was light, but strong. "My spear will slay them if they attack us."

Iluna stopped and gave him a look. "When we arrive you are to do exactly what I tell you. There will be no blood spilled, if I can help it."

"They have spilled the blood of an entire clan. If one of them should die, then we shall have some vengeance."

Iluna blinked. "Is this Anton or Zodor I am speaking with?"

Anton looked down at his feet. "Anton."

"Vengeance is the path to savagery. I will not own it. You will do as I say, or I will enchant you. We had an agreement."

Anton gave a curt nod, and Iluna continued down the mountain.

They stopped only briefly, twice to rest and fill their water skins from the mountain creeks, and then from the river, and to eat some loquat berries and hazelnuts that Anton had collected earlier. The raven was never far. He would fly ahead only to circle back and squawk every now and then, as though letting them know they were on the right path. Iluna said little. She'd warn him of a thorny bush ahead or a steep drop in the terrain, but mostly she was silent. As they descended, the vegetation changed ever so slightly. Closer to the river more orange fruit trees and loquats grew. And the forest became darker still, with taller oaks and elms.

They skirted a bend in the riverbank and the raven perched on a branch, waiting for them. Strips of pink streaked the sky to the east.

"It is time to prepare," Iluna went to the river and filled her skin and drank deep before sitting on a river rock. "Eat. We need our final nourishment before we face them."

Anton sat next to her and took the last two orange fruits from his satchel. He peeled one and gave it to Iluna.

"Thank you," she said, taking it from him.

He touched her hand with his, as they held the fruit. "You're welcome."

They ate the orange fruit and the hazelnuts. Then Iluna walked to the river and splashed water on her face. She turned and stood in front of him. "The enemy clan is through the trees that way." She pointed to the south-west. "We will stop at a place close enough for you to watch, but you are not to make yourself known."

"I want to help you; I have my spear. I can defend you as you do your magic."

"I said – there is to be no blood spilled. If possible, anyway. And you *will* help me, Anton."

"How?"

Iluna frowned. "How, has not been revealed to me. It is important that you do not follow but stay where you are. If I have to spend energy to stop you, it will hinder my actions with the enemy."

Anton took a deep breath. "Very well. I promise to stay in my place."

"Thank you. Now, once we leave I do not want us to talk again. I will cast a shield for us in the Otherworld that will protect us, but if we talk someone might hear. They have powerful magics and strong hunting tools. They could easily overpower us if we are not careful."

"I thought you were more powerful. That's what you told Izhur and Cypra; I heard you say it."

Iluna's eyes looked to the ground, revealing her doubt. "It has not been tested. It is not known for a certainty."

"We could turn back now; it's not too late. Let's convince the others to help us fight them."

"You're forgetting your brother and the Grand Soragan. They

will not allow it. No, this is the only way. Are you ready? Remember, we're not to speak once we leave. Is there anything else you wish to say?"

Anton's eyes drank her in. "I think you're wonderful."

Iluna shook her head. "Let's go."

∞

PINK CLOUDS DOTTED the dawn sky. The raven flew low and perched on a low branch of a pine tree. He sat so still he looked like a carving made from ironwood. Iluna squatted next to him and gestured for Anton to do the same. She gave a signal that this was the spot where he was to stay. He nodded. Then she looked through the needles of the pine and he followed her line of sight.

Anton saw them – the enemy. Their encampment was huge. Their tents were large, but plain in colour. Every one looked the same, as though they had been sewn from the one skin of leather, made by the same hand. They were pitched in perfect formation, in lines.

When he saw the people, Anton almost uttered the Mother's name. He'd never seen such people. They were tall, with pale skin and golden hair that they tied back in elaborate weaves. Their clothes were made of a material not leather, not grass, something altogether foreign. They spoke a strange language.

But what caught Anton's eye more than anything was their hunting tools – spears, axes, knives, short and long, and some he had no name for. All had a sharp, dark metalic sheen, different from the bronze and stone of his people. Some of them were practising the hunt; their knives flashed in the first sunrays. Why were they performing the hunt on each other?

He looked again. There were no women. Every one of them

was a man; all tall and strong. How was Iluna going to face them? His heart raced. She needed protection.

Her eyes were closed now; her lips moving, silently. He remembered her doing exactly this when they were children and he had caught her in the forest. She'd cast her spell and the mountain lion had come out of nowhere to hunt him. He'd never run so fast in all his life. She had power, but would it be enough to overcome them? He swallowed. They looked so strong, and they had their own magics. They were powerful, Iluna had said. Suddenly Anton didn't want to be here. He should have told her what he wanted say at the cave. They could be far away by now; away from this chaos.

Iluna touched his arm, and he looked into her eyes. Anton wasn't sure if he could see fear there, but he knew it was time for her to go. He covered her hand with his own and gave it a squeeze. He tried a smile, but Iluna stood and then she was gone. He looked through the pine trees.

She walked into the camp. No one had seen her yet. She stopped, very near the first tent, and drew a circle in the dust.

The raven quorked; he watched her, too.

Iluna stood in the circle she had drawn and extended her arms outwards, towards the tents.

Suddenly one of the enemy clan saw her. He clutched a long knife close and yelled in that strange tongue, and hundreds came from everywhere.

"Who among you knows my language?" Iluna shouted but her voice seemed so small compared with the strong calls of the man.

Anton's eyes scanned them, his heart pounding.

It seemed the entire camp bustled, edging closer to Iluna. There were hundreds and hundreds more. Anton had never seen so many people. Not even at Agria.

"I speak your tongue." A man in a long black robe stepped forward. His hair, gold and silver, fell loosely over his shoulders, contrasting sharply with the black robe. "Who are you, little girl, and where are your people?" The man's eyes looked over Iluna's shoulder toward the pine. Anton held his breath. Could he see him?

"My name is Iluna of the Wolf; we are Ona's people. I have come to beg of you to turn back. We are a peaceful people; please let us be. We have bled and hurt from your past attack. Please show us mercy, leave us be."

The man squinted. "I am Gudmund of Nordesa." He spoke their language, but he said the words differently, and Anton had to concentrate to understand him. "Where is Yuli or Xaroth? Are they with you?" Gudmund held up a hand as if searching. Anton silently cursed his brother.

"I am alone, aside from my raven."

The raven quorked and took flight, circling above Iluna, and coming down to land on her shoulder. This seemed to cause a ruckus and the men spoke excitely to each other. Another man wearing the dark robes similar to Gudmund pushed through the mob. He spoke to Gudmund, their voices elevated until they were shouting at each other. Finally Gudmund put his hand up and a large clap like thunder pierced the air. Silence followed.

Anton swallowed. Magic lingered; he could smell it.

"We have heard of you, Iluna. You are the evil witch of your people." Gudmund smiled. "You may have a great gift, but you know nothing of our power." Other men, all dressed in the black robes came to stand beside Gudmund. There were ten of them – their Soragans perhaps.

"We will not turn back, girl. The gods have shown us the way. We march this very morning. By midnight we will have conquered your people, and your lands."

Anger bubbled in Anton's blood, but he remained silent and still, as promised.

"And what of the bloodshed you will cause. Have you no remorse?' Iluna's voice carried softly.

Gudmund shook his head. "This is the path set out for us by

our gods. Many of your people will die tonight. It has been fore-seen." Gudmund shouted a guttural word and the hundreds moved as though they were one, lifting their hunting tools in preparation. They were readying to fight her.

"You will be our first sacrifice to the Holy Ones," Gudmund shouted and a man lunged at Iluna. He threw his arm up with the knife to strike.

"No," Anton whispered, forgetting to be silent.

But the raven was quick, he'd flown and dived and plucked the man's eye before his knife found its target. The blade dropped and he screamed with pain.

Iluna's arms went high and a breeze swirled through the throng lifting her hair and her robe. "You will return!" Her voice grew loud, it boomed, no longer the innocent voice of a young woman.

"Guzaarrrrr!" Gudmund's voice boomed, too, and the throng of men rushed forward, hunting tools held high. But darkness filled the sky. The daysun was suddenly, silently, blackened. Anton jumped at a touch on his shoulder – a black feather. He looked up. A dark cloud grew closer. Only it was no cloud, but hundreds and hundreds, and hundreds more ravens – scores of hundreds. They swirled and swooped as one, and plunged into the throng. The men screamed, and dropped their knives and spears. Then they ran. She had broken them. Anton smiled. Yes, she could win this after all.

"I do not wish your death." Her voice boomed louder, over the squarks and screams. "I just want you gone!" And the cloud of ravens rose up like a wave of the ocean and struck again, bringing more screams from men with eyes plucked or gaping wounds in their faces. Much blood had already been spilled.

The ten men moved as one, throwing their arms to the sky. There was a crack in the air and each raven stopped where it was and fell. Ravens rained down, dead.

Gudmund shouted a command and men, injured or no picked up their tools. The fight wasn't over yet.

The armed men came at her again, and they struck with their knives and spears, but each strike bounced off her. Iluna's back was to him, but Anton could see her hands, up in the air. She was protecting herself with some kind of magical shield. The men couldn't touch her, but they kept trying, striking time and time again.

Gudmund and the other robed men stood in a circle now. Hunched over, their chant grew louder. One of them suddenly turned, grabbed a fighter, and sliced his neck with his own knife. Blood gushed everywhere. A white light formed, becoming brighter the longer they chanted.

Gudmund turned and held fire in his hand. He shouted another command and the men stopped striking Iluna and ran back toward the tents. He whispered to the fire he held, and then threw it with great strength toward Iluna. It flared when it hit her, and caused a bright flash that made Anton close his eyes. When he opened them Iluna was laying on the ground. His heart stopped, but then she moved, and stood, stumbling. She was tiring; the magic draining her.

"I have tried to warn you," she said. Her voice back to normal, she sounded weary. "The deaths of your men will be on your head, Gudmund."

Gudmund smiled then, and threw back his head, laughing.

Anton heard a growl; it came from behind. A bee flew past, followed by another. Then he heard the growl again. Slowly he turned, and came face to face with a mountain lion. Its blue eyes looking him over, it padded closer and its nose sniffed at his skin. Anton's heart thumped in his ears. The lion was twice the height of a man, its saber teeth as long as his own head.

Another growl came then and the lion looked behind him and Anton risked a glance. Wolves stood in the shade of the trees. A buzzing in his ears made him twitch; mosquitoes were every-where. He swallowed, and slowly turned to look at Iluna.

Her arms were up as though appealing to the very sky.

"I've destroyed your shield, little girl. It's time for you to face your gods." Gudmund gave the order and the men ran forward once more.

Iluna brought down her arms and the lions and wolves sprang from the forest. Hundreds of animals now attacked and the horde of men ran back in fear. One lion clawed a man throwing him backwards. Another tore a man in two with powerful jaws. Then came more – wolves, jackals, cats, bears, foxes, stags and oxen. They thundered out of the forest and plunged into the throng of men. Gudmund had formed a circle again with the others, and their chanting began once more, but bees, mosquitos and wasps stung them, breaking their concentration. Bats, hawks and buzzards filled the sky. Snakes and water dragons slithered and stung, and the men started to run.

Gudmund broke with the other robed men, who had started to flee as well, but he seemed to resist the throng of stings, his mouth still murmuring the words. He cut his own wrist and a spear came to life before him. It lurched through the air and plunged into Iluna. She fell to the ground. Blood gushed from her leg. Anton didn't think – he acted, and ran to her. The spear stuck out of her thigh. She was in pain, but still murmuring her spells, her chants.

"Iluna, let me do this. I'm sorry." He grabbed the spear and pulled. It came out and Iluna screamed. Anton took three large strides and threw the spear at Gudmund. It landed with a thud, deep into his heart. The man gazed at Anton, a questioning look on his face. "Yuli?" he said, before falling and dying.

The animals continued their attack, killing, chasing. The enemy now retreated, panicked. Anton ran back to Iluna. She was cold, she'd lost much blood, but her eyes fluttered open. "Hold my hands," she croaked.

"Of course, Iluna. You've won! You've done it."

"Not yet." She grabbed his hands and moved her lips. Anton could feel his energy draining. She was using his life force to feed her spells. With every heart beat he grew weaker.

The ground moved. Clouds in the sky swirled as the ravens had done before. The ground shook with earthquakes; lightning and thunder filled the sky. All around him the dead ravens were coming back to life, flying fast to join the chase. Was it the end?

The enemy was fleeing, a funnel of wind chasing them down. And then a white light flashed; his energy left him and Anton closed his eyes.

YULI

*Y*uli's blood raced as he told the Grand Soragan the news. They met in their usual place. A small chasm in the mountain, some distance from the encampment. The Grand Soragan's enchantment ensured that no one would ever stumble upon them.

"You're sure? There's no one left?" Xaroth's voice hissed.

Yuli swallowed. "No one. I reached their camp at midday; I ran all the way. There was no one left. Only the dead and the remnants of their camp remained. It looked like they left in a hurry – those who survived. When I sent out my essence to look for them I sensed they headed south. Back the way they had come."

The Grand Soragan snarled. "All that work." The lines in his aged face seemed deeper, and dark bags circled his eyes. He was spending too much energy controlling the others. Yuli glanced around for Sethra. She was usually on hand to give up her blood, or more, but not now. It was just the two of them.

Yuli blinked. "How did this happen? I don't understand. We had an agreement. They were to launch their attack this very night!"

The Grand Soragan nodded, vaguely, his mind elsewhere.

Yuli had become part of the Grand Soragan's scheme the day he agreed to be Xaroth's unofficial prentice. He had kept up his training with Izhur for appearance's sake, but it was the Grand Soragan who had taught him everything he knew, who gave him the skills he now enjoyed – power thrice as strong as Izhur's.

Since their first meeting two winters past, Yuli had learnt to use the blood of an animal to drink and cast powerful spells; how to send out his mind and travel with his essence through the Otherworld – a skill only practised by the most powerful of Soragans, after much training and meditation. But now he could do it easily. During his hermitage, Xaroth had taught him in person, and he'd introduced Yuli to the Nordesans.

At first Yuli had been wary. Their tall fearsome appearance had frightened him. And he knew what they were capable of; the Otter had all perished. But he soon saw their way was better; their magic stronger.

Their way of life made more sense. They didn't roam from place to place, but stayed in one area and built villages and towns and each man would own land. Their women were more beauti-ful. He had also learnt their language – a sophisticated tongue with a broad cadence of words and rules. Xaroth had planned a life amongst them in their new world that was to be built in Ona's Valley. And now it had all gone wrong. The Nordesans had disappeared.

The old Soragan studied the floor of the chasm, muttering to himself.

"I just don't understand." Yuli thumped the ground with his staff. "What made them leave?"

The old Soragan snapped out of his musing and looked at Yuli with those unsettling small eyes. "It was the witch."

Yuli scowled. Of course. It had to be her. She must have found out about them and used her evil magic to scare them away. Then another realization dawned. Yuli swallowed. "She has that kind of power?"

The Grand Soragan turned and his robe twirled as he limped to the back of the chasm. He snapped his fingers and the oil pots came to light. A rabbit remained tied there – its nose twitching and its eyes revealing its terror. The Soragan grabbed the frightened animal by the back of its neck and took out his ceremonial knife from his robe. In one swift action he slit the rabbit's throat and held it twitching and convulsing above his head as he drank in the blood. He wiped his mouth and handed the corpse to Yuli.

When he first had to drink blood, so fresh and warm, Yuli was disgusted and vomited the sticky substance up, but now he almost yearned for it. He took the rabbit willingly and drank his fill.

"I'm going to find them in the Otherworld."

Yuli nodded.

"You deal with the witch," the Soragan said, his voice like death.

Yuli didn't need to hear the words twice. He turned and marched out of the cave sending his essence out as he walked. He concentrated on the clearing up in the mountain forest, but no sign of her lurked there. He sent his essence further through the forest, under trees, around boulders, but still no clue arose.

Yuli snapped his essence back like a whip. Where was she? He walked along the river. The camp's drumbeats were clearer now that evening had set in. Maybe she was at camp, hiding among the people. Yuli stood still, and sent his essence through the large encampment. It took him longer to search through the thick black web of bands that connected most members to Xaroth, allowing the Grand Soragan to have so much control. But, Iluna wasn't there either.

Yuli frowned, not sure what to do next. Then his lips twitched. His brother had been causing their mother grief of late. Since he'd bonded with Hennita, Anton had hardly been home.

The new couple had set up their own tent, as was the custom, but Anton had barely shared it for more than a conversation. He'd not even consummated their bond yet. And why wouldn't a young hunter such as Anton eagerly take his new wife?

Yuli squinted as he recalled the clearing that night. His brother had been looking for Iluna too.

Anton must be with her.

Yuli closed his eyes and sent out his essence once more.

ILUNA

"*I*luna."

Everything was black. That was her first aware-ness. Then pain shot through her leg – a deep stab. Her muscles twitched, and she screamed.

"Iluna. Shhhh. Ona, help me."

Her eyes fluttered and Anton swam before her, his face panicked. She tried lifting her head but another bolt of pain struck, and she screamed again.

"Don't move your leg. I've stopped the bleeding; we can't risk it starting again. Here, I want you to try and drink this. I found some paleheart flowers along the river bank. It will help with your pain."

Anton lifed her head and brought the warm bone pot to her mouth. Iluna took a sip. Bitterness filled her mouth but she drank the whole thing down.

"I'm thirsty," she croaked.

Relief lit Anton's eyes and he smiled. "It's good to hear you talk. I've been so worried. I wasn't sure whether I should have left you here and raced back to get Amak. Here, drink."

He filled the pot with more water from the skin and lifted her head again. The water was cool, instantly quenching the dryness in her throat. She finished that cup, too. "More." Then a bolt of pain pulsed and she scrunched her eyes shut until it passed.

"The paleheart should take effect soon and stop the pain, but it will make you sleepy, too." He refilled the pot. "Should I get Amak when you sleep? You'll be safe here."

Anton's small fire lit up the cave walls. Yes, they were safe. Aside from the pain, Iluna was exhausted. She could barely think to answer Anton's question. Her gift had taken all her energy.

"The enemy clan, are they gone?" she whispered.

"Yes. You're amazing, Iluna. I've never seen such magic! Better than any evenfire tale."

Iluna frowned, the pain was easing slowly. "What happened to me?"

"It was that dark wizard, Gudmund. He tried to slay you with a spear. It pierced your leg. You've lost a lot of blood, but I managed to bind it and staunch the flow. I carried you back to this cave. Well, after I woke. It was strange, everyone had gone. I found some mallowroot and I've bathed the wound with that to try and stop any infection. But alza would be better. I should return to camp to get some. Or even better, Amak."

Iluna reached out a shaking arm. "Hold my hand."

Anton's palm was warm and his essence calmed her – almost in the way her raven did. "My raven, where is he?"

"Outside somewhere. I think he is keeping a lookout. He followed us up the mountain."

"Is it night or day?"

"It is night now. Imbrit, Atoll and Goda are all in the sky."

Anton's thumb caressed her hand as he held it, the type of thing lovers did. Iluna closed her eyes and drew a little of his energy. He was a strong hunter and seemed to have endless essence. She focused on her leg, healing the muscle and flesh and dimming the pain, just a little. She breathed more easily and opened her eyes.

"Thank you." She sat up.

"Iluna, no, you're not ready yet."

"It's all right, Anton."

He frowned. "You're not in pain?"

"It's eased, must have been the paleheart flowers."

Anton smiled.

She looked at her wound. Anton had wrapped it with reeds; tight. Blood had dried in small clumps all over her leg.

"Could I have the water please?" She was so thirsty she could almost finish the skin.

"Well, should I return to the camp? Tell the others we are all safe now?"

A chill swept through the cave and Iluna shivered. "No. We are not yet safe. There is still Xaroth and – your brother."

"Oh." Anton picked up a stick to poke the fire.

"Is there anything to eat?" Iluna was suddenly as hungry as a wolf in winter.

Anton smiled and peeled an orange fruit before handing it to her. They ate for a while. The orange fruit tasted sweeter than any other.

"About Yuli," Anton said. "What's this ceremony Izhur spoke of?"

Iluna wiped juice off her chin. "I'm not supposed to tell you. It is meant to be a secret only Soragans share. I'm not supposed to know it myself, but Cypra and Izhur, they've told me all the secrets, or I've learned them myself. Could I have some of the hazelnuts now?"

Anton reached out and took her hand, it was warm and soft. He grabbed a handful of the peeled nuts and placed them in her small palm, closing her fingers around them and smiling into her eyes.

She shook her head, but a warm glow bloomed somewhere inside. She smiled back and popped a hazelnut into her mouth.

"But, it seems to me that the Grand Soragan and Yuli have had their own secrets. Surely I can know this secret. Yuli is my brother."

Iluna finished her mouthful and looked at him. "It is called a binding ceremony. It has not been done in many summers. Not since Cypra was young. They will bind Yuli with his totem."

"What does that mean?"

Iluna pursed her lips. "Are you sure you want to know this? It is kept secret for a reason. You may not believe it if I tell it to you."

"Tell me."

"When he binds with his totem he becomes that animal, physically changed."

Anton's mouth fell open. "You're not jesting with me?"

Iluna shook her head. "I rarely jest."

"You mean, he turns into an animal? Like in some evenfire tale?"

"Yes, but his mind will remain unchanged, providing he has the strength to control it."

"Will he be that way forever? Until he passes to the Otherworld?"

"No, he will be able to change back, as long as he succeeds the first time he will be able to control the shift at will, though it will expend much energy."

"There is a chance he will not succeed? What does that mean?"

"It means he could die."

Anton swallowed; his amber eyes suddenly sad. "Well, what should we do now? Should I fetch Amak? I'm worried about your leg."

Iluna took a breath. Her leg would be fine. She would heal it properly when she was stronger, later. "No, not Amak. But Izhur and Cypra. I enchanted them before they left here. I had to make them forget everything or Izhur was likely to do something stupid and face the Grand Soragan himself, in front of the other

Soragans, too, no doubt. But by dawn the enchantment will have worn off. I need you to find them and bring them back here. Together we will work to face Xaroth and Yuli."

Anton nodded. "Dawn isn't far off. I should leave."

"Yes."

"Is there anything you need? I'll leave my satchel. It has more orange fruit and hazelnuts. None of your favourites though."

Iluna raised an eyebrow. "And what do you suppose is my favourite?"

"The moonberries, of course." His grin showed all his beautiful teeth.

"You are observant."

"I am a hunter."

He stopped smiling then and Iluna watched his lips, the line of his jaw, his eyes – amber and beautiful. She brought a hand to her brow. It must be the palehearts, finally taking their effect. "I'll be fine here. But please, help me outside. I want to see my raven."

Anton frowned. "I don't think that's wise. I don't think you should leave the cave."

Iluna flicked her hand. "I'll be quite all right. Just for a little while I want to see my raven. Then I'll come straight back in and get some more sleep."

Anton took a deep breath. "All right. But, please, not for too long."

He helped her up. Iluna felt weightless as he wrapped an arm around her and helped her to stand. A wave of dizziness circled through her head, but Anton held her tight and her leg only pulsed dimly. She took a step and with the hunter beside her she slowly made it outside.

"Thank you. I'll summon him when you go."

Anton still held his hand around her waist. He looked down on her. The golden highlights of his hair where the daysun had lightened it shone almost white in the moonrays.

"I don't want to go now." He put his other hand around her

waist, too. It was warm. Iluna felt safe, happy, but it was a luxury she couldn't waste time on.

"You must. We need Izhur and Cypra."

Anton nodded and swallowed. "I know. I just don't want to. I don't want to leave you."

Iluna put a hand on his chest. It felt like warm carved rock, but she could feel his heart beating and she pulled away and stepped back out of his embrace. "Please let go. Let's get it all over with."

Anton frowned, looking down at his feet. "I will be quick," he said and turned to go.

"Anton, wait."

"Yes?" His eyes lit up.

"The thing you wanted to tell me? What was it?" She'd remembered his promise to tell her, and her curiosity flared.

He smiled. "Let's meet again when you are well. I will tell you then." And he left, without making another noise.

YULI

*Y*uli ran through the forest, the rabbit's blood still firing his veins. Goda's nightsun had descended out of sight now. Soon the eastern sky would brighten. He had sensed his brother much earlier in the night, and then promptly lost him. Anton's essence had blinked out like a late night oil pot, but now it burned close, and there was someone with him – Iluna.

Her essence was weaker than usual. A smile twitched Yuli's lips. Perhaps she was injured. It would make sense. Gudmund and the other mages were more powerful than any Soragan. No one could attack the Nordesans and remain unscathed.

Yuli crested a rise and came to the mountain's peak. Up here he could see everything. To his left, way down in the middle of Ona's Valley, the evenfire flickered small, like a distant star. To the right was darkness, only the red glow in the west lit the sky, the remnants of Goda's nightsun. Or Thardun, as the Nordesan's referred to it – their god of war. Yes, their gods were better, too. Yuli's people didn't even have a war god. That is why they could never protect themselves.

Voices sounded close as he descended the other side of the

mountain. Yuli pulled his essence around him like a warm cloak and snuck through the trees, being careful with his footing so as to not alert them to his presence. He had done this many times when spying on Iluna and it was easy enough to hide from her, especially when she was always so focused on summoning that stupid bird.

He glimpsed them now, and crept forward on all fours, like a wolf, shrubs and bushes camouflaging him. But Anton was gone. When Yuli reached out he sensed his brother running down the mountain, returning to camp no doubt.

Yuli paused. Had she detected his presence? A quick rush of panic distracted him. He'd seen the dead she'd left behind at the Nordesan's camp. There had been much bloodshed. Many had died of gruesome injuries. Some had their eyes plucked out, other's their throats, and others still had been torn in half. Yuli frowned. How had she done it?

He stilled his breathing and dissolved the panic, taking control of his senses. He would be just as powerful soon. The Grand Soragan had promised. He peered through the bushes to where Iluna now stood. She was studying the bird, in some sort of trance. The bird, perched on a low limb of the tree, was looking around. Yuli hoped it didn't sense him, like last time.

But then it squawked.

"Spurn it!" he muttered. Iluna spotted him and her eyes widened.

She fears me. Good. It gave him a boost and Yuli stepped forward. That was when he saw the cave behind Iluna. It distracted him momentarily. He'd not known there'd been a cave here.

"What do you want, Yuli?"

He kept his body relaxed, and forced a friendly smile as he bent to pick up a rock half the size of his hand. "I've been walking this night. I wanted to visit some new friends I'd made, but when I came upon their camp, they were all gone."

Iluna was breathing hard. She stumbled as though unbalanced and looked behind her toward the cave.

Yuli frowned. Something was wrong with her. Her essence was weak. *Good.* He smiled. "I don't suppose you know what happened to my friends? I wanted to introduce them to my mother."

Iluna's nostrils flared. "You don't scare me, Yuli. You know I am more powerful than you. You've seen the proof of it now. Just leave. Run back to your twisted master. Spill your blood and practise your evil magics. It will do you no good. Your new friends are no longer a threat, and I will tell the other Soragans about you and Xaroth, and undo the spells he has woven over our people – spells that have blinded and ensnared them." She stuck her chin up. "You and Xaroth are finished."

Yuli smoothed a snarl on his face, relaxing his muscles. He needed to resist anger. He must remain in control. "I'm curious about the bird." He nodded toward the black demon as he lobbed the rock in the air in front of his chest, catching it again with his hand.

Iluna squinted. Her eyes darted back and forth between the raven and Yuli.

She didn't trust him. And well she shouldn't. *Witch.* He sent out his essence to the rock until it thrummed in his hand.

"He is your totem, no?"

Iluna's eyes widened.

Yuli laughed. He knew her secret – a dangerous thing for an enemy to know. "What a suitable creature for a tamatu. You'll always be our tamatu, Iluna."

His essence continued to fill the rock that now buzzed with magic.

Iluna stumbled again and her hand went to her head. She took a step back, toward the cave. "Just go, Yuli. Leave me alone."

"Very well. Your wish is my command." He took a low bow and when he came back up his arm rose behind his head. "I'll leave you quite alone." He threw the rock. The raven squawked and took flight, too late.

"No!" Iluna screamed.

But the rock met its target. Of course it did. He had embedded it with enough essence to kill an entire family of people let alone one bird.

The thunk of rock meeting bone greeted his ears with satisfaction. Feathers shot up and floated down in circles. Yuli watched with a smile as the bird fell from the sky and landed with a thud on the ground; blood pouring from its impacted head. He laughed, and then turned to Iluna only to see that she also lay on the ground, as though dead.

He watched her chest, but it did not rise or fall. He smiled. That task was easier than he thought it would be. So much for all of her power.

IZHUR

*I*zhur walked past the evenfire pit. The cooks were busy stacking dry wood, and getting ready to fan the coals. Above, the sky transitioned slowly from blue to pink, and soon to purple. Dusk was nigh. People milled about the encampment getting ready for the festivities. It was the second-last night of Agria – the night of the long dance.

He avoided others as best he could, but being a Soragan, this was proving difficult. Many wanted to greet him, to wish him well or to ask for good omens.

"Will you be dancing tonight, Soragan Izhur?" Old Gelda of the Ox asked. Her cheeks shone like red summer plums when she smiled.

Izhur pursed his lips. "No, Aunty, excuse me." Dancing was the last thing on his mind.

Finally, after evading the bulk of the tents, he came to the old dead tree that marked the outskirts of the wolf encampment, and just beyond it stood the small weathered tent shared by Iluna and Cypra.

Izhur paused and took a breath. Anton had brought the news early that morning. The knowledge of the enemy clan, and

Xaroth and Yuli's part in it, all came back to him through a fog in his memory. Iluna had told them – him and Cypra at the cave, before she took the knowledge from them and sent them back down the mountain, ignorant. He shook his head trying to shake off anger and frustration. He understood why she'd done it, but he still wished she hadn't. Izhur had an ill feeling Iluna's troubles were far from over.

Anton had led Izhur and Cypra back to the cave atop the mountain that morning, and they'd found her lying on the ground at the cave's entrance – her raven dead beside her. Something had killed it.

At first they'd been afraid she was dead also. But both her pulse and her breathing were present, though slow. Anton scooped her up in his strong hunter arms and carried her down to the camp.

Cypra and Izhur had tried everything to wake her, in this world and the Other, but Iluna remained out of reach, in a trance. She had defeated the enemy clan, Anton told them. But now she slept, and no amount of shaking or tugging at her essence would wake her. And she was wounded. Amak had bathed her leg with alza and mallowroot as soon as they'd returned to camp, but there was no assurance it wouldn't fester. She needed medicine, Amak told him.

The gossips had been whispering all day, casting sidelong glances at Iluna's tent. Some held their hands, four fingertips touching, and took a wide berth as they walked past. Izhur had no care for what they thought. All would be revealed soon enough, and then Iluna would have all the love she deserved. She was their saviour, and finally everyone would see it.

Izhur opened the tent flap, stepped inside and took a sharp breath. A woman sat by Iluna's side, bathing the girl's forehead with a wet sponge.

"Ida."

She looked up. Dark rings lined her eyes. These days her silk hair was streaked with grey, but her beauty still took his breath.

"Tell me she'll be well again, Izhur." Ida's voice wavered.

"I wish I could. But I don't know if I can believe it myself. She is in a deep trance and I am unable to bring her out of it."

Ida sponged her forehead again. "She has a fever."

"Yes, but there is little we can do for that either, not unless she wakes and Amak can give her medicine."

"How did it happen, Izhur?"

Izhur thought of the raven, dead by Iluna's side. "I don't know. I think someone may have – done this to her."

Ida nodded. She put the sponge back in a clay pot filled with water and rose petals, then stood and faced Izhur. "Yuli has gone again. I haven't seen him since yesterday."

Izhur swallowed. "You're worried."

Ida looked back at Iluna. "Yes. I don't know my son now. Not since his hermitage. He is not the Yuli we sent away."

"I'm sorry, Ida. I have failed you."

Ida took a deep shuddering breath. "Don't blame yourself, Izhur. Some great evil has befallen my son. I know it. There is nothing we can do about it." She nodded toward Iluna. "Look after her, please. Don't leave her alone. She needs protection."

Izhur nodded. "Cypra and I have been watching her."

"And my eldest son, I hear."

Izhur looked to the ground. "Yes. Anton. He's been a great help."

Ida nodded. "But when this is over he must return to his wife. You must tell him, Izhur. He'll listen to you."

Then she opened the flap of the tent and left.

∞

Izhur was the last to enter the Soragan's tent. Inside, smoke from burning sage and cinnamon made a thick haze. Red coals from the fire pit in the tent's center added to the smoke. The air was already hot and humid. It was to be their second last meeting, and bound to be a long one. They were still to reach an agreement regarding the celebration for the following night – Agria's last. It was tradition for the Soragans to use the energy of the eight clans to enact a powerful chant – one that would bring good fortune for a group, or an individual.

Xaroth had been pushing for Yuli to undergo the binding ceremony, but now everything had changed, surely. As soon as Iluna woke she'd be able to break the control Xaroth had over the other Soragans and together they could tell them about this enemy clan. Nordesans they called themselves; Anton had told him that.

Izhur scanned the circle. All were present, except for one. Yuli had still not returned. Izhur squinted as he took a cushion for his seat. The longer his prentice stayed away the more Izhur grew convinced that Yuli had something to do with Iluna's trance, and the death of her raven.

"We are all assembled," Xaroth spoke. "Shall we begin?"

"Quite," Hentyl said.

"My novice is not yet present," Izhur interrupted. "Has anyone seen him?" He stared at the Grand Soragan, but Xaroth's eyes remained lifeless black beads.

"We will start without him. Yuli will be along directly. We have urgent matters to speak of." The Grand Soragan's quiet voice cut through the murmurs of the others.

Izhur raised an eyebrow. Did he know where Yuli was?

"No doubt you want to talk about Yuli's binding ceremony, Grand Soragan?" Jana spoke, sounding like the sycophant she'd grown into. "I for one am in agreement. If you have had the visions, as you say, that is enough proof for me that Yuli is meant to go through with it. It will be an exciting time for all of us. I have only heard of such a ceremony, like many of us here. I've not witnessed the skill, and it will be useful to have another person with such a gift."

Izhur rubbed a temple. There were many nods around the fire. He watched Belwas, but the old Bear nodded along with the others. Izhur frowned. Even Belwas had surrendered to Xaroth's influence.

"Yes, I agree." Hentyl added. "Let us go through with the binding ceremony. How should we acquire all the energy that will be needed?"

Would no one speak against this absurdity? Izhur felt more alone now than during his own hermitage.

Xaroth wore a smug smile as he raised his hand. "Thank you, Soragans. But I want to defer our discussions about Yuli's ceremony, for more pressing news has come to hand."

Izhur squinted. Surely he wasn't about to tell of the Nordesans.

"News has come to light about the enemy clan who attacked the Otter over two winters past."

"What? The enemy?" asked Tyvan.

"I thought they were gone, no longer a threat." Talso of the Lion looked as though he wanted to flee in the next instant.

"Yes, you assured us of it, Grand Soragan." Belwas looked displeased.

Izhur swallowed. Where was Xaroth going with this?

He flicked a tongue over his lips. "I have toiled long and hard every night to find them. I had no wish to cause you all concern. But, you see, I've long had a premonition that the enemy would come for us this very Agria."

There was uproar in the tent as the Soragans raised voices, trying to be heard. Tyvan stood, his eagle feathers sticking out of his head in their usual ostentatious manner. "We must fight. We must take our revenge."

Xaroth held a hand for silence. "Please. Let us resume our civility, brother. Hear me out."

The others quieted and Tyvan resumed his seat.

"Yesterday I meditated until the daysun took her leave. My visions in the Otherword were fruitful and I learned of the enemy clan. They were camped not a day's walk from Ona's Valley."

There was a sharp intake of breath, and Xaroth held his hand for silence once more.

"I left our encampment as soon as we broke our meeting last night. Yuli accompanied me. Together we faced them and ran them off."

Izhur frowned. It was a lie. He looked to the other Soragans; they wore expressions of relief, gratitude. They all believed the Grand Soragan's tale. Even Belwas seemed to be swallowing it. What was Xaroth up to? Izhur was tempted to speak out now, but it would do no good. Xaroth still held them all in his power.

"So they have gone; they are not a threat?" Hentyl asked, his elderly voice shaking.

Xaroth squinted. "We took one of them as prisoner. I have ordered Yuli to bring him to us. His name is Gudmund and he carries proof that one of our own has betrayed us."

Another outburst of gasps and exclamations filled the tent as the Soragans voiced their anger. "Who has dared to betray us?" Tyvan shouted.

Xaroth silenced them once more. "I propose a Grand Council."

"What?" Izhur asked, his voice tight.

Xaroth ignored him. "Summon all your people, Soragans. We will listen to the evidence as one, and we shall judge as one – before the evenfire, this very night."

Izhur swallowed. There'd not been a Grand Council since he was a boy. The memory of it brought a bitter taste to his mouth. He recalled a sickness had taken hold in one of the clans and at

Agria it had spread through the entire camp. It caused coughing and nausea, and within three days most people afflicted had died. They'd called a Grand Council then to decide the fate of the twelve remaining sick but not yet dead. By rights, everyone had a voice, but mostly it was the Soragans and elders who spoke – Xaroth more than any other. The twelve had burned – a sacrifice to spare the rest of them, and Izhur's father had been among them.

Izhur's hands balled into fists. He flung open the tent flap and marched out into the night, leaving the others to talk it out. He needed time. He needed Cypra. There was much to discuss.

ILUNA

*I*luna.

Someone called to her. Only it was more like many hushed whispers than one single voice. She walked toward it. Her arms ethereal, made of light, she watched them fold back heavy green vines that pulsed with strong essence. She was in the Otherworld.

Keep walking. You're almost here.

Dark wings fluttered up ahead and Iluna followed. Was it her raven? The voice was similar. Sadness gripped her heart when she'd remembered what Yuli had done. He'd killed her friend.

Shhh. No tears. Just keep walking.

She parted more of the heavy vines and branches. Ahead, in a clearing, or perhaps a cave, stood a woman, or a man. The figure's face shimmered and changed, never remaining the same. Sometimes it appeared as a human, sometimes the raven, now its skin looked more like the bark of an oak. When she blinked and looked again, a woman's face smiled at her.

Ona? Iluna said.

The woman smiled again before the oak bark covered her

skin, amber leaves falling gently, and then changed to the dark feathers of the raven. *Perhaps I am she. But I am also that which your people call the Malfir.* The many voices whispered again.

How can that be? Iluna frowned.

The entity before her changed again and now stood as a man with dark hair and darker eyes, his laughter filled the world like rolling thunder. *I am everything. The beginning that was; the end that is to come.*

And, my raven?

Was never yours, it said, its skin changing to black feathers once more.

What is—

No more questions. Come give us your hand. Watch. Learn.

Iluna stepped forward and reached out touching the black feathers of the god. A force stronger than any known essence assailed her and she gasped ...

... she saw everything.

A vast knowledge fed her. First, the foreign clan. Their camp spread out as far as the eye could see, tents pitched in perfect lines. In amongst them a small group gathered. Mages they were called. She knew this now. They wore black cloaks, and there was Yuli, meeting with them, his beads of wood on show. They planned the attack. Iluna could understand their language now. Yuli spoke to them with his heavy accented tongue, and she learnt more of his treachery. He'd been in league with this foreign clan for some time, meeting with them often during his hermitage.

The vision skipped back again, through the cycles of the past. Yuli in their summer grounds in a trance. In the Otherworld he was linked with the Grand Soragan who communicated to him all the lessons of dark magics from the foreign mages. That was how Yuli had grown stronger, more powerful.

Further back still, Yuli stood at the altar in their winter lands, the snow lay in a blanket that covered the hard grey rock of the chasm. He made a promise to the spirits of Malfir and blood dripped from his hands. In that instant, the essence of his light turned black.

The cycle turned once more, and it was now many summers in the past. The Grand Soragan was younger, his features less worn. He traveled in earnest, and in secret and met with one of the mages, Gudmund. They spent a day and a night talking of plans for the future in which the Nordesans would take the lands of the Otter, and Xaroth would be shown the secrets to more power. He knew the sacrifice he was offering.

Further back, time turned, and the Grand Soragan was even younger. He'd just finished his prenticeship and now set off on his journey to his hermitage. He was heading toward a set of caves to the south, a full two eightnight's journey from his clan's summer lands. But when he arrived, it was occupied by the foreign clan. They tried to attack and kill him, but having achieved the power to bind he transformed into his totem – the snake – and escaped. But it was short-lived for the clan threw their dark spears and one struck the snake through the tail. He changed form to his natural state, the spear still wedged firmly in his leg.

The Nordesans took him in, and healed him. They wanted to understand this new magic. They began to learn each other's language. The Soragan stayed there for the entirety of his hermitage, and that's when the plans were first made. The Nordesans were in search of new lands. Their country had been taken from them by a powerful people who built large structures they called 'fortress' and 'temple'.

The Nordesans did not travel the lands to follow the seasons; rather they stayed in the one place. But their homeland was now occupied; they'd been driven out.

Xaroth burned with a desire to learn all of their magical secrets. A scene played before Iluna – the Nordesan mages sat in a circle, one of them stood in the center with an ox, a beautiful creature with large dark eyes and a glossy coat. In a flash the mage took a weapon and slashed the beast's throat. Blood spilled, running over the ground and the ox went to its knees. The mage took an ornate silver cup and filled it with the blood. Xaroth's eyes were frightened, but he drank the substance down; blood trickled over his chin. He was one of them.

He grew used to the taste of blood, and then he came to desire it, and the lust-magic, and the power it brought him. He learnt to bend light and travel through the Otherworld, and finally to control the will of others.

Then the mists swirled and Iluna traveled further through the cycles of time, right back to the beginning when there was just the light and the dark. They met with a great explosion, mingling together. Little bits of light lingered in the darkness, and shadows formed on the light, but all was in balance. Things began to take shape. A round rock circled a star and a moon and a sun. On that rock water came together and fell from a sky and creatures were born. The mother, Ona, lived in the same space as the Malfir, but she always in the light, and they always in the dark.

Awake.

And all the knowledge of all the universes was hers.

∞

"Iluna."

Iluna came out of the trance as one would a dream. Not knowing quite where she was or what had happened.

"Iluna?"

She opened her eyes and the glow of an oil pot made her blink.

"Thank Ona, you're awake!"

Her eyes looked up and she saw a young hunter, his golden tips of hair illuminated in the soft light.

"Are you well?" He put his face closer to hers and his amber eyes showed concern.

"Anton," she whispered, reaching out and touching his cheek with her hand. His skin was warm.

He held her hand with his own. "Here, let me help you."

He grabbed her arms and she sat up. Iluna felt giddy and nauseous and bent over to the side. She vomited into the clay pot beside her.

"Here, drink." Anton handed her his water skin and she took it and rinsed her mouth before drinking the skin dry, her thirst suddenly overbearing.

"Thank you." She wiped her mouth and handed the empty skin back to Anton.

"I'll just get rid of this." He stood and took the clay pot with him outside. When he returned he was carrying another skin of water. He sat by her side and reached out to steady her, holding her shoulder. "You're not well. What happened?"

Iluna blinked. She no longer felt nauseous and with every breath she was feeling less dizzy. She tried to recall what had happened, and then it all came back in a flash of memory.

She scowled and ripped her shoulder away from the hunter.

"Your brother – he killed my raven!"

"What?" Anton frowned but his voice was smooth and gentle.

"My raven," she cried, "he's dead because of Yuli. He killed it with a rock and his evil magics." She sunk her face into her palms, the memory bringing all the emotion with it.

Anton put his hand back on her shoulder but she slapped it away.

"Iluna, please."

"Leave me." She lay down and rolled over; tears soaking the wolfskin beneath her.

"Shhhh. Iluna, be calm," Anton said. "Shhhhhh, it's alright. It's alright. Just breathe. That's it, shhhhh."

Gradually her breathing lost its jagged edge and slowed. Bit by bit her memory of the visioning returned to her – along with parts of the knowledge. She gasped. Anton had his own part to play in this long circle of time. The tears stopped and she rolled over to look directly into his amber eyes.

"I'm better now," she said.

Anton stared at her. His face bespoke a hunger of some kind and his eyes had that look of hope she'd seen before. Suddenly he kissed her, with lips soft and warm, and a physical tingling erupted in her belly. He stopped as abruptly as he had started and brought his hands to his eyes. "I'm sorry, Iluna."

She reached up and touched his face with gentle finger-tips. "Tell me what you wanted to say at the cave."

His cheeks burned. "I had an idea, no doubt a foolish one."

Iluna sat up and held his hands in hers. "Tell me."

Anton took a deep breath. "I thought we could run away – you and me. Find our own lands somewhere."

Iluna smiled.

"We would be happy, just the two of us. We'd find a valley as beautiful as this one, with a river and a nice cave. Or we could make our own tree-dwell. I would hunt and gather enough for both of us. And your magic would protect us. And you'd no longer be a tamatu." He breathed hard, excitement shining in his eyes. "We could—"

"Kiss me again," Iluna said and Anton blinked.

They kissed and rolled to the wolf skin, their breathing heavy and fast.

"Wait." Anoton managed between kisses. "I have to tell – Izhur is worried."

But Iluna knew her future, just as she knew her past.

"We won't take long, my love," she whispered, for she knew that Anton was her match. The raven had shown her that, too.

Anton's eyes burned and he embraced her with a fire in his arms, kissing her hard. "I love you," he whispered as he kissed the soft warm flesh of her neck.

"I know." She smiled as she held him and watched the flickering flame of the oil pot.

IZHUR

*I*zhur found Cypra at the evenfire. She stirred a pot of broth over the coals but stopped when she saw him approach.

"You look as angry as eight bears in spring, Izhur. What's happened?"

Izhur took a breath as he looked over his shoulder. He needed to be calm. "Is Anton with her?" he asked Cypra, keeping his volume low.

"Yes. I was just about to bring him something to eat. He won't leave her side. Izhur, what is on your mind?"

"Come. Let's get back to them. We must talk."

The space around the evenfire was very crowded now as people came to share in the evening meal. Izhur and Cypra walked past Ida who sat with her bond-daughter, Hennita. Anton's new wife had puffy eyes, red and swollen. Izhur pursed his lips and marched on, Cypra hurrying with him. They could worry about Anton and his wife later.

Finally, they reached the tent and entered.

"Thank the mother," Izhur whispered when his eyes fell on Iluna. She was sitting up, drinking from a steaming cup, Anton at her side. "You're awake." Izhur choked a little on the words, and reached out to touch her forehead. "Are you well, child?"

"I am well, Uncle. Anton only just fetched Amak and she brought me this medicine. I feel good now. But my raven," her voice caught, "Yuli killed him. We had a strong connection and, when he died, I was drawn into the Otherworld. There is much I learned there." A tear ran down her cheek and Anton put an arm around her. She rested her head on his shoulder.

Both Izhur and Cypra glanced over them before giving each other a knowing look.

"I see things have advanced between you two," Cypra said, one eyebrow raised.

Izhur brought a hand to his temple. "Anton." He breathed.

"I know, Izhur. But it is too late now, and you said yourself time is scant. What do we do now?"

Izhur stared at him a moment longer before nodding his head and sitting down on the reed mat. "Xaroth is calling for a Grand Council."

"What? What is he scheming now?" Cypra sat beside him.

Izhur relayed to them the discussions in the Soragan's tent. "Xaroth claims Yuli has captured one of the enemy; someone called Gudmund."

"Gudmund?" Anton looked up, his hunter eyes narrowed. "But that's not possible. I slew him with my own hand."

Iluna put a hand over Anton's. "No doubt the Nordesan mages have restored him. Their dark magics have such power."

"Izhur, this does not bode well." Cypra's eyes were full of fear. "I remember what happened at the last Grand Council."

Izhur nodded. "As do I, and something tells me this council may follow the very same path. Iluna, are you well enough to overpower Xaroth? We need to break his hold on the others."

Iluna looked down at her hands, her dark hair a mess around her shoulders. She appeared every bit the little girl he had protected all these years, but she was their saviour, and a grown woman. If it wasn't for her, many would be dead now. Izhur took a deep breath in an attempt to stop the anger from bubbling up. He had to remain calm if he was to bring about justice.

Gradually Iluna shook her head. "Not yet." Her dark eyes filled with tears. "I simply don't have the energy. Perhaps tomorrow, or the day after, but now, I don't think I could overpower him, as well as this Gudmund – and Yuli." She glanced at Anton who squeezed her hand.

"What if Cypra and I were to help you? Feed you energy through the Otherworld. Could it work?"

Iluna considered this. "As a last resort, perhaps. But it won't be enough to best them – not if they work together."

Izhur turned to Cypra. He knew by her look of fear that they were thinking the same thing. Izhur took a breath and exhaled. "Iluna, this Grand Council – I've a very ill feeling about it. It may go badly for you."

"I know, Uncle. I know what you're thinking." She shook her head. "But it's a blur to me. I can't quite see our way through it. During my trance I was given a lot of knowledge, but it only comes to me in fragments."

A shout from outside made them jump. "... a Grand Council, assemble yourselves."

Izhur swallowed. "It is time."

"The Grand Soragan has called for a Grand Council. Assemble at the evenfire. A Grand Council ..." the voices repeated.

"Let me take Iluna," Anton's voice cracked with emotion. "We could run, hide. We'll be far away before they're even ready to begin this farce."

"It won't do any good, Anton," Iluna said. "They will find me sooner or later. There'd be plenty of willing volunteers to track us if we left now. No, we must attend like everyone else. Come, help me up."

∞

Izhur watched the assembled clans from his spot in the circle around the evenfire. People were quiet, calm, as they sat in formal lines according to clan. Could it be that Xaroth's influence extended to all of them now?

"Brothers, Sisters, in the name of Ona, our great mother, I have called this Grand Council for we have a grave decision before us." Xaroth stood tall, his twisted staff at his side. He looked even older now; deep wrinkles lined his skin. Yet his voice carried effortlessly to every person present. "The enemy clan, the very one that attacked and killed our brothers and sisters of the Otter, have returned this Agria."

Panic sounded in the shouts and gasps of the throng. The essence around the evenfire roiled. Izhur took a deep breath. The excitement was almost tangible.

"They were camped very close to Ona's Valley, preparing to attack us. It is only due to the vigilance of myself and Yuli that we became aware of them, and managed to run them off. But, sadly, they were drawn to us through one of our own, a traitor."

More gasps. Izhur closed his eyes for a moment.

"Who is this traitor? Show him to us. We will burn him," somone shouted. Izhur couldn't see who, the flames of the evenfire blocked his view.

Xaroth held up a hand. "We have captured one of the enemy. Yuli, bring him forward."

From beyond the evenfire Yuli came forward holding a man in front of him who had his hands tied with leather. The man was very tall, with long gold hair streaked with silver; it hung over his broad shoulders. He walked obediently toward the evenfire and slowly turned to face the throng.

"One of their leaders," Yuli shouted. "His name is Gudmund

and he speaks our tongue, because he has been taught by the traitor."

"Gudmund," Xaroth intoned. "Do you deny you are the leader of this enemy clan?"

The tall man looked at Xaroth and lifted his chin. "I was the leader of the Nordesans." Gudmund spoke their Onan language but the words sounded very different. Still, he was easy enough to understand and every member of every clan listened intently. No one moved.

"We came here to slay your people and take your lands."

"Kill him," someone shouted.

"And how did you find us?" Xaroth asked, ignoring the calls of his own people.

Gudmund snarled. "One of your own showed us, through the trickery of the Malfir."

There was uproar at this. "Who is this evil person? Show us!"

Izhur swallowed. So this was Xaroth's trick. He looked for Iluna in the crowd. Would Anton have taken her? Hidden her?

"Her name," Gudmund's nostrils flared, "is Iluna."

The uproar boomed and someone sounded the drum, beating it in a wild rhythm. *BOOM DOOM, BOOM DOOM.* Movement rippled in the throng and the crowd parted. Ulath and Ugot held Iluna between them and pushed her in front of the Grand Soragan. She stumbled. Her leg pained her still.

Izhur stood; he had to stop this! "Xaroth, how do we know he is not lying?"

But Iluna spoke before he could finish. "It is true, Soragan. I am the traitor."

Izhur blinked. No! What was she doing?

"Yes, she's a witch." A woman's scream cut through the din, and the drumming stopped. Hennita rushed forward. "She has stolen my husband from me with her charms!"

"My baby was taken!" another woman yelled, and Izhur saw Ayla from the Eagle, tears streaked her cheeks. She'd lost her baby to a mountain cat on the journey to Agria. How could she think Iluna had anything to do with that? "It was the witch who took my daughter. I saw it!"

More people came forward. All of them shouting injustices and spitting at Iluna's feet; some calling her the Malfirena. Ugot stared at Izhur, a smug smile on his stupid face.

More shouts came out then, and the anger and rage of the crowd grew like a beast with a life of its own until someone shouted, "Burn her! Burn the witch!"

"Brothers, Sisters." Xaroth's voice carried through the chanting and quelled the fire of their rage the way rain blinks out an oil pot. "This is a fortuitous moment. Our own Yuli must undergo a powerful ceremony, one that will give him the strength to protect us from such dangers in the future. But this ceremony will require much energy. Burning the witch will indeed give us the energy needed for Ona's work to take place. At dawn we will invoke the ritual – an ancient one. Yuli will bind with his totem, and we will be protected by him. At dawn, the witch will burn!"

They took up the chant again. "Burn her! Burn the witch!"

Izhur looked to the purple sky, his mouth open. What had they done?

ANTON

*A*nton lifted the flap of the weathered brown tent and peered at the sky with tired eyes. The nightsun descended slowly. He closed the flap and looked back at Izhur and Cypra who sat huddled over an oil pot. "It is almost dawn."

Izhur nodded. "You know what you have to do?"

"Yes," Anton replied. "But are you sure this will work? Cypra, how can you know if you've never done this before?"

Worry and fear mingled on Cypra's face, creasing her brow. "It's our only hope, Anton. Don't be concerned with my role in this. I am after all, a very experienced Soragan. At least I was before they took my clan. I know what to do. The fact that I've not done it before doesn't mean I won't succeed. Just be sure you get the message to her."

Anton nodded. "Yes, Soragan."

Cypra smiled. "You best go now. People will awake and assemble soon."

"And remember to come back for her satchel. She will need it," Izhur said.

Anton glanced at the satchel. They had packed it full with Iluna's few items, her tunic, cloak and bowl, a water skin, her little bone carving of Shephet, and as much food as they could jam in.

"May the Mother watch over you," Izhur added.

Anton took a breath then opened the tent flap, and stepped into the night.

The encampment was quiet now. Most had gone to their sleeping mats to restore their energy. The Grand Soragan had told them they would all have to give of their essence if the binding ceremony was going to be a success. The excitement of the coming events had run through the clans like chain lighting. Older people recalled Dream Day tales of Doom, and told long stories to their grandchildren of humans transforming into lions and dragons. Everyone wondered what animal Yuli would transform to.

A wolf, Iluna had told him, twice the size of an ordinary one. And what terror would his brother wreak then? But Anton had no time to wonder about it. He had gone with Izhur and Cypra as soon as the Grand Council had finished. The Grand Soragan had ordered a group of hunters to get a stake ready for burning, and to tie Iluna to it. It had torn his heart to leave her, but Izhur had insisted, and he'd left with him and Cypra to discuss Izhur's idea. At least they had a plan now.

They had to get her out, far away, Izhur had said. That was the only way to save her. The hatred and distrust people felt for Iluna was irrevocable, thanks to Xaroth. It made Anton angry to think of it, but a future hope dimmed his rage. They would run away after all. They'd live together, in a distant land, just the two of them. They'd be happy.

He had to hurry. Anton quickened his pace, but a hand on his shoulder stopped him. He spun on the spot to see the familiar form of a muscled hunter standing solid before him.

"Father."

Zodor put a finger to his lips. "Follow me."

Anton swallowed. No, he would not be stopped. Not now. "Father, I can't – I—"

Zodor's eyes burned. "Follow now." He hissed and stalked off toward the river.

Anton took a deep breath. Years of training to be the obedient son was ingrained into his very skin. The nightsun still lingered high enough. There was time, just a little. He bit his lip and followed his father.

Zodor crossed the river and sat on a large boulder on the other side. Water gurgled and bubbled over a shallow ford of rocks – a calming sound. Anton put both arms out to balance and jogged over the ford until he stood before his father. "What is it, Father?"

Zodor held his hands in front of him, fingertips touching and thumbs crossed – the sign of warding against evil. Anton's nostrils flared. Did he think Iluna would curse him out here?

"You're going to try and save her, yes?" His father's voice was flat.

Anton bent his head. His pulse raced. He'd never been able to lie to him. "Yes, Father."

Zodor nodded sharply and looked up to the sky. "You have a plan? With Izhur? Cypra?"

"Yes, Father. We have a plan."

"And do you think it will work?"

Anton doubted it, now that his father knew. "I don't know. It probably won't."

Zodor stood, rubbing his hands together. "Much evil has befallen us, son. Too much. It has to stop."

Anton rubbed at the stubble on his cheek, concentrating hard on stopping the tears that blurred his vision. Iluna was as good as dead now, and there was nothing he could do to stop it. He wouldn't be able to get her the message. The nightsun danced dangerously close to the horizon. He shouldn't have gone with his father.

"It has to stop now," his father continued. "So tell me. How can I help?"

Anton blinked. "What?"

Zodor put a hand on Anton's shoulder. They stood face to face, Anton as tall as his father.

"Iluna saved me that night. Your mother has told me all. Although, somewhere deep inside, I knew it. She is a good girl. She's never been the ill omen that Xaroth spoke of. No, that title belonged to another." Zodor's eyes flicked to the camp across the river. "So tell me, son. How can I help you? We must save her."

∞

Finally, Anton took his seat at the very back of the throng, near a wattle bush. Its pungent scent filled the air, but hid Cypra well enough from everyone else. She sat crosslegged now, with eyes closed, her breathing deep and regular. Both the nightsun and the moon had descended past the western horizon. Atoll's star danced just above it and a red glow lit up the clouds to the east. The last day of Agria dawned.

In front of the evenfire a large stack of dead wood had been gathered and Iluna was tied to a stake in its centre. Her head was bowed making her hair appear even messier than normal. Her shoulders slouched – she looked tired. He knew she was still recovering from her attack on the enemy, and her leg pained her. Anton tried to calm his heart, but Izhur had stressed the amount of energy this kind of magic took, and Iluna was exhausted. At least he'd got the message to her. His father had helped, distracting the other hunters who finished building the stack for burning, so that he could talk to her. She knew their plan and her part in it.

Fellow clan members now sat around the evenfire, taking up

their usual positions. The ceremonial drum started a steady beat and the buzz of excitement grew. Anton clutched a stick and snapped it in half. These people, his people, they were the monsters, blindly following Xaroth's rule.

Yuli stood at the front facing the crowd, his pale robe crisp and clean. Anton's lip curled into a scowl. His brother's greed had much to answer for.

Izhur sat in the circle with the other Soragans. Gudmund also sat among the Soragans, his hands bound, not that he was truly their prisoner. It had been part of his secret agreement with Xaroth and Yuli; he wanted to see the magic that was about to unfold. Anton grimaced and turned back to Cypra. She nodded.

The drums stopped and silence descended. The Grand Soragan stood with the help of some of the prentices. He limped forward to address the crowd. He seemed just as exhausted as Iluna, but his voice never faltered. "This dawn we shall renew an ancient ritual – one that has not been performed for generations. We will show to Ona and all the Benevolent Ones that we still have much to offer."

There was a cheer and the Grand Soragan held his hands out for silence. "Each of us will go into trance. Every man, woman and child needs to offer up their energy if we are to be successful and witness Yuli bind. We Soragans will draw your energy to help with the ritual. Exhaustion will follow, but with this new power Yuli is to acquire, we will have more protection from our enemies in the future."

Gudmund sat still, his eyes watching all with ardent fascination. Anton frowned. He wanted to shout, to tell them all to wake up and see how they had been fooled. But he sat quietly. He couldn't risk the plan.

The drumming started once more and the Grand Soragan spoke to Yuli briefly before putting his hand on Yuli's brow. Then Yuli lay on the ground. This was probably where Yuli began his trance to dream of his totem, or whatever he had to do. Iluna would be doing the same now. She hadn't moved. Her head still hung low. When he looked over behind the wattle, Cypra had her eyes open, watching. Soon she would also go into a deep trance.

Xaroth and the Soragans sat in their circle. Their eyes closed as they chanted to the drum's beat. Then everyone else joined in, closing their eyes and concentrating. The hum of over ten one hundred people held a power of its own. Anton kept his eyes open. He would watch all.

Yuli twitched every now and then, and, as the trance went on, the twitches became more violent. Xaroth opened his eyes and nodded to Ulath. The young hunter took his cue, and with a burning stick from the evenfire he walked toward Iluna. Anton's heart raced. He turned to the wattle. Cypra gave him a slow nod. *Be calm,* it said. But when he turned back the fire stack had been lit and panic swelled close to his heart. If the plan didn't work, Iluna would burn. He looked back at Cypra. She had closed her eyes, her mouth whispering her own chant.

It had begun.

Even from where he sat Anton could see the gleaming sweat on Cypra's face. Izhur had said this would be difficult for her. She had to collect all the essence of all the clans and Soragans and guide it to Iluna somehow.

The beat grew stronger and so did the chant. Anton could feel something. Like a spark in the atmosphere, the way lightning ignites static energy that lingers in the air.

Something was going to happen.

The flames at Iluna's feet grew higher, but she hadn't moved. Suddenly one of the Soragans went down, as though he fainted. Anton panicked, not knowing what it meant. He looked to Cypra but she was deep in trance now, the sweat shining on her brow.

Another Soragan went down. Izhur was still sitting upright in the circle, deep in trance like the others, but his robe clung to him and his long hair stuck slick to his head. Then the chanting lifted higher, louder and Yuli, unbelievably, seemed to float in midair, as though someone had him on a rope and pulled him up. Anton's breath caught in his throat. This wasn't meant to happen to Yuli! The flames around Iluna grew higher. It wasn't working!

There was a murmuring now and others also opened their eyes to see the floating Yuli. People pointed and whispered. A low rumor spread through the entire crowd as eyes opened and looked in wonder at the miracle before them. But the chant from the Soragans remained strong and the drum continued to beat.

Darkness radiated from Yuli's core, and thorny black tendrils wound around his torso and limbs. A sudden nausea bubbled in Anton's stomach, but a light came from the east and when Anton looked he had to put his hand over his eyes to shield them, for it was like looking into the daysun – worse. The brightness grew until it was impossible to see anything at all. Anton closed his eyes and still the light penetrated through the flesh of his eyelids making him see red. He scrunched his face.

Shouts of panic sounded around him as people questioned what it could be. "Where's Yuli?" someone asked. "Has he turned?"

Then it stopped, as though someone had extinguished the fire, and a scream pierced the dawn – a woman's scream. It came from the front and was vaguely familiar. Anton blinked. The white light had gone and his mother stood and ran to the front where her son now lay. She bent and picked up Yuli, cradling him in her arms. He was limp. And, judging from his mother's wailing, Anton guessed his brother was dead. The Soragans were all lying on the ground, spent – even Izhur. The Grand Soragan was just coming to – blinking and looking around – when a loud squawk echoed thorough the valley.

People screamed and pointed up. Circling above them in the dawn sky, a large raven flew. Its feathers shone blue and purple in the golden rays of the early morning sunshine. It was larger than any beast they'd known and its squawks almost deafened them. It circled again and swooped low and a breeze whipped up the evenfire as it passed. Then it flapped powerful wings and glided up, toward the mountains.

Anton smiled. He looked at the fire stake. The flames engulfed it fully now, but Iluna was gone. Anton stood and turned to Cypra. She lay on the ground behind the wattle. Her face was grey, and she wasn't breathing, but a gentle smile lay on her face.

"Thank you," Anton whispered.

He allowed the chaos of shouting and movement to swirl and bustle around him as he ran for the bush where he'd hidden their satchels and then made his way up the mountain path.

ILUNA

The golden light of dawn filtered through the trees, illuminating different shades of green. At the clearing, the little white flowers that surrounded each moonberry had now covered their treasures in full, and the berries would only be on show again once the moon returned to the sky.

Iluna stood in human form, her breathing still labored after the flight, her first. Being a raven seemed oddly familiar to her, and her senses buzzed with energy. The power that had opened to her was like a vast ocean of essence that she could draw on at will. In the form of the raven, breaking Xaroth's bonds had been easy. Each dark link she'd snapped with her essence as she'd flown over the encampment and the black tendrils had withered and died like a cut vine in the summer sun. Most of the clan had fallen under his direct control, but his influence was now destroyed. At least they'd know their own minds again.

Now that she had transitioned once, she knew she could do it again, easily – and she would need to shift soon. It was time for her to leave the clan, and never return. She just had to wait for Anton.

When he finally stepped into the clearing he was panting,

having run up the mountain path. He stopped to gaze upon her nakedness, and a broad smile lined his face.

Iluna went to him and wrapped her arms around him in a hard embrace, her head on his chest. His heart raced.

"Come, we must go, Iluna," he said, stepping back. "They will be tracking us soon, if they haven't started already." His eyes darkened. "It killed, Yuli."

Iluna took a sharp breath. "I am sorry."

Anton shook his head. "It was his own fault. If he wasn't so greedy for power he wouldn't have undertaken such a dangerous ritual."

Iluna looked to the ground, fearful that he would think it because of her that Yuli died. But she knew Yuli wasn't meant to bind; he would never have been successful, even with the dark magics.

"And Cypra," Anton continued, "it took her, too; she has passed."

Iluna took a deep shuddering breath. She knew it was true the moment she sought Cypra in the Otherworld. She was gone. A tear fell from her cheek. "She did it for me. She gave all her essence so that I would succeed." How was her own life worth more than Cypra's?

Anton put a hand on her bare shoulder. "It's what she wanted, Iluna."

Anton drew her close, wrapping his arms around her, and Iluna allowed a few tears to fall before blinking hard to cut them off.

"Come, we must hurry," Anton said, stepping back. "I have your satchel. Do you want me to carry it? You should put a tunic on."

"Anton." Iluna's voice was barely more than a whisper.

"I know my way over the other side of the mountain. There is a cave we could go to. It will give us shelter for a night, but we have a long day ahead of us. Many long days." He picked up his spear and satchel, and took a few steps out of the clearing.

"Anton," Iluna said, a little louder.

Anton stopped and turned.

"I have to go alone."

Anton's face distorted into a shadow of despair. His brow furrowed, making him look like a lost little boy rather than the hunter he was.

"I am sorry." Iluna took a deep breath to try to override the pain in her heart. "I love you. You are my great love, and just when I have found you, I must leave you."

Anton shook his head. "Then don't do this. Let us go together. I want you, Iluna. All I want is you."

"I know." Her voice was soft, but her heart hurt with heaviness, and the tears had won out and now lined her cheeks. "It seems that way now, but in time I will not be enough for you."

Iluna had seen it in the visioning. Since her trance, pieces of knowledge continued to flash in her mind. If Anton was to come with her he would grow to resent her, blame her even for taking him away from his clan. He had grown up with the respect of every clan member – the son of a great hunter who was now a great hunter in his own right. That kind of esteem was something he had become accustomed to. It was in his fabric to expect it. His place was with the Wolf as an important clan member; it was quite simply who he was. She couldn't take that from him, as much as it would break her heart to say goodbye, she had to do it.

"Well, come back with me. Please, Iluna. Don't leave me." He blinked with glistening eyes.

"It's too late, Anton. Too many despise me, distrust me. I will always be their tamatu, and I will not control their minds the way Xaroth did." She wiped a cheek. "And what of your wife?"

Anton snarled. "I don't care for her."

"Anton, you know it wouldn't work. No, it's time for me to leave."

ADERYN WOOD

Anton brought both hands to his eyes, defeated, his shoulders shaking.

"Anton, kiss me." She went to him and pressed her naked body into his. They kissed for a long time before she pulled him down to the soft grass of the clearing. She wanted to lay with him one more time – a desperate goodbye. She sat astride him and kissed the tears from his cheeks and the soft skin under his ears. His arousal was immediate and their love making a fiery mix of love, passion and sadness.

When it was over she kissed him once more on his tender lips, then stood and picked up her satchel, placing the strap over her head. It bulged with the food that they had packed for her, but in raven form her cargo would be light.

"Xaroth will be spent today, his power at its lowest. You know what you must do," she said.

Anton nodded.

"Tell Izhur I've always loved him, as a daughter loves a father."

Tears fell openly from Anton's eyes. He sniffed.

"I love you, Anton. I always will." She turned, stepping away from him before more tears could fall. Then she focused and began the incantation, imaging the raven as she did so. It came quick when it happened and through the eyes of a raven she saw the sad form of Anton as he reached out and said goodbye. She squawked and in two wing beats flew above him. She circled, and Anton grew smaller and smaller. Then she turned north and picked up her speed. The snow on the highest mountain peaks sparkled in the morning sun.

ANTON

*A*nton stumbled through the camp. People were still in the grip of chaos as Soragans and clan members tried to understand what had happened.

Izhur was comforting Belwas when Anton found him. The Bear's Soragan sat on the grass staring into space and shaking his head. "I don't understand," he kept muttering.

Izhur put a hand on his shoulder. "Belwas, it's all right. Xaroth's influence has been broken. Iluna saw to that. She has such power now."

Anton told Izhur what Iluna had said, that she loved him as a daughter.

The Soragan nodded quickly, pursing his lips. "I would have liked to have seen her one more time, just one more time," he muttered, his eyes following the line of mountain peaks above.

"She told me Xaroth would be weak now, very weak."

Izhur looked up at him, eyes narrowing. "Can you do it?"

Anton clenched his jaw. "Nothing will stop me."

∞

No one had known where the Grand Soragan had slithered to – no one but Sethra. Anton spotted her poking around the even-fire, scratching her head as though lost, but when he'd asked her where Xaroth was, a look of fire and determination set in her eyes and she pointed to the east, along the river.

"Find him, hunter," she said, her eyes squinting with hatred.

The Grand Soragan's trail had been easy to discover. His limp and the heavy use of his staff clearly indicated in the pattern of tracks along the riverbank. Anton had not come this far upriver before. He frowned, wondering why. Trout lept from the river; it would have been a good fishing spot during Agria.

But trout were not his prey now.

Soon the tracks brought him to a deep chasm cut far into the mountain, dark and cool. At the back of the chasm Anton spotted Xaroth lying on his back, on the rocky floor, seemingly asleep.

Anton crept forward with his spear and noiselessly bound Xaroth's feet and hands, the way he would a boar. Then he stuck the point of his spear's head to the Grand Soragan's throat and pierced the scaly skin so that it broke; blood fell on his Soragan's beads.

Xaroth's eyes sprung open, his small pupils widening. He laughed – a dark sinister cackle full of mirth. "Retribution is what you seek, hunter."

"Be silent," Anton snarled.

"I can give it to you. I can give you your revenge on Gudmund, and all the Nordesans. I will lead you to them."

"Silence!"

"To retrieve our people."

Anton stilled his spear hand.

Xaroth smiled, revealing stained teeth – reddish brown. "Yes, they have our people, the children of the Otter. They took them prisoner. Many long to return to us. Let me free and I will lead you to them."

Anton shut his eyes. His hand gripped the spear. Perhaps he could save them and get his revenge on the Grand Soragan later. He could help the children for Cypra. Then he remembered Gudmund. The Nordesan remained in their custody; Izhur had him under guard. Perhaps they could use him to find the children. But would he cooperate? Anton took a deep breath. He musn't allow the Soragan to trick him. Iluna had told him Xaroth was now at his weakest. She meant for him to kill the Soragan while he could.

A noise distracted him. Like a whisper, or a hiss. Anton looked to his right. Xaroth's staff lay about an arm's length away on the rocky ground. Golden sunshine lit up the top of the chasm revealing the multiple colours of the rock. Some of it shining like gold.

Anton closed his eyes. He had to make a decision. He wanted to find the Otter children who were taken, but Xaroth couldn't be trusted. He shook his head.

The hissing sound returned, and Anton opened his eyes. Xaroth was gone, and so was the staff. Only his stained Soragan's robe and beads remained. Anton blinked, in front of him slithered a snake the size of a man. Its head reared up and its tongue flicked out.

Anton stood as quick as a cat. "Great Mother."

The snake struck and Anton jumped back as far as he could, but the snake came at him, and his heart leapt up to his throat. Anton jabbed the giant in the head with his spear and all his strength. The snake hissed and slithered in a circle toward the back of the chasm. It flicked its tongue, its small black eyes watching him. Blood trailed along its head. Then it reared and opened its mouth revealing long sharp fangs, as long as Anton's forearm, dripping with venom.

Anton swallowed and tried to steady his shaking hands. He'd

faced bears, mountain ox, and wolves, but nothing like this. His heart raced. His palm was sweaty and the spear slipped in his shaky grip. Fear was taking over.

The snake opened its mouth all the wider and came for him. Anton whispered a quick plea to Shephet, and gripped the spear. The snake reared backwards ready to strike and Anton saw his chance. He let go a hunter's cry and threw the spear with all his might. It pierced the snake's open jaw and plunged into the roof of its mouth before lodging into its brain. The snake fell with an unnatural scream and a thud, dead.

Anton breathed heavily and let loose a roar filled with anger and grief that echoed around the chasm, again and again. The sunlight above now shone more brightly, and when he looked back at the rocky ground the snake had gone, but Xaroth remained, his naked body still and lifeless.

Anton took a breath and went down to his knees before the corpse. "Ona, please forgive me. I did this for the Otter clan. I did it for my brother, Yuli. For Cypra, for Golldo, for Sethra, for all our people who came under the spell of this evil man. And for Iluna. Please, look over her."

He grasped the handle of the spear, lodged firmly in Xaroth's mouth, and ripped it free, wiping the spearhead on the Soragan's robe. Anton rubbed his swollen eyes and stood up, still catching his breath. Sunshine lit the wall at the back of the chasm in full. Gold, jade and other colors mingled and sparkled. Anton paused a moment, steadying his breathing and taking in the beauty of the rock.

When he finally walked out of the chasm the sunlight reflected on the river, and trout leapt to catch the dragonflies that buzzed happily in the morning sunshine. *Yes, a good spot for fishing. I will return later today and catch a worthy meal for Mother. And for my wife.*

. . .

THE END

* * *

WANT TO KNOW WHAT HAPPENS NEXT? READ ON...

Did you enjoy *The Raven?* Why not help spread the word about this series by posting a quick review on Amazon and/or Goodreads.

While 'The Secret Chronicles of Lost Magic' is a collection of standalone fantasy novels set in the same world (rather than a series), there will be a trilogy of short stories called 'Iluna's Song', which follow Iluna's journey after the events in *The Raven.*

The first story is called, *The Doom of Arlg-Teg*, and is now available exclusively for Aderyn's Newsletter subscribers. Sign up now to Aderyn's Monthly Newsletter to receive a free copy of *The Doom of Arlg-Teg*, or if you'd prefer, a free book in another series by Aderyn Wood.

Also, be sure to check out Book Two in The Secret Chronicles of Lost Magic, *Dragonshade* – a must for lovers of long epic fantasies.

Happy reading!
Aderyn.

ACKNOWLEDGMENTS

Thanks to Peter for his steadfast faith in me and constant encouragement.

Thanks to my parents, Ian and Pat, for allowing me to go off with the fairies as a child. Also to my brother, Barry, who understands what it means to love fantasy fiction.

A good book is impossible to write without quality critique - thank you D.A. Ravn, Julie Angel, Judy L. Mohr, Shamsi Ruhe and Pam Collings for their invaluable feedback.

A special thanks to Tairelei for her tireless efforts to create yet another perfect cover design.

ALSO BY ADERYN WOOD

DRAGONSHADE (THE SECRET CHRONICLE OF LOST MAGIC)

In the sweeping desert realm of Zraemia, an ancient prophecy stirs – the Great War to Come will turn the world to ash, and one king will rule all.

The enemy king aspires to the seat of supreme ruler, and with the weight of a mighty army at his back, most would concede his ascension. But one ruler stands in his way. His daughter, Princess Heduanna, is a natural-born seer who receives visions from the goddess – divinations that foretell a different fate for Zraemia.

Beyond the Sea of Death, a fierce ally awaits, in a strange land of forests and mountains. The goddess has revealed the wild people who call it home will fight for Zraemia in the Great War to Come. But if Heduanna's interpretation is wrong, thousands will perish. The visions take their toll on Heduanna, and as the goddess grows distant, the enemy-king's army becomes more powerful by the day.

Alliances are pushed to the brink as a war like no other looms – a war that could tear the world apart. For from the shadows, a dark new order is building, one that hungers for the blood of battle, and a king of their own,

When the gods speak, ancient cities burn.

THE BORDERLANDS TRILOGY

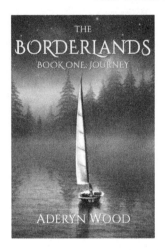

Dale has never felt a sense of belonging. She despises the bullies and snobs at school, and her family are difficult to like, let alone love. Rhys, a new boy at school seems to take an interest in her. But can she trust him? When the only friend she has ever had, Old Man Gareth, is murdered before her eyes, she is set on a frantic journey and a lonely adventure; the Borderlands beckon. But what are the Borderlands? Will she make it to them? And if she gets there, will she belong?

The Borderlands: Journey is a magical fantasy adventure that fantasy fiction fans, particularly older teens and the young at heart, will enjoy. It is the first book in the Contemporary Fantasy series 'The Borderlands'.

* * *

THE VISCOUNT'S SON - TRILOGY

The Viscount's Son tells the story of book conservator, Emma, and her online project - to transcribe an ancient and mysterious text. The trouble is, Emma's colleague, Jack, believes the medieval 'diary' is a fake. Emma decides to translate the text and leave it up to her readers to decide - so what will you think? Follow Emma's journey to discern the mysteries of the medieval memoir.

The Viscount's Son may or may not include a mysterious vampire - that's for you to find out! But all fans of dark vampire fantasy fiction will probably enjoy it.

* * *

ABOUT THE AUTHOR

From high fantasy to paranormal, Aderyn's stories cover the broad spectrum of Fantasy. Inspired from childhood by the wonder and mystique of Susan Cooper's *The Dark is Rising* and the adventures in Tolkien's *The Hobbit*, her love of the Fantasy genre has been life long. As a writer, Aderyn brings characters and places to life in stories filled with magic, mystery, and a good dollop of mayhem.

Aderyn studied Literature, History and Creative Writing at university, travelled the world, and taught English before becoming a full-time writer. She is also a part-time farmer passionate about self-sufficiency and poultry. She lives in a cosy cottage on a small farm in Victoria, Australia with partner Peter, their dog, cat, and a little duck called Snow.

If you'd like to be informed of the next installment in the 'Chronicles' collection consider subscribing to Aderyn's Newsletter.

For more information
www.aderynwood.com

Made in United States
North Haven, CT
10 February 2023